MOSTLY ME

Rachel Edmunds

Chapter 1

I used to hate rich people and I used to hate private schools. I hated that some people are born with the advantage that they can get a better education just because they can afford it when some of us can't. Yet, in the future, if I had a child and enough money to pay for a private school, would I send them to one? Yes. Absolutely. Why wouldn't I? They'd have more opportunities I would have wanted for myself.

It's bullshit and it makes me an absolute hypocrite because I was currently hauling a box of clothes into my new dormitory room at Darwin school which is (you guessed it) a private school. Don't be fooled: I could in no way whatsoever afford to go here. I worked my ass off at a state school to apply for a bursary to cover the costs of going here. The only reason I applied was because I wanted to get the best education I possibly could and if I could get it for free, I would work my hardest to get there.

And here I was. My GCSE predicted grades along with my interview and recommendations were enough to get me in and then I lived up to those predicted grades and got straight As and A*s. It wasn't easy but I have always been naturally studious and when I want something this badly, failure isn't an option. The only worry I had was that I would never, ever fit in with the students here and it probably wouldn't be hard for them to work out that I don't have any money.

It's supposed to be confidential that I'm a 'free student' but it won't take long for people to notice that while they put their books in their Michael Kors bags, all I have is the plain black rucksack I've been using since year seven. Ok, I'm generalising and ironically being the pretentious one here. Luckily, the school has a uniform, even for the sixth formers and I was going into lower sixth to start A-levels. It's a pretty traditional uniform, just plain blue skirts and blazers with white shirts and I don't have to wear a tie because I'm a girl. We all had to wear them at my last school and I hated how masculine I looked.

Even if these two years turn out to be absolute agony living and studying with all those posh kids, at least it wasn't for that long and I'd come out of it with amazing grades hopefully and it'll look great on my CV and no one would need to know that I didn't pay.

My room was so much bigger than my one at home and I had my own desk, no more having to work at a kitchen table and since I wasn't paying for the electricity, I could study as late as I wanted with the light on instead of having to light candles to read by. The bed was the same size - still a single which I guess was standard for any dorm room but it was a lot nicer than my old shabby one at home.

I sat on the bed pulling out clothes from the box and sorting them into piles of tops, bottoms and underwear when someone walked right into my room.

"Oh shit. Sorry. Wrong room," they said. It was a very athletic looking guy with tousled light brown hair and a sheepish grin that didn't look sorry at all. This wasn't even the boys' boarding house - what was he doing in here? "My sister's room is just next door. I'm Horne." He stuck out his hand for me to shake. I quickly pushed over my tops pile to cover the underwear.

"Horn?" I repeated, confused, as I shook it.

"Nathan Horne," he said. "And you are…?"

"Um, Emily. Green."

"Nice to meet you 'Um, Emily Green', are you new?"

I rolled my eyes at his mocking of me. "Yeah, I'm new."

"Where did you go before?"

Before I could even consider whether to tell him I went to a state school or lie and tell him somewhere else, a girl's face poked round the door.

"Nate, what are you doing flirting with the new girl already?" she asked.

"I'm not!" He put his hands up in defense.

"Sure you weren't," she said sarcastically as she came into the room and pushed him out the door. "Ignore him." She closed the door behind him. "Don't let him charm you before term even starts," she said, sounding exasperated.

She came over and sat on the bed besides the piles. "I'm Bea. Beatrice. That was my ape of a brother." Her soft brown hair matched his and I could see the family resemblance in the face it framed. They were both admittedly quite attractive. "Do you know anyone here?"

"No, I'm not from around here" I said. Darwin School was just under a hundred miles south of my home.

"I've been here since third form and my room is next to yours so I can show you around, introduce you to people and whatever you need. Just shout me whenever. You can hang around with my friends Hannah and Megan until you get bored of us and make other friends."

It was a nice offer of her and I was glad she was acting so nicely towards me right off the bat since by the looks of her alone, I would have written her off as a bitchy queen bee. Or queen Bea.

"Thanks, I'll probably take you up on that." I offered a small smile and she seemed to take this as a cue to leave which was fair because we both had unpacking to do. As she got to the doorway, she paused and said, "Hannah and Meg will be in my room from like seven thirty for a girls' night and you're welcome to join us if you want. We'll swing by your room when it's time for dinner and show you where the dining hall is."

True to her word, Bea knocked on my door just a few minutes before 6 o'clock and when I opened it, there were two other girls I assumed were Hannah and Megan. The girl with tresses of curly black hair and a particularly snub nose introduced herself as Hannah and the other girl, a redhead with a very obvious birthmark on her cheek, had to be Megan.

"A blonde!" Hannah screeched upon seeing me. "Now we've got the whole set." Then she hugged me as if we'd known each other for years and this was only a reunion after the summer holidays. I laughed awkwardly and wasn't sure whether to hug her back but she withdrew before I had the chance.

"Don't worry Emily, you'll be valued in this friendship for more than just your hair colour. Don't mind Hannah being fucking shallow."

Bea linked her arm through mine. "Come on guys, I said we'd show Emily where the dining hall is. There's two but there's one that's for boarders for breakfast and dinner and there's another one we eat at for lunch during term time with the day students. The boarding one is between the boys' and the girls' houses but don't worry about a jacket because there's a cover running between them.

Until she said this, I hadn't even realised it was raining but now I could hear the pitter-patter of droplets hitting against the window panes.

"Cool, I'm starving. Does you brother board too?" I asked

Bea, thinking about that boy I'd encountered earlier in my room.

Bea rolled her eyes. "Yes, unfortunately for me and he wouldn't have it any other way because he literally *lives* in the damn campus gym. Every single girl in this god forsaken school is drooling over him and *you* are not going to be another one of those brainless bimbos."

"Hey, ok," I laughed. "I might be blonde but I'm not dumb." We started walking down the corridor and down the stairs. When I arrived here earlier, the Dean of the girls' boarding house told me that it was split into the east wing for the lower school and west wing for upper school and each floor was a different year group with sixth form students on the top floor. There was an elevator but from the signage, it looked as though it was only for disabled people. I'd better get used to climbing several flights of stairs.

Since I didn't know my way around that well, I was expecting to go out the main doors I came into the building through but with my arm still linked through Bea's, she led us to a door behind the stairs out the back of the building to a path that ran towards what was presumably the boarding dining hall and I could see a path from the boys' boarding house going the same way. The overhead cover protected us from the rain as we walked towards the other building.

When Megan opened the door to go in, the heaviest aroma of good food wafted over us and my mouth immediately began to water. "That smells so delicious," I said.

"You totally can't beat the food here," Hannah said as we edged around the side of the room filled with many circular tables towards the serving bar. There were only around 20 other students in the dining hall and they all seemed to be younger than us. We grabbed a tray each from the stack and slid them onto the rack skirting the bar and waited behind the short queue.

Probably because it was a Sunday, and it was traditional, they were serving a roast and after we got our plates filled, we sat at what I would guess was their 'usual' table.

"So Emily, what subjects are you doing?" Megan asked while spearing a roast potato on her fork. I'd worried about choosing my A-levels for quite a while, not sure which would be the best to do but finally I'd settled on: "Fine art, maths and English lit." I thought it would be good to do maths and English with a bit of creativity on the side. "How about you guys?"

"I'm all performing arts based," Megan said, still chewing her potato. "Not as fancy as you."

Hannah smiled, "I'm doing literature as well, plus psychology and history."

"I'm doing classical studies and history and psych," Bea said. She scrunched up her nose as if she'd rather she wasn't doing those subjects. "My mum studied them here and she said I should too. It all sounds pretty boring and hard while my dumbass brother is allowed to just fuck around kicking a ball on a playing field until he probably gets awarded a scholarship somewhere. He wants to go to America for uni."

"Lucky for some," I said, hoping my cheeks weren't blushing as I was relating to getting into somewhere for free. So far, it hadn't been that hard to just play along with the rich girls and I didn't plan on giving away my secret so soon. Maybe in the future if I trusted them… but not now.

The three of us went back to Bea's room after dinner for her aforementioned 'girls' night'. I really hoped it wouldn't go on for too late into the night since classes start the next morning and I wanted to be fresh-faced and show that I was eager to learn, not turning up with bags under my eyes and too sleepy to pay attention to anything.

Bea's room was already elegantly decorated with printed

pictures of memories with her friends collaged on the wall over her bed and she had plenty of rugs and beanbags to go around.

"Hello, what's this?" Hannah asked excitedly as she pulled out a bottle from under Bea's bed. It was a clear bottle with a red lid which I recognised as Smirnoff even before reading the name.

"No," Bea said firmly, snatching it from her and putting it back in its hiding place. I knew for sure we weren't allowed to have alcohol in our rooms, the Dean had said so specifically and we weren't even old enough to buy it. Plus I'd also been told we were not allowed to ask upper sixth students to buy alcohol for us. As if I would. "I'm saving it for the party on Saturday, don't waste it on the first night."

"What party?" I asked.

"End of first week party. Happens for sixth formers every year," Bea explained.

"And you're allowed to drink?"

She laughed. "No, it's not like an official school thing, everyone just does it. It's wild, you'll love it. I've been looking forward to it since I started here when I was like, what, thirteen? It's in the boys' sixth form common room from what I've heard."

"How have you heard? We've only been back for five minutes," Megan joked.

Bea shrugged. "That's just what Nate said but it could always change. Moving on from you trying to steal what little alcohol I could smuggle in here, what should we do tonight?"

"Makeovers?" Megan instantly suggested.

"Don't you think that's a little childish?" Bea laughed. "We aren't thirteen anymore."

"It's fun," she sighed and stuck her bottom lip out, pretending Bea had upset her.

"How about just face masks, doing our nails and whatever

then?" Bea compromised. "There's no point dolling up just to take it off by tomorrow."

I was relieved they had settled an option that involved nothing too crazy or anything likely to keep us busy for too long. However, I wasn't so sure about this party they were talking about on Saturday. It sounded like something they assumed everyone would be going to and a party they described as 'wild' didn't really sound like my scene. Hopefully I'd find some way to avoid it.

But then again, it was a Saturday night, as long as I didn't have too much homework which I wouldn't expect to have after just the first week, I would have the whole of Sunday to sleep off any potential hangover I may have.

Megan and Hannah were already rifling through Bea's belongings looking for things to use tonight and it wasn't long before an assortment of face, nail and hair care products were littering her floor. I noticed Hannah eyeing up my tattered looking fingernails - I had a bad habit of biting them when I was nervous and I'd been justifiably nervous about the transition to this school so they were bitten almost down to the quick.

"We need to sort these out." She swapped places with Megan so she could sit next to me. Taking a file to my nails, she smoothed the edges until they were all the same shape and then proceeded with a lick of light pink nail polish. She said we would put a topcoat on so I wouldn't damage them as easily but while they were drying she asked, "don't you ever get acrylics?"

"No, I don't really like them and they look too long anyway."

"Just get short ones," Bea said matter-of-factly. "They're still cute."

The truth was I'd never even considered spending money on something as pointless as false nails. The money my mum and I had was to put food on the table and clothes on our backs, not to waste on luxuries we couldn't afford. Things were different before Dad left. We had money then, not as much as these girls, but enough. Probably the same as most people. But when he left Mum for the younger (and uglier in my opinion) accountant working in his office six years ago, our main income had gone and mum had to work three jobs to support us.

"Maybe," I non-commitantly answered in response to their nail related suggestions.

By eight o'clock we were all looking like ghosts with our faces covered with white sheet masks pasted onto our faces. It actually felt quite nice and soothing to actually indulge in the skin treatments we'd gone through that evening but all good things must come to an end and the Dean cut short our enjoyment by telling us that for the first week back, we had to be in our own rooms by nine p.m. Reluctantly, we washed our faces off and Megan, Hannah and I said goodbye to Bea and went back to our dorm rooms.

There wasn't much to do once I'd changed into my cotton pyjamas so I turned off my main light and switched on the desk light that had come with the room and started rereading one of the books I would be studying on my literature course. It was King Lear and I'd developed a taste for Shakespeare during GCSE after having to study Macbeth so I'd read a fair few plays borrowed from the library during the summer holidays.

Even though it was still a bit early, I put my bookmark into the book after the first Act was over, pulled my curtains shut and climbed into bed. The next day couldn't be too bad when this evening had been such a breeze and I'd barely even been trying. As long as I kept going as I was, everything would be fine.

Chapter 2

My alarm clock woke me up in the usual way: by giving me a damn near heart attack. It was one of those analogue ones with the bells on top that rang so loudly and suddenly, it doesn't give you any time to mentally prepare for it. After a few years of using it, my response wasn't to fiddle around on the back for the off switch since that would take too long in my sleepy state, but to quite simply jam my finger between one of the bells and the ringer to stop it hitting it until I could turn it off.

7:00 am. I needed to give myself enough time to wake up, shower, get dressed, have breakfast and anything else I might find I needed to do before the assembly at 8:30 in the school auditorium. It was for the whole school so the girls from yesterday would show me how to get there but I thought I could vaguely remember from when I came to visit during an open day a while ago. From there, I was sure someone would be able to direct me to my literature classroom for my lesson at 9.

I had two hours of literature in the morning and an hour of maths after lunch. According to the timetable I'd been supplied with, I didn't have art until tomorrow so I had plenty of time to locate the art studios. I half-rolled out of bed to the en-suite bathroom, switching the light on and finding my yawning face reflected back at me in the mirror. My hair had come loose from the ponytail I'd slept in and stray tendrils swept over my cheeks. Not in a cute way.

After making sure to turn on the extractor fan, I stepped out of my pyjamas and turned on the shower to the hottest setting. Every time I shower it always felt like if the water wasn't scorching, it wasn't hot enough - anything less and I'd be cold with goosebumps to show for it. Of course, at home I had to take short showers since I did this and it wasn't fair to waste so much money on hot showers but since I wasn't paying here, I saw no reason not to indulge in a long, hot, steamy shower for once.

The water cascaded over my body and I worked shampoo into my hair, scratching at my scalp by the parting of my hair because sometimes I was prone to getting a bit of dandruff and I didn't want to look flaky. I massaged soap over my body while I let the remaining shampoo run out of my hair, then went in with the conditioner so it wouldn't frizz. I could have stayed under the spray all day but I didn't even know what the time was and I didn't want to lose track of time and be late so I got out and dried myself off, wrapping my hair into a towel turban.

My uniform was hanging ready in my wardrobe and I pulled it on before settling at my desk to brush my hair and dry it. On my bedside table sat my wristwatch which I fastened around my wrist and lastly I put on a pair of plain stud heart shaped earrings that I'd owned for years. I studied my reflection in my desk mirror. I looked alright. No different to anyone else.

Opening my bag, I placed in a notebook for my English literature lesson and a new exercise book for maths along with my copy of King Lear, just in case I'd need it. My pens and highlighters were already sorted into my pencil case so I put that in there. I filled my water bottle up and couldn't think of anything else I'd have to use during the day.

As it was, there came a knocking on my door while I contemplated adding anything else and I opened it to find Hannah on her own.

"Hi!" she said. "I'm about to knock on Bea and Megan, are you ready?"

"Yeah," I replied. "I'll just grab my bag and then we can go."

"But anyway, if Miss Fisher doesn't let me audition for Elle Woods because I'm ginger, that's basically discrimination against looks which is everything that Legally Blonde is against," Megan explained solemnly while gesturing with a piece of toast.

Somehow on the way to the dining hall, we'd got onto the subject of the school musical which Megan was dying to get the lead in. While I could see that, indeed her unusual hair colour didn't make her the ideal candidate for an Elle Woods, I admired her argument.

"You could always wear a wig, I guess," I said while absent-mindedly stirring my cereal.

"Exactly!" Megan said. "I was born to play Elle; it would be a crime to cast someone else."

"Tell Fisher you can wear a wig then, but it'll probably be between you and airs and graces," Bea said.

The whole table groaned. "It's a girl in our form called Rosie Ayres but you'll know her when you see her. She's beautiful, blonde and her nose is always stuck in the air. She also reeks of Daddy's money." I thought she sounded exactly like the type of person in this school I'd want to avoid and I was glad the others had the same sort of opinion of her.

"I used to be best friends with her," Bea said and then stuck a finger in her mouth, pretending to gag on it. "Vom."

* * *

"Do you think I'd need to bleach my eyebrows?" Megan asked out of nowhere as we took seats in the assembly hall.

"Why would you do that?" Hannah said.

"To match the hair for Elle obviously."

Hannah shook her head, exasperatedly. "You're committed I'll give you that." Personally I thought bleaching her eyebrows was the worst possible idea since it absolutely wouldn't match her natural hair while she wasn't wearing the wig and that's assuming she even gets the role in the first place.

"There is a distinct lack of lead roles for gingers. I'll write a dissertation on that someday, mark my words," Megan said. This seemed to be the last word said on that matter as the assembly hall had been filling up, the earlier students having consisted of the boarders and by the current time (8:23 am), the day students from first form through to sixth form. There were only around seven hundred students which compared to my secondary's population of over a thousand, seemed quite empty.

By the time 8:30 rolled around, everyone rose from their seats for the headmaster. He was a stern looking man but despite that, he had a smile like he knew how to have fun. I remembered him briefly from a little introductory talk he gave before I took an exam to get into this school. His name, as he introduced himself, was Dr. Hilton and he expected hard work this year, respect towards staff, respect for each other and absolutely nothing that wasn't already a given. The whole assembly seemed pointless to me. On the positive side, it gave me a whole half hour to wake up properly before my first lesson and I stifled my yawns in my sleeve and wasn't surprised to see a few other people doing the same. It was the first day back after all.

Hannah was almost dozing off by the time it ended and I think I might have made her jump a little bit when I touched her on the shoulder to ask her to direct me to the room B-12 for English since she was in that class as well.

"It's in that building over there with the shitty broken elevator and a bazillion stairs," she said as we filed out the fire exit doors in the side of the hall as there were too many of us to all leave through the entrance doors at once. Trust me, you'll get super buff thighs climbing those. You'll be able to crush a boy's head with them in no time."

I let out the most unladylike snort in reaction to that peculiar statement.

"It would be a miracle if a boy got anywhere near my thighs in the first place for that to happen," I joked.

"You're kidding right? Look at you, you'll have boys begging for you in no time. You're new, you're a novelty. Not to mention naturally pretty. Give little miss Ayres a run for her money." I was genuinely surprised to hear Hannah call me pretty; I'd never been complimented like that in my life and I'd definitely never received that much male attention. But anyway, I wasn't the most appealing bachelorette at the school when most of them have bulging purses and I still haven't told anyone I'm here on a bursary.

It hadn't occurred to me that in a new environment with new people, I might be perceived differently. Hannah was right. Whether people decided they liked me or not, I was a novelty in the school. We walked up to the doors for the building Hannah had said English was in and as she held the door open for me, I saw the elevator that she'd mentioned and also noticed a sign on the wall informing that room B-12 was on the top floor.

She was right about the stairs, they spiralled around on themselves so much it felt like I was climbing a lot more than I probably really was. Having reached the top, Hannah was already pushing through a classroom door.

"Did you miss me?" she asked with a fake pout at the

teacher stood by a board at the front of the room. I managed to catch the door she'd thrown open before it swung closed in my face. There were already two students sat at the desks: one boy and one girl.

"I treasured every second of peace I got from you Hannah," the teacher (named Mr. Groves according to my timetable) said. Hannah laughed and grabbed me by the arm to lead me to a table where we pulled out seats.

"Isn't he dreamy?" she asked quietly.

"What?" I laughed. "Mr. Groves?" I looked at the only other boy in the room and quickly deduced that it was very unlikely she was talking about him.

"Yeah, you should see him when he's acting Shakespeare, it's so hot." She pretended to fan herself with a book she'd gotten out of her bag. I covered my mouth with my hand to hide my laugh. I couldn't believe my friend had some sort of crush on our teacher but when I looked at him properly I guessed I could kind of see what she meant. He was pretty good looking but he was a teacher after all.

"Don't go getting any illegal ideas," I cautioned.

"Too late."

Before she could go any further with her fantasising, Mr. Groves came over to our desks. "Are you Emily?" he asked.

"Yeah, that's me," I said.

"Pleasure to meet you ," he said, holding out his hand for me to shake. "It's nice to have new faces in the class. Try not to get too caught up with certain bad influences in the room." He cast a look at Hannah. "I jest, I jest."

"He's like that fit teacher from *Pretty Little Liars* that gets with Aria," she said as he walked away and she rested her chin in her hand pretending to swoon. I'd not seen that show but I could imagine what she was getting at in regards to a student-teacher relationship.

"Do you really have that bad of a reputation?" I asked,

referring to what the teacher had said when he came over.

"The *worst*," she said but in a voice that suggested that she, too, was just kidding. "He loves me really."

It was well past nine o'clock by the time all the students that were supposed to be here had arrived and I expected people had been a little lax on timekeeping considering they were probably seeing a lot of their friends for the first time in a while during and after the assembly, especially those not in boarding.

"I'm going to just run through an overview of what we'll be studying during the two year course, so if you'd like to make a note in your notebooks as I speak, please feel free." Everyone that hadn't already set a notebook on their desk got one out and he proceeded to explain about how the A-level course was set out with two plays for drama, two novels for prose, the poems we'd study and briefly (because he didn't want to overwhelm us already) outlined the coursework we'd have to tackle in the second year.

The first component we'd look at was drama so we'd be studying *King Lear* first and I caught Hannah wiggling her eyebrows suggestively when he said this as she mouthed 'Shakespeare'.

The bell rang to signal the end of the lesson at 11 o' clock and Hannah said we should go to the sixth form common room for the hour before lunch started. It was a cosy room and we sank into a sofa in the middle of it.

"Ooh, watch out," Hannah said as she jerked her head towards a girl who'd just walked in from another door to the side of us. She was tall, slim and matched exactly the description of Rosie that I'd been given earlier.

"Ayres and graces?" I asked under my breath.

Why yes, however could you tell?" Hannah whispered back. "Oh my god…"

"What?"

I followed her open-mouthed gape to Rosie who had walked over to a boy I hadn't noticed was in here and was kissing him full on in front of everyone. It wasn't just any boy either, it was Nathan.

Hannah whipped her phone out of her inside blazer pocket in a less than a second and was already sneakily angling the camera towards Nathan and Rosie. As soon as she'd got the photo, it was sent into a group chat with Bea and Megan.

"I guess Bea didn't know about those two, then?" I asked.

"That's so gross, no."

Rosie and Nathan had broken apart at this point and she had linked her arm into his and was looking around smugly as if marking her territory.

"Do you want to be added to this group chat?" Hannah asked. "What's your Snap?"

My heart jumped at that innocent question. It was a kind gesture but I didn't have a phone let alone a Snapchat account. I hadn't been sure whether I was going to be honest or lie if these kinds of questions came up but now it was actually happening, I found myself quickly saying, "my phone broke, I'm getting a new one soon," as an excuse.

"Oh, ok, I'll add you when you get it then."

I breathed a small sigh of relief at avoiding having to tell her but then I felt ashamed that she'd treated me with nothing but kindness and openness and I'd lied to her. To take my mind off it, I looked at the messages flooding into the group chat on Hannah's phone. Bea was clearly disgusted and very, very pissed off at her brother. Megan didn't seem as angry but she did share the disgust, with the occasional message of 'vom' and 'ew' in between Bea's tirade of messages with appropriate emojis to accompany them.

Forty minutes later we were meeting for lunch in the dining hall and Bea was picking at a muffin while throwing dirty looks over at Nathan and Rosie who weren't even looking in our direction anyway. Eventually, she'd had enough and she texted him: **you're joking right? You and bitchface are a thing?**

For a minute, I thought she wasn't going to get a response but then Rosie stood from their table sharply and marched right over to Bea who folded her arms as she saw her coming. Rosie flicked her long blonde hair over her shoulder and said, "no, babe, we're not a thing, as you call it but if you wanna chat shit about me, you can do it to my face next time, ok?"

I felt my mouth fall open in shock at how forward she was but Bea only arched an eyebrow and shot back, "so you just snog the face off anyone do you? Well, *babe*, he's probably riddled with STD's so if you wanna get on that, be my guest."

Rosie snorted. "You'd know," she said before turning on her heel, walking back to Nathan and tugging his arm to lead him out of the dining hall. Nathan looked annoyed and glared at Bea, then caught my eye and rolled his eyes as a smile came onto his face. Rosie saw and unlinked their arms and pushed through the doors.

Most of the dining hall had just witnessed what went down and it was deadly silent until Megan and Hannah burst into laughter and I found myself joining in as everyone went back to their business and soon even Bea, who was still red in the face, was cracking up.

Chapter 3

The following day, news of Rosie and Nathan as a couple had spread across the school, including the altercation between Bea and Rosie in the dining hall. It was even mentioned in the maths lesson I had that afternoon.

A boy called Donnie had asked me about it since he said he noticed me at the table with Bea when it had happened. I didn't want to get to involved since I didn't know whose side he would be on and, as it was, he told me he used to be friends with Rosie years ago so I didn't say any more than just that Bea was annoyed her brother was dating her. Or not dating her. Whatever.

This afternoon, however, I only had one art lesson for two hours. Most of it was spent doing ice-breaking activities and basic drawing tasks. It was a small class of only myself and five other people: four girls and one boy. People whose timetables didn't fit us into the bigger class. We were briefed on our first theme of work which was portraiture and we started sketching each other.

"If you're new, you won't have heard of the party on Saturday night," the boy, Steven, said, looking up from his charcoal sketch of me.

"I have heard, actually." I smudged the shading of his cheekbone with my finger. "Are you a boarder?"

"Yeah, I'll see you there then."

I still hadn't been sure whether I was going to go or not but the girls had been talking about it as if it wasn't really a question of my attendance. It was a rite of passage to go to this annual crazy party.

The rest of the week passed in a hurry with Bea getting more and more irritated every time she saw Rosie near her brother. They were still apparently just friends, 'with benefits' according to Bea but apparently even the thought of them just being friends was enough to annoy her.

Surprisingly, the alcohol she'd kept stashed under her bed had survived the whole week until Saturday. To be honest, I'd thought it would last twenty-four hours tops. This went into her bag as we were getting ready that night after what felt like hours of hairstyling and outfit choosing, borrowing and changing.

The boys' dorms were just the other side of the dining hall but I hadn't been there before - not that I'd had any reason to. The sky was darkening from some heavy grey clouds forming overhead as we walked over there. Lovely British weather. It was a lot colder down south, I was beginning to realise.

There were already a lot of people over there as Hannah had held us up for almost half an hour after she'd changed her mind over how she wanted to wear her hair and decided she wanted to straighten her naturally curly hair which took the whole team of us to help her with.

A table was filled with alcohol and Bea added her bottle to the collection. There were plastic cups stacked next to them and Bea took four and started filling them with something. I didn't really drink, like, at all but I didn't want to seem boring so I took one when it was given to me.

It tasted shit and I could barely even walk in my borrowed heels, I didn't want to think how wobbly I'd be walking by the end of the night. All of a sudden, someone's hands were pressed over my eyes from behind me.

"Guess who?" they said.

"I don't know," I said, squirming away, feeling uncomfortable. It was Steven who stood behind me, along with Donnie from maths. "Oh, hi guys."

Hannah nudged into me. "Damn Em, how many boys have you managed to pull in less than a week? Save some for the rest of us."

I could feel the heat seeping into my cheeks. I definitely wasn't trying to 'pull' anyone, especially not anyone I had to take classes with for two years. Besides, I was way too awkward to even attempt flirting.

"I'm *kidding*, stop looking so stressy," she said.

"No, we're both her boyfriends," Steven said, throwing an arm around my shoulder.

"It's polyamorous," Donnie said.

I didn't even know how to respond to their teasing but I didn't need to because Nathan had just entered and clearly wanted to talk to Bea as he made a beeline for her.

"Wow, did you have to have surgery to get Rosie removed from your hip?" Bea asked before he could even get a word in.

"Very funny. Stop telling people we're dating. We're not and I don't appreciate all the rumours flying around."

I felt awkward being caught up in the conflict and I sipped tentatively at my drink even though I could feel it going straight to my head. When Bea was mixing drinks, I hadn't been paying much attention to what she had been putting in it. I zoned out while they continued their argument and looked around the room instead, fixating upon a group of people playing beer pong.

"Hey, Emily?"

"Huh?" I was startled as I realised I was daydreaming and

Nathan was trying to get my attention and I hadn't even heard whatever he'd been saying since the noise was so loud in here.

"Oh, sorry it's '*um*, Emily' isn't it?"

"Very funny," I said, mimicking his tone of voice when he'd marched in to have a go at Bea. "What were you saying, I didn't catch it?"

"Was just asking how you were getting on settling in and everything." He crossed his arms and rubbed his bicep as he waited for my reply.

"Yeah, right, well, good, thanks," I spluttered like an absolute idiot. It was at this moment that Rosie walked in behind him.

"I think we're gonna go enjoy the party rather than talk to you all night, *if you don't mind*," Bea said as she dragged Hannah and Megan away by the elbows. The drink she had in her hand knocked against Megan's elbow as she did this and the cup squished and spilled all down her arm. "Fuck's sake," she muttered.

"As if just asking you to leave Rosie alone was gonna work," Megan laughed. "Where are we going?... oh." I followed the trio to the beer pong table at which I found Donnie had already escaped to.

"Want to give it a go?" he asked me. I shook my head; I'd never tried so I probably wouldn't be any good and I'd already drank almost all of my drink while the awkward exchanges were going on.

"I will." Bea took the ball from him and missed her shot at the cups completely. "Oops."

"Try again," he said as he picked it up and handed it back to her.

"I guess it's all about being focused on your target, right?" she said. She looked around like she was looking for someone and then threw the ball into the crowd. I followed the projectile and watched it hit someone on the back of the head. Rosie turned around and upon seeing us, glared. Donnie instantly pointed an accusing finger at Bea.

"Wasn't me," he said but he seemed to be more joking about it than seriously trying to rid himself of blame. After all, he did say they were friends once. Maybe she had a soft spot for him. Definitely not for us. She raised her eyebrows as she turned away as if she couldn't think of anything more immature.

"What's your deal with her, anyway?" Donnie asked Bea.

"The deal is she's a bitch," Hannah answered for her.

"She thinks she's so much better than everyone else," I found myself saying. It was like I'd been indoctrinated into their school of thought. "Seriously thinks she's all that." I'd never really disliked anyone before but since Bea and Rosie hated each other and I was friends with Bea, I had to on principle and besides, Rosie had probably decided she didn't like me by now anyway.

"You don't even know her," Donnie said. "Maybe you should get to know her before you make any judgements."

"Yeah, get to know her," Bea said through a snort and she pushed me lightly towards Rosie's direction. "Go be bezzy mates with Rosie-wosie."

"No thanks. Hard pass on that one."

Roughly three hours later, I'd imbibed more alcohol than I had before any other time in my life put together than I had tonight and I'd spent the last twenty minutes sat in a large circle playing the stupidest game of spin the bottle (involving much kissing) and I noticed Rosie hadn't wanted to join in until a certain someone else did.

I was fervently hoping it wouldn't land on me at any point and so far, I'd been lucky. That was, until the game changed to a more risky version of truth or dare which even then, people quickly deemed to be too boring after people stuck to truth and it was soon just a game of dares.

It was quite fun to watch unfold, I had to admit, with victims having to do some things such as giving someone else their unlocked phone, letting them do whatever they wanted and not be able to know what it was they did; someone jumped from the balcony at the top of the common room and broke the table the beer pong was set up on; and a girl got a radical new haircut with a pair of nail scissors. I wondered how we were allowed to get away with this party if alcohol was supposed to be banned.

As the dares heated up, I took a five minute break to go locate a bathroom and when I got back everyone in the circle was looking at me.

"What?" I asked self-consciously as I smoothed down my dress with my fingers, making sure the skirt of it wasn't tucked into my underwear or anything.

"The bottle landed in the gap where you were," Megan said, pointing to it. The neck was indeed pointed to where I had been since Megan and Bea hadn't bothered to close the gap when I left.

"That so doesn't count, it's closer to Bea," I said.

"Nope, it's definitely you," Bea persisted.

"Fine," I said. "Who spun it, what's the dare?"

"I did." The voice came from Nathan, opposite me. Oh god, what would he come up with? Something to tease me, probably.

"You gotta streak and run around the whole campus once, including the sports fields."

"STREAK?" I shrieked.

"Naked," he said.

"Yeah, I know what it means. No way," I said, very aware of all the eyes on me now. "Not a chance."

Rosie leaned into the middle of the circle to spin the bottle.

"It is a stupid dare, we'll skip."

"No, we won't," Hannah said, snatching it from her. "We'll change it. Not naked, just underwear *and* Nathan has to do it as well."

That still didn't seem like much of a better deal to me. Yet, I could see a glint in Bea's eye now that she knew how much this was going to piss Rosie off and the look she gave me was pleading.

"It's not that bad, no one's allowed to take photos or anything and it's already dark and raining anyway so no one will see."

"You have to be joking," I said but she didn't seem to be and Nathan was already holding out his hand.

"I'm down if you're down," he said.

Maybe it was to impress my new friends; maybe I didn't want to be the first to turn down a dare; maybe it was to spite Rosie; most likely I'd just drank way too much, but fine. I'd do it.

I shook his hand.

"I regret this already."

Standing outside the front doors of the boys' boarding house with the wind and rain hitting my barely clothed body, I honestly could not tell you how I'd got there. I had my arms folded over my chest whereas Nathan was beside me confidently resting his hands on his hips.

"Will all be over in like five minutes," he said.

"Depending on how fast you run," Steven countered as he came out the doors. "Not everyone's built like you."

"Ok, it will all be over in like ten minutes," Nathan rephrased. "Doesn't really matter, does it? Just a bit of fun."

Nathan had convinced everyone to let us keep our shoes on but somehow wearing shoes made me feel even more naked than I would without them. Not that I would want to run around barefoot, though. Someone had already got an earful for recording on their phone but some of Nathan's friends were making sure no one else was getting any ideas. They weren't even my shoes; I for sure would have tripped and sprained my ankle in the heels I was wearing so I was borrowing one of Nathan's friend's.

I wouldn't have gone through with it if I hadn't trusted in the social authority of Nathan and his friends.

"You ready Em?" he asked.

"Guess so. Don't really know where we're supposed to be going."

"Just follow me."

"Ohhh god, ok."

He started running off along the path towards the back of the dining hall and I followed, keeping my arms covering my chest and hoping I wouldn't contract pneumonia within my first week at school.

We went around the back of the dining hall and then the girls' dorms. Thankfully by this point, no one was in sight anymore and with Nathan a few metres in front of me and not looking, I dropped my arms and started running faster and less awkwardly.

"Having fun?" Nathan called back, casting a quick look over his shoulder. I resisted the urge to cover myself and realised that maybe, yeah, this was kind of fun. Definitely not how I imagined the night going, but fun nonetheless. Plus me spending some private time with him would be sure to annoy the hell out of Rosie.

"How far are we going?" I asked as we started to skirt around the buildings at the edge of the school campus. "We're not really going around the playing fields and everything, are we?"

"Yeah! No short cuts Em, we gotta do this properly."

I sighed and started picking up speed to overtake him.

"Oh, thanks for the view."

Was he flirting? No, it was probably just his personality. If he's got a girl like Rosie, he doesn't need to waste time on someone like me. I couldn't lie though, I myself had had a good view of his back muscles from behind. Obviously I wouldn't have had the boldness to say anything.

Just to test the waters I responded, "Yeah, thought we should swap. Not fair that I get all the good views." I cringed immediately at how bad I was at flirting back. I'd basically just used his own words back at him. It wasn't anything I'd attempted to do before.

"Well, I can't complain," he said anyway.

We were coming up to the edge of the school buildings and would have to start going around the fields. All the running had started to make me feel a bit short of breath so I slowed down.

"Think I need to take a break a sec," I said and rested against the edge of the building I thought, but wasn't sure, was a science block.

"You ok?" He asked stopping behind me.

"Yeah just need to catch my breath. Feeling sort of dizzy as well, just need-" My stomach flipped suddenly and I vomited against the wall, turning away from Nathan. "Oh fuck… sorry…"

"It's ok. It's alright," he said. His fingers scraped my hair away from my face.

"I'm fine."

"You done?"

"I'm *fine*."

"Sure?"

I gave him a look that told him how much his questioning was annoying me. This situation already extremely embarrassing as it was and now I'd been unable to even hold my alcohol. "We should go back, here, let me help you."

He put his arm around me and guided me back the way we'd came. Slowly we approached the boys' boarding house only to find all the lights in the common room were now off and groups of girls were walking towards us, or, back towards the girls' boarding house.

"You're in *trouble*," one of them drunkenly teased us.

"Ughhh shit. I didn't even think about what Rosie would think," Nathan said, pushing his wet hair back.

"Not with Ayres," the girl said. "The Headmaster, hmmm, perhaps."

"What?" I asked but Nathan was already pulling me onwards.

"We are in the shit," he said.

He was right. Very right. And so was the girl we'd come across. Just outside the front doors of the boarding house was Dr Hilton looking angry.

Fuck. The party was shut down after all.

Chapter 4

After being allowed a moment to put our clothes back on in the now deserted common room, we had to meet Dr. Hilton in an office in a small building nearby. It went about as well as you'd expect: he expected better of Nathan who should at this point be setting an example to the rest of the school now he was in sixth form and that I was allowed to be here due to the generosity of the charity that pays for my bursary and if anything like this were to happen again, he would call our parents.

"You go here on a bursary?" Nathan said.

"Yeah." I rubbed my hands over my arms which were covered in goose bumps to warm them up. There was no point trying to hide it now. If Nathan knew, everyone would find out. He'd probably tell Bea and then she might wonder why I didn't tell her or Megan or Hannah.

"I didn't know that. Guess I don't speak to Bea enough besides arguing."

"Bea… doesn't know. No one knows."

"Why not?" He looked at me out the side of his eye and I looked away.

"Embarrassed, I guess. I thought I might tell her at some point but I really don't know. Never mind, everyone's going to know now." I laughed shortly and felt tears stinging in my eyes. His hand took my bare arm by the elbow and he led me to a bench nearby. We were only halfway through the campus and Dr Hilton had told us to go straight back to our dorms. I wasn't sure I wanted to break any more rules getting in trouble out late with Nathan.

"I'm not going to tell anyone if you don't want people to know."

"Really?"

"Of course not, why would I do that? If you want to tell anyone, whoever, if or when you decide you do, that's your decision and it's certainly not anything to be ashamed about."

He was smiling what I'm sure was supposed to be a sincere grin but with his hair dripping wet and flopping into his eyes, the squinting was making it seem a little more like a grimace.

"Thanks."

"You're good fun, Em, money can't buy good character."

"I'm not really fun; I'm just drunk." The headache that was starting to form in my forehead lightly pounded its agreement.

Nathan laughed nonetheless. "Well, I'd like to get to know you better when you're sober. What's your Snapchat name? I'll add you when we get back to dorms."

"Don't have snapchat," I admitted.

"Phone number?"

The look on my face seemed to tell him everything.

"You don't even have a phone?"

I raised my eyebrows. He may be understanding in his words when he talks but I could still feel the underlying judgement.

"You don't have a phone. Ok. No problem because I have a spare one. I'll get it to you tomorrow."

As much as I would have loved to have a phone - killed to

have one, even - there was no way I could accept that.

"Why do you have two phones?" Is that what it's like to be rich? To have far more than you realistically need when some people don't have half as much.

"It's just my old one. An iPhone 6 if that's ok. I don't really use it anymore anyway."

I tried to make a joke to dismiss the awkwardness I was feeling. "You know what they say about people with an extra phone don't you?"

"What?"

"Drug dealer."

At least that's what I'd gathered about the type of people I'd been to secondary school with. Half of them had grown up on the wrong side of the tracks and clearly it was easy money. It probably was a stupid joke to make, playing straight into the stereotype of the dodgy state school that some privately educated kids seemed to have.

"That was a joke."

"Yeah?" he teased with a toothy grin. "Do I strike you as the type?"

"No, not really. Guess I just don't know how to say I can't use your old phone. It's yours, that's not fair. I can't afford to pay to use it anyway."

"You don't need to pay. It's on a contract for a year still and it would get more use if you used it and then it would be getting the money's worth for it."

"Well… when you put it that way…"

Nathan stood up abruptly. "Exactly, no more arguing. It's yours. Now come on before Rosie gets it in her head that I'm cheating on her."

"I thought you said you weren't together."

"Ahhhh. Fuck's sake Emily, I don't even know what we are but like I said, I'm open to getting to know you."

I couldn't tell if he was telling the truth and this revelation that he really might actually be with Rosie pissed me off somehow.

"So you want to get with two girls at once? You shag her and talk to me at the same time?"

He frowned deeply. "What? No, of course it's not like that. You don't know what you're saying. Let's get you to bed before you're sick again or pass out or something."

"I can get myself to bed on my own, thank you," I said haughtily as I started marching off towards the boarding house. "Stop following me," I said when I noticed he was.

"Boys' dorms are the same way, I'm not following you," he said flatly. Once I was about to enter the girls' boarding house, I heard him yell from a distance, asking if I still wanted that phone but I ignored him and closed the door behind me.

In the morning, I'd never, honestly never, been more grateful it was a Sunday and I didn't need to do anything. No classes, no compulsory socialising and having to show my face to anyone considering how embarrassed I was about last night, not to mention how bedraggled I looked.

Nathan's friend's shoes were on the floor along with Bea's slinky silver dress that I'd borrowed and my underwear and bra, still wet through, were in a heap. My head hurt more than I imagined it would. Up until now, I'd never had much experience with getting drunk or dealing with hangovers. A towel from my bathroom was also hung over my desk chair and although I couldn't remember it, I must have used it to dry off before getting into bed.

I wasn't sure how long I stayed in bed after I woke up but it was long enough to replay last night in my mind at least a dozen times, cringing harder each time. Why did I flirt with someone so obviously taken; someone who was dating someone my friend hates so much; and also happens to be someone that is my friend's brother of all people? A recipe for disaster for sure.

By the time I faced up to actually checking my alarm clock, it was past 11 o'clock and I'd definitely already missed breakfast so I'd have to wait until lunch but I really wasn't looking forward to that either. Begrudgingly I dragged myself into the bathroom and turned the shower on. While I waited for the water to get hot, I took my hairbrush from the shelf above the sink and dragged it through my knotted hair which was still damp from the rain.

After my shower, I brushed my teeth and washed my face before getting into some clean clothes of comfy jeans and a plain white jumper. At this point, I noticed a crumpled piece of paper that had been shoved under my door and I picked it up to find a note scribbled from Hannah:

Hey hope ur ok we're going into town. we tried knocking but think you were asleep. If u want to find us later we'll probs be at the cafe but its up to you - Hannah x.

Darwin school was situated on the edge of the town of Hillsborough which was miles from home so I had no idea what the town looked like since I hadn't had a chance to explore it and I didn't have a clue which cafe the note was talking about so I didn't stand much chance of being able to find them.

It would have been nice to have gone with them but maybe today just wasn't the day. Besides, I had homework I needed to do anyway for all my subjects and I hadn't managed to get it done yesterday.

Although I wasn't thrilled with the idea of going out and seeing everyone, I didn't want to stay in my room all day either so I decided to put my sketchbook in my bag and head to the art studios which were always open to get some work done.

Steven was there as well as a few other people but I pulled

up a chair at Steven's table opposite him. As soon as I made eye contact with him, he burst with laughter.

"You gave us all a good laugh last night. I had you pegged for a shy girl who wouldn't get in any trouble but there you were stealing Rosie's man from right under her nose and out frolicking with him after dark'.

"I wasn't stealing her man and I definitely wasn't frolicking - whatever you mean by that!"

"I'm joking Emily," he said as he returned to his drawing.

"Ok," I sighed as I got my sketchbook out and started planning out the work we'd been assigned during the week. I worked on this for about an hour and a half until my rumbling stomach told everyone in the studio that I needed to get lunch now.

Steven accompanied me to lunch and I was pleased to find that Nathan and Rosie were nowhere to be seen for once. I did receive a few looks from other sixth formers but I ate as quickly as I could then left to go outside at Steven's suggestion that we should do some drawing on the fields outside.

We'd been settled in the grass peacefully for quite a while doing easy portraits of each other and passers-by in the sun while some boys played rugby nearby when one of them came over to us after their game finished.

I looked up to see Nathan in the striped white and green uniform with a sports bag slung over his shoulder.

"Look, I'm busy right now and really not in the mood for whatever you've come here for," I said, peering up at him with my hand covering my eyes from the sun.

"I was just going to ask if Dan could get his shoes back sometime soon," he said. I felt a bit awkward at assuming it was going to be something to do with last night.

"Oh," was all I could manage as I closed my sketchbook

and gathered my pencils up from the grass. "Yeah, I'll go get them."

I said goodbye to Steven but as I was walking away, Nathan came with me. I'd been hoping to avoid him for as long as I could but evidently that wasn't meant to be.

When I opened the door to my dorm, I was going to quickly get the shoes and escape him as soon as possible but he seemed to be intent on bugging me with his presence as he came over and sat on my bed.

"Can I see any of your drawings?" he asked and nodded to my sketchbook I was putting onto my desk while he rifled through his sports bag.

"No."

"Well, here you go," he said, producing an iPhone from the bag and dropping it onto the bed, then delving back into it to pull out a charger by the cord. "It's completely wiped but it's got my number in it and I put my Snapchat username in the notes for when you make an account so you can add me."

"I don't want it."

"Just because I said something stupid yesterday doesn't change my offer. I'm sorry if you think I was messing you about or something."

That little ball of unfamiliar anger from last night returned in my stomach. "Oh I *think* you were messing me about? You *know* you were." I was looking him straight in the eye but at these words, he broke his gaze and looked down at his hands.

"Yeah, ok. That's fair. But I'm not with Rosie. Like *definitely* not with Rosie at all. I don't know exactly what we were before but now… we're definitely… not."

"So you've come to me instead? What am I? Second preference?" I sank onto the bed a good distance from him and snatched up the phone - just out of curiosity. Once pressing the home button on it, however, I discovered it was passcode protected.

"1 2 3 4 5 6. And, no, I don't think you're just another option. Me and Rosie are just better off as friends and like I said before you got mad at me, I think you're interesting. But she is kinda aggy with me right now."

"Cos of me?" I'd keyed in the passcode and scrolled through the home screen. It wasn't a bad phone to be honest. It had a crack down the screen but beggars can't be choosers and I did want the phone really.

"Because of us, yeah," he said, rubbing his palms together as he watched me going through the phone. I was only half listening to what he was saying because I was already thinking how useful it would be to have a phone I could revise from since the laptops I'd been borrowing from the school had to be locked away at the end of each day and I was pretty much the only person who used them anyway since everyone else had their own.

"Don't say 'us' like we're a thing... or something..." I was losing my train of thought as I opened up the Snapchat app. Just as I was about to type in my email address to create an account, he said, "do you need to use my email address?"

"I've got my own email address, thank you very much. Patience with you is what I'm running short on."

"Has anyone told you how sexy it is when you talk like that?"

I was so ready to lash out at him and kick him out my room but the teasing tone of his voice was making him try not to laugh and he was visibly cringing at what he was saying.

"Shut up," I whined and swatted him on the shoulder.

"Here," he said, taking my - his - my phone and adding his username into my Snapchat contacts as if I couldn't have done that myself considering he said he'd put his name into the notes already. He clearly did want to spend time with me. Maybe it wasn't too bad.

He did apologise for last night, even though the whole conundrum could have been avoided if I hadn't rose to doing such a stupid dare with him. But then on the other hand, he's the one that proposed it so he's more at fault than me even if we both were... a little bit. And him not being with Rosie anymore was a change to the status quo that I hadn't been expecting.

"How come you're not with Bea and that today?" he said, giving my phone back. I absolutely did not think about how it felt when his fingers brushed mine. Truly, I did not think about that at all. Especially not how warm and surprisingly soft they were against my own.

"Why do you think? Mentally recovering from the fact that I'd nearly blown everything I worked for getting into this school before I could even make it to the second week of classes."

"It's actually not that big of a deal. Things like that happen every year in first week; if it was anything out of the ordinary, Dr. Hilton would have been a lot harsher than he was. We got off really lightly. A little warning, practically nothing. Last year a guy who's in upper sixth now, who shall remain unnamed, was caught shagging his girlfriend's sister during the end of week party *and* she was underage. Bit of skin exposed and running around is the least of the headmaster's concerns this time each year."

And here I thought I'd been special in the scandal we caused last night.

Chapter 5

The week that followed was far more normal. Absolutely no drinking, no dares and no Nathan most importantly. I hadn't bothered to try to message him or speak to him and he hadn't tried to contact me either, though I was grateful for how handy it was to have a phone.

It passed in a blur of classes, homework and visits into town. There was only one run-in with Rosie which I wasn't there to witness, in which she apparently accused Bea of setting me after her brother just to spite her. Bea quickly told her how ridiculous that accusation was seeing as I hadn't even talked to him since Sunday and that was that.

The first week was a bit of a blip but I'd been studying hard ever since, especially in maths which I was beginning to struggle with. The art teacher, Mrs. Hayes, however, was impressed with the portrait work I'd produced and suggested that I help out with painting the sets for the school's plays.

That was how I found myself having to work with Rosie on a rainy Tuesday evening, mixing brown paint and painting bricks onto a panel that would be the background for a school hallway in the Legally Blonde production. I'd expected that to be awkward in itself since we were the only two people in the hall for a good couple of hours but she actually hardly acknowledged me.

In fact, it was me who struck up the conversation first. "I hear you're auditioning for Elle, right?" The boredom made me do it.

"Yeah."

She didn't say anything else but kept painting methodically. "Cool…" I said. "Megan's going for Elle too, so watch out."

"I'm not worried."

I laughed in surprise. The sheer rudeness was unmistakably more evident than her reply being just about confidence.

"Well I've heard her singing and she's pretty good," I tried.

Rosie put down her brush. "I've heard her sing too. Not voluntarily, might I add. But even if she could outdo me in auditions, who looks more the part of Elle? Me or her?"

"…You I guess." I hated that she was right.

"Precisely. That's why the part is as good as mine."

There was silence for at least ten minutes before any conversation started up again and she knew exactly what she was going to say to get at me.

"How have you settled in to Darwin? Bit crazy to start off with isn't it?"

It was obvious what she was hinting at. She was still pissed off about Nathan because he hadn't taken her back and she just wanted to embarrass me by reminding me of that damn night. I laughed it off.

"Certainly is a different experience to my last school, that's for sure."

"Why? You're still not spending any money are you?"

My heart jumped. My stomach did a little flip. She couldn't be implying what I thought she was implying. She couldn't know about that because only one person knows about that and he said he wouldn't tell anyone. I believed that he wouldn't tell anyone. And if he did tell anyone, he would know that Rosie is the last person I would want to know.

"What?… What do you…?"

"You have a full scholarship, don't you? Boarding and all. That's *nothing* to be ashamed of," she said in such a snarky voice that it was very clear she thought it was something to be ashamed of. "What *is* shameful though, is not even telling your best friends."

"I was going to tell them," I said as heat rushed into my cheeks. "Although it's pretty shameful your stupid boyfriend can't keep a secret. Oh. Sorry. He's not your boyfriend is he? He's just your boy toy or whatever he is. I should have known he'd run his mouth to you."

"Oh you want to talk about running mouths?" She picked up her brush still heavy with paint and angrily flicked it at me while she spoke. "I'll show you just how well I can run mine." Specks of paint flew onto my face and clothes. Luckily I'd been wearing overalls instead of my uniform.

She stalked off, throwing me one last wink at the door. "Watch your back."

I went to the nearest toilets to wash the paint off my face and it was as I was rinsing my hair under the tap that my phone started buzzing persistently. My hands were wet and I couldn't be bothered with any more dramatics even though I knew full well Rosie had just gone off to 'run her mouth'. Once the paint was mostly out, I finally dried my hands and took my phone out my pocket.

There were several missed calls from Bea and texts from all the girls but it was Nathan's that stood out at the top of my notifications: **I'm sorry.**

Sorry, was he? I trusted him, like an idiot, and all he did was screw me over. I'd never felt so pissed off in my life. I saw my eyes welling with tears in the mirror and I shut myself into one of the cubicles. I flipped the toilet lid down, sat and pulled my knees up below my chin and started sobbing.

My phone still had Nathan's text open and I replied: **Why the fuck did you do that???**

Opening the messages from the girls, they were all just full of surprise, as was expected but not of judgement, as I'd worried about. But I'd still wanted to be the one to tell them, not have them hear it from Rosie who apparently had sent around a text to pretty much everyone.

Where are you? Need to talk? - from Steven.

No I replied.

When I stumbled out of the memorial hall into the rain half an hour later, it was Donnie from my maths class that I bumped into right outside the door. He was still in uniform with his bag slung over his shoulder and an umbrella in hand, probably returning from the library.

"Are you ok?" He switched his umbrella into the other hand to cover me too. I was ready to lie through my teeth but it was futile to deny it. Either he knew already or he would soon. "Have you been crying?"

My eyes were still red and my eyelashes were clumped wetly together still so it was hard to pretend I hadn't and I found the tip of my nose begin to sting as it always does just before I cry. I thought I was all cried out but here I go again.

"Come on, come to my dorm. I don't want to stand out in the rain all evening."

I wanted to refuse but I didn't want to see Bea, Megan and Hannah just yet even though I knew they were fine with it. I just felt bad for keeping it from them and surely it would just be awkward.

"Ok."

Once I was in his room, I took my overalls off because I was worried that some of the paint on it might not be dry and I didn't want to stain anything so he let me throw it into his bathroom.

There were several trophies on his shelves and I noticed they said "Peter O'Donoghue'.

"Your name's not actually Donnie?"

"No, it's Peter, obviously." He had noticed me looking at the names on the trophies. "But it might as well be Donnie."

I picked up one of the trophies and inspected it. It was from a maths challenge.

"So, what, you're a maths whizz?"

"Yeah, can't find me a problem I can't solve." He took the trophy, gave it a spin and blew the dust off of it. Besides from when he'd chastised me at that party about judging Rosie without knowing her, we hadn't really spoken that much since in class. He'd struck me as a quiet type, though he had no need to be and I could see the pride in his smile as he returned the trophy to the shelf.

"Anyway, do you wanna tell me what's wrong?" he asked as he took his laptop out of his bag and started fiddling around on his desk for the charger.

I sat on the edge of his bed. "I don't think you're really the best person to talk to about it," I admitted. He used to be friends with Rosie and she's the one who'd just created a massive drama, bitchy as it was, how was I supposed to know whose side he would take? This was the second time I'd had to tread carefully while talking to him about her.

Donnie looked disappointed. "Oh."

"No, I mean, it's not personal. Well, it is personal but not to you. Except maybe it is… inadvertently… I don't know."

Donnie shook his blond locks with a confused grin. "How can it be anything to do with me?"

I was going to have to tell him about what had happened but I didn't know if I wanted to talk about how I felt. I didn't know if I could separate the two.

"Checked your phone recently? I asked.

Donnie felt around in the pocket of the blazer he'd hung over the back of his desk chair and took out his phone. He tapped the screen and seemed to be reading. Hs eyes flicked up to me. "Ah."

"Not quite how I'd put it but yeah. Ah."

"That's…" He gestured with his phone. "… shit." He sat next to me on the bed. "It'll blow over though. It's not the end of the world though, is it?"

"Maybe not for you. I'm gonna get the piss taken out of me. I just wanted to keep it low key and tell who I wanted, not the whole school."

"But you're not the only one on a bursary, are you? There's at least two or three in each year and you can tell who some of them are."

"Why, because we look poorer than you? Isn't that nice. It's not like their names are being dragged through the mud right now."

"I can't help having money any more than you can help not having twenty odd grand to spare for a stupid school."

I groaned and buried my face into his pillow, hoping I wouldn't get paint on it but really not caring too much.

"It's the important things that count and make people like you."

"What important things do I have going for me?" My voice came out muffled from the pillow.

There was a long pause. "You're smart, clearly, or you wouldn't have got in in the first place. You didn't have to buy your way in. I think that makes you better than any of us."

"I'm not even smart, I'm not as good at A-levels as I was at GCSE. Well, art is going well and English is ok but I *suck* at maths. Someone else should have got my place."

"If you need help in maths, I'd be happy to help you out. Tutoring or something."

"Mmm," I said into the pillow.

"What is that? A yes or a no?"

"I think you're changing the subject."

Donnie laughed. "Maybe a little bit. I'm just trying to make you feel better but I mean it, I will help you with maths if you want it."

I turned over so my face wasn't squished into his pillow anymore. "Ok." I did want to do the best I could in school, after all. Even if I did have to deal with girls like Rosie and boys like Nathan at the same time. Donnie got out a box of tissues and I patted my eyes dry, even though I hadn't cried as much this time.

"Do you still want to talk about it or do you want to be distracted?" he asked.

"What distractions can you suggest?"

He shrugged. "Watch a movie? In here, we don't have to go down to the common room if you don't want to see anyone."

"Ok."

Someone knocked hard on the door.

"Emily are you in there? Open up, Donoghue." It was Nathan's voice.

I shook my head at Donnie and mouthed 'no'.

'Hide' he mouthed back. He quickly pushed some things out of the way under the bed and encouraged me to get under there. If I could speak without being heard, I would tell him that I thought it was very undignified. Donnie pulled a corner of his duvet to hang over the edge of the bed to hide me. My bag was shoved into my face a second later.

"Donnie! I need to talk to her."

"Calm down man." Donnie opened the door and I saw Nathan's feet as he walked in.

"Someone said they saw her with you. Where is she?"

"She just left like two minutes before you started trying to break my door down."

Nathan stepped into the bathroom for a brief few seconds. "Sure she did, well there's her fucking painting clothes or whatever the fuck they're called and your bed sheets are all messed up so there's one obvious thing that's happened here."

"What? No, we aren't shagging."

"How do you explain it then?" Nathan asked, sounding angry. I clasped a hand over my mouth to stop myself laughing. "There's used tissues on your bed, Donoghue."

"I was… having a wank… before you interrupted."

"You're saying Emily left two minutes ago… and the first thing you did was wank over her."

"Not over her, but I was going to have a wank, yeah. That's why I didn't answer the door straight away."

"Oh, that's why? I thought it was because you were hiding her under the bed, along with her bag, which I can *see*."

Shit. The corner of the duvet was flipped up and Nathan crouched in front of me. "I think we need to talk."

"We do not need to talk," I said whilst trying to extract myself most ungracefully. "There's nothing I want to say to you, except this." I slapped him across the face but he barely flinched, although I could see a red mark rising. "You fuck me over again and again. I don't want to hear what you have to say about it. I don't want to hear your pathetic excuse. Just go." My palm was stinging.

Nathan looked almost genuinely hurt but he didn't say anything.

"I think she wants you out of my room, buddy," Donnie said.

"Fine. I'm sorry Emily."

I looked at him and felt nothing. "Go."

He left but not without saying he'd message me later.

"Damn, that was feisty," Donnie said. I burst out laughing. I wasn't feisty at all, just very pissed off and I'd been waiting until we weren't in a serious moment to take the mick out of his cover story.

"Having a wank Donnie? Oh my god."

"I thought that would have been quite a good excuse actually if I'd gotten away with it. It's your fault he could see you under the bed."

I wasn't so sure it was a stellar excuse considering it did make him sound very dodgy if he had been about to bash one out just after I'd 'left'. If I wasn't so mad at Nathan I would have found it funny how he strung Donnie along with it even though he knew where I was.

I scrunched up my tissues and dropped them into his bin. "I'll take you up on that movie unless you've changed your mind. I don't want to have to hear from Bea or Nathan for a while." I lay down on his bed and threw my phone onto the floor at the far side of the room. So what if it breaks? - it's only a pity present from Nathan.

"What do you want to watch?" He opened his laptop and put it at the bottom end of his bed next to my legs.

"Surprise me."

"Can't go wrong with a classic Harry Potter. You like those movies?"

"Love them." I really do.

Donnie set up the movie and reclined next to me and I pushed his pillows up against the headboard so we could lean up against it or there wouldn't be enough room for the laptop with both of us on the bed. "Thanks for being so nice. I wasn't even sure if you were just going to tell me to suck it up when you found it was Rosie I was upset about."

"Rosie isn't the nicest girl around, I know but she usually has her reasons for what she does."

I frowned at him.

"Not for this though," he said quickly. "I'm sorry she did that to you." If only he'd stopped talking at that point. "But you must have done something to provoke her?"

"All I said was that Nathan was her booty call not her boyfriend or whatever and she was already getting at me about the bursary before I said that so she started it." I didn't want to argue over this anymore and we were talking over the movie so I shushed him when he started to reply. "Just watch the film."

We only watched for about half an hour before my back started hurting from the angle we were leaning at so I slouched down until I was laying properly and tugged a pillow down with me.

"Can you even see the screen like that?"

"No."

"Had enough?"

"Yeah."

Donnie flipped the laptop closed and lay it on the floor beside the bed.

"Do you want to go?"

"Not really."

"You're not really saying much, you've been pretty quiet."

"Mmm." I rolled onto my side, facing away from him.

After a moment's hesitation Donnie's arm snaked around my waist.

"What are you doing?"

Donnie nuzzled his face into my hair as he pulled me into the curve of his body.

"Do you want me to stop?" He whispered.

"Not really," I laughed and I rolled back the other way to face him. His arm was still around my body and his face was very close to mine. It was so close, his eyes were distorting into one unless I focused. He was a charmingly good looking boy, it was funny how he could look so odd close up but I realised I probably looked the same to him. I pulled my head back a little bit, hoping I wouldn't look too strange.

He was like the opposite of Nathan. Blond instead of brown hair, almost golden in the light. His eyes were like sparkling blue pools. Nathan's brown eyes didn't sparkle. They were more brooding and dark. Donnie wasn't anywhere near as built as Nathan was but he wasn't skinny either.

And why am I in the arms of a boy who is looking at me like he really wants to kiss me and maybe I want to kiss him a little bit too when all I can think about is Nathan even when I'm mad at him? Extremely mad at him. Never-going-to-forgive-him level mad at him.

"What are you thinking about?" He asked.

"You," I lied.

There was only a few centimetres distance between us for him to close and his lips were on my lips.

And then I really wasn't thinking of Nathan.

Chapter 6

I didn't spend the night at Donnie's. It would have looked really dodgy to everyone, especially since Nathan knew I'd been with him so it would be difficult to deny. After getting back to my room and dropping my things off, even though it was pretty late at this point, I made sure to drop by Bea's room. I know I said I didn't want to face her but having someone who can prove I didn't sleep in Donnie's room was probably a good idea.

She was perfectly nice about the whole thing but she said that Nathan had been bugging her about making her get me to talk to him but when I told her he was the one who spilled my secret to Rosie, she took back what she said. "Fuck him. Why's he always got to be such a dick? Yeah, don't talk to him." She asked where I'd been all evening and I told her I'd bumped into Donnie and that he'd just been cheering me up and how Nathan barged in to ruin everything.

"Donnie was cheering you up for a fair few hours, huh?" She raised her eyebrows suggestively.

"My lips are sealed," I said, making my way to her door so we could both get some sleep soon. Bea smiled knowingly as we wished each other good night.

Nathan had tried to call me during the night but I must have slept through it. He'd left me mixed messages being both sorry and hoping I was 'having fun with O'Donoghue'.

His attitude annoyed me so much I finally found myself replying to him with **at least he was trying to cheer me up not being the one who started shit in the first place.** He read the message instantly and I only had a second to notice the read receipt pop up before the screen changed and he was calling me.

Fuck it, I might as well hear whatever he's got to say and get it over with. I tapped answer.

"Nathan I have *just* woken up. Please do not piss me off this early in the morning."

"Just want to talk Greene. Is Donnie still with you?"

"No I'm in my room. Did you think I'd stay there?"

A pause…

"Do you want me to answer that?"

"Do you want me to hang up?"

"Ok, sorry, look I fucked up. I know I did. Real bad and I know you won't believe me but I am really, really sorry and I want to make it up to you and I don't know how but just let me talk to you in person. You don't have classes this morning and I'll skip mine, we'll go into town and we can get lunch."

"Do I even get a say in that?'

"No."

"Wow."

"Please."

"Fine."

He was so cocky and arrogant. I'd really been looking forward to maybe seeing Donnie during my free morning. There was always the chance that things might be weird between us now but I didn't get the impression they would be. He's a very sweet boy and such a gentleman. Unlike someone.

I didn't bother putting my uniform on since he said we

were going into town so I'd just change into it later. I was going to go down for breakfast but then I'd remembered Rosie's text and decided I couldn't be bothered dealing with that just now.

Nathan was waiting for me outside the dining hall looking sheepish.

"You've got so much explaining to do," I told him. "And it better be good but I'm not holding out much hope."

We started walking down the road towards the town and I crossed my arms, showing him that just because I was giving him a chance, doesn't mean he has an easy shot at being forgiven.

"I didn't even mean to tell Rosie in the first place. It just kind of slipped out in conversation," he said, gesticulating as he talked.

"What kind of conversation were you having where it's easy for 'by the way, that girl you hate, she's on a bursary and she'd love you to know that' to slip out?"

"It wasn't like that. She was upset and being all accusatory and asked why I broke up with her or whatever you want to call it just after being with you that night so she thought something went down between us so I told her what actually happened and that's when I sort of realised that I'd said something I shouldn't."

"So when you say you broke up with her, is that you admitting you were a couple?"

We were in the town centre and Nathan was walking into the park so I followed in and we sat on the edge of a fountain. Secretly I thought that was a bad idea of his because if he were to say anything that really wound me up…

Nathan wrung his hands together. "Yeah I said we should stop seeing each other after that night and she didn't take it very well and clearly she thought it was because of you."

"*Did* you break up with her because of me?" That was a

very personal question to ask but I felt like I had to know. He had said before how he wanted to get to know me and although he does fuck up a lot, he has his nice moments like when he gave me the phone and he tried to apologise as soon as he'd realised what Rosie had done. And I'd slapped him in the face.

Nathan looked at me for a moment too long for me to believe him when he said, "no, it was about her. She was being all psycho and I didn't want to put up with her attitude all the time so I said we'd be better off as friends and then she got all teary and manipulative but it didn't matter, I was leaving her." He'd almost completely avoided my question.

"Can I ask you something, though?"

What could he want to know about me? If it had anything to do with me 'provoking' Rosie like Donnie had suggested last night, Nathan was going in the fountain.

"Depends on the question."

"Why did you go to Donoghue's when it happened. I didn't even know you two were friends."

"We're not friends. I mean, I think we're friends now. I hope we are, we just happened to be in the same place at the same time after I finished in the memorial hall and he invited me to his room because it was raining."

"Ooh because it was raining; valid excuse."

Don't tempt me Nathan Horne, that fountain is calling your name.

"Ok, because he's not a dick and I was crying, he invited me to his."

"And then you didn't spend the night at his but he did give you a hickey on your collarbone so now everyone's going to think you did."

"What!"

I pulled the neck of my jumper away and craned my neck awkwardly and saw that he was telling the truth. I hadn't noticed it when I was getting dressed because it was out of my line of vision but there it was: the bruised purple skin.

"Oh my god, we just kissed. We didn't do anything like… bad. It *was* just kissing."

"If that's all it takes to cheer you up, you should have told me sooner," he said, kicking a stone towards a nearby pigeon and frightening it. "It hurt a bit to find you in the arms of some boy you hardly know. Guess I hate to admit it but I was kind of jealous."

I put my face into my hands. Why did he have to be so forward and open about his feelings especially when he knew I was starting to like someone else?

"You don't have the right to say that."

"I know."

"You're saying you like me yet you're the one that fucks things up, Nathan."

"I know… but I am trying to do better by you."

I didn't know what to say because despite his flaws and his responsibility in telling Rosie something so personal, I couldn't fault him for being honest and he had been making an effort. It was me who never sent him messages after he was kind enough to give me a phone which I use *all* the time and me who didn't accept his apology.

My stomach rumbled and Nathan asked if I was hungry. Grateful for the change of subject, I said I didn't have breakfast and he said he'd buy me something from the food van nearby.

"Brunch," he said, handing me a hot dog he'd bought and we went to one of the park benches to sit and eat. It was much comfier than that stone fountain.

"So since I poured my heart out to you *and* bought you a hot dog, do you think you can forgive me? I'll even talk to Rosie and see if I can get her to apologise."

I considered it. "Forgive maybe, but I won't forget." I gave him a sly smile. "And I think pigs will fly before you could convince Rosie to apologise to me.

"If that's the best I can get, I'll take it. Do you need to be getting back to school soon?"

"Well I was going to be painting sets this morning for Legally Blonde but since Rosie was there last night, I don't want to tempt fate in case she's there again. Plus if she wants to make more work for herself by driving people away, she's more than welcome to do that. I don't have anything to do until art this afternoon, which you already knew, you stalker."

"You slapped Bea's brother and then lipsed Peter O'Donoghue?" Hannah said when it was just me and the girls in the common room that evening. "Fucking hell, think Rosie might have actually done you a favour pushing you towards Donnie. He's a catch when you think about it."

"That's *my* catch, get your own. You can take Nathan."

"Ew. None of you are dating my brother," Bea said, waving her hands and dismissing the idea.

"You tell him that because he basically admitted earlier that he broke up with Rosie because he had feelings for me."

"What, after he spoke to you, like, once?"

"Must just be the allure of my charm," I laughed and flicked my hair as Rosie does. It's her signature move. "Anyway Donnie's tutoring me in maths now so I need to go meet him at the library."

"What an exciting date," Megan said sarcastically.

Donnie was waiting in a secluded corner of the library even though it was near empty at this time. He was still in his school uniform but his shirt was unbuttoned at the top and his tie was loosened.

"Missed me?" I asked as I pulled out the chair next to him and set my books onto the desk. He swung his feet out of the way.

"More than you know."

What a flirt. "I'm just here to learn me some maths, don't let last night give you the wrong idea."

"I'm offended you think I would have such dishonourable intentions. I too, am only here to tutor you in the art of mathematics."

"Where should we start?" I asked and we were soon focused on integration problems that I still couldn't wrap my head around, even with Donnie's help. He was very patient and showed me where I was going wrong as I worked, although he did laugh at my silly mistakes.

"I'd been hoping to see you at breakfast or lunch, where were you?" he asked. I was glad he was the first one to start getting bored because I was tired from staying up so late the night before and I couldn't do maths even if I'd slept for a hundred years.

"I had lunch in town."

"With Bea?"

"With Nathan."

Donnie frowned. "I thought you hated his guts."

"Yeah, well…" I clicked my pen absent-mindedly. "He had a lot to get off his chest."

"Don't let him trick you with his puppy eyes and big muscles. Horne is trouble."

"I know, he's not fooling me; I just thought I should hear him out, at least just to get him off my back for a while."

We went back to the maths before we could start arguing over whether Nathan should be even be allowed to say he's sorry.

"Can we talk about last night?" he said. Well, that reprieve only lasted two minutes but maybe I wanted to talk about last night too, just a little bit.

"What about it?"

Donnie shrugged. "It was nice and all and I hope you don't think I was taking advantage of your… emotional vulnerability. I was just wondering… did it mean anything to you?"

Emotionally vulnerable, as if Rosie and Nathan making me angry meant that my other feelings weren't valid, but to be honest, it was just a bit of a weird night. Did it mean anything to me though? I agreed, it was nice. It had been a while since I'd done anything with a boy. In secondary school, I'd had a couple of boyfriends but nothing that lasted and they weren't serious or physical in any way. Nothing was more important to me than getting the grades to get into the school I was in now.

There was a natural attraction to Donnie, undeniably but as far as a few kisses meaning anything… I wasn't sure they did. That's just what you do when you find yourself in bed with a boy, isn't it? It just happens.

"Did it mean anything to you?" I countered. Maybe it would be easier if I knew how he felt first.

"Do you think I'd be asking if it didn't?" He smiled sheepishly as if I'd missed what was right in front of me.

"Oh."

"…Oh? That fills me with confidence, thanks Em." He scratched the back of his neck and leaned his chair back on its legs in the way that makes teachers tell you the story of a boy they knew who cracked his head open.

I closed the book I was working in. It was evident there wasn't going to be much more maths going on. "No, I mean, it's not that it didn't mean anything to me. It's more that we don't really know each other that well and it's early days and things."

"Ok, I understand that," he said, setting his chair right again. "But I do want to get to know you better so then maybe hopefully it can mean something to you too."

Where had I heard that before?

He continued, "The way I feel is, you got charmed - don't deny it - by Horne as soon as you saw him, as all girls do, so he's got in before me and even though I'm the one that got to kiss you last night and he's the one that got a slap, I still have this gut feeling that I don't have as much of a chance with you as he does. Girls always go for the bad boy."

I wish he hadn't said that and articulated it so well because it was exactly what I'd been trying not to think about. I couldn't help it, Nathan is a complete idiot but behind his cocky exterior he has shown that he really cares and Donnie had been nothing but kind so I really couldn't explain why my thoughts always keep drifting back to the wrong person.

Donnie was right, so I said nothing.

"Yeah, that's what I thought," he said, packing up his things.

"I'm sorry," I said as he walked away.

Chapter 7

Donnie admitted he was overreacting retrospectively and a few weeks later, we hardly even thought about how childishly he'd behaved back then. We'd spent quite a bit of time together, not just in his tutoring sessions but outside of school. I found it a lot easier to be open about how I felt towards him and Nathan and we hadn't kissed or anything since that night in his room. Sure, there was the odd brush of his hand against mine when it shouldn't and I noticed how often he looked at my lips when I talked but there wasn't anything that went past friendship.

I supposed I had forgiven Nathan as time passed and Rosie backed down but unsurprisingly, I never got any sort of apology from her. Nathan made his feelings very clear too but I didn't forgive him easily. It wasn't until we were both drunk at yet another party that anything new happened between us. In fact, I was the one that kissed him and I found that I didn't regret it in the morning and I decided to let bygones be bygones regarding anything to do with Rosie.

Things escalated from there, we got much closer, enjoyed each others' company more often but while the chemistry between Nathan and I was much more palpable than between me and Donnie, I wasn't ready to take that step and be serious with him just yet. There was still a part of me - I call it the common sense part - that was leaning towards Donnie. I knew he wouldn't hurt me whereas with Nathan there was that little niggling fear that he'd done it before and he'd do it again.

I felt kind of bad for Donnie when Nathan convinced me to skip his tutoring one evening to go for a run with him instead ("you need to keep fit, how often do you even exercise?"). Running did seem like more of an attractive option than maths which was still just as torturous as I'd found it before having Donnie's help.

I was going to let Donnie know that I was going to cancel. I really did intend to and I told Nathan so and was just typing my message out but then he was kissing me and pressing me up against the wall of a building until his sports coach was telling him to 'get a room' as he walked past us. Naturally I forgot to finish the message.

Donnie wasn't too annoyed about having waited for me in the library for ages and he strangely seemed perhaps even happier when he found out it was because of Nathan. I soon found out why.

"Don't shoot the messenger," he said in maths class the next day. "But you must have heard talk about Nathan and Rosie by now?"

"What kind of talk?" I asked and scribbled out the whole problem I was working on. I'd gone very wrong somewhere and it was snowballing. I pretended I wasn't going to be bothered by whatever these rumours were but I knew that I was going to be and as I started redoing the maths question, I tried to settle my face into an impassive expression.

"That they're back together or hooking up or something. Definitely seeing each other a lot more lately."

"Really?" For all I knew, that could be Rosie starting those rumours just hoping I'd hear them since she hadn't had a go at anyone for a while. I personally hadn't heard of anything like this and I hadn't even seen them together at all.

"Yeah and I know for a fact that he sneaked over to her room on Friday night because someone on the football team saw."

I put my pencil down, otherwise I'd end up being the clichéd movie character who breaks their pencil with the amount of pressure they put on it after hearing something they didn't like. Me and Nathan weren't together, granted, but I thought we weren't going to see other people. He knows that I wouldn't do anything with Donnie because of him so I thought the same went for him and Rosie. Guess I was wrong.

Donnie was reading me, I could feel his eyes burning into my forehead as I looked down at my work. He said all that on purpose to see my response and I'm not mad about it - I would have wanted to know that Nathan is seeing her. I trusted that Donnie was telling the truth about him going over to see her because he always gets his facts right before he spreads any gossip.

"I'm sure Nathan had his reasons but I don't think there's any need to assume they're seeing each other in that way. He would have told me if he still had any feelings for her and he's said for ages that he doesn't."

I didn't believe a word I was saying but I didn't want to give Donnie the satisfaction. Inside, I was fuming and the only reason I wasn't whipping out my phone right now to text Nathan about this was because it would invalidate what I just said.

"Ok. I just thought you should know."

"I'll ask him about it but with the amount of stupid rumours that go around this school, it's not concerning."

"If you say so."

* * *

I didn't get the chance to speak to Nathan for a while because he'd gone on some sports trip or other and I'd decided to ask him in person so I'd wait for him to get back but it was going to be a little while before then.

In the meantime, the sets for Legally Blonde were all painted, luckily Rosie hadn't spent too much time working on them so I didn't engage with her again. Auditions were today and Megan was getting ready warming her voice and though it was beautiful, it was starting to drive me mad. Yesterday, we'd only just about managed to convince her not to bleach her hair. Hannah was hiding the box dye Megan had bought in her room.

Bea, Hannah and I sat on folding chairs in the memorial hall while the auditions were taking place and largely ignored all of the other girls auditioning for the role of Elle except Rosie who we made exaggeratedly horrible faces to each other while she was singing, hoping to throw off her confidence. Megan's audition was just as good, if not better than Rosie's performance so hopefully she was in with a shot for the role. It was all she talked about these days so my fingers were crossed for her.

I got a call from Nathan that night and I contemplated bringing up the Rosie rumours then but he was being so sweet on the phone that I didn't want to spoil the mood. Although, once I mentioned Megan and the Legally Blonde auditions, he asked if I'd watched Rosie and how I thought *she* did.

"Why are you still so interested in her life? I thought you were done?"

"Just being friendly."

I was lying on my bed on my stomach, elbows in my pillow while we were talking. "Maybe ask Rosie next time instead of going through me. I don't have or want anything to do with her. Pretty sure you still have her number, give her a call instead."

"I wanted to call *you*."

"And talk about *her*? We need to have a serious talk when you get back here by the way."

"About what?"

"Her," I said and hung up the phone before he could hear in my voice that I was going to get upset. Bea wasn't thrilled with how close her brother and I had gotten but she was also ten times happier that he wasn't consorting with Rosie anymore so it was deemed acceptable, especially as "you're keeping your options open with Donnie too though, aren't you? That's good."

Megan was adamant that the cast list was going to be put up on a notice board tonight ready for people to see their roles tomorrow but she wanted to sneak out and see for herself before everyone else. Reluctantly, I pulled my coat on and trudged out to the memorial hall again. The door was locked, unsurprisingly, but Megan was picking it with two hairpins and it looked like she'd done this countless times before. The eye roll Bea gave me affirmed this was typical Megan behaviour.

"There it is," she shined her phone torch onto the board and gasped. "That bitch."

Rosie had been casted as Elle and Megan, shining her torch down the list to her name, was Vivian, Elle's enemy. How typical. "I can't believe this."

We assured her on the way back that she was obviously far better suited and apologised for not supporting her with the hair dyeing but I'm not sure that *that* was the thing that clinched it for Rosie.

The next day, we decided to go into town to cheer her up and watch a movie at the cinema. "It's just not the same," she said when the movie ended in between throwing popcorn into the air and catching it in her mouth. Or missing more often than not. Hannah seemed to think retail therapy would raise her spirits where a chick flick had failed and we trailed from shop to shop, trying on clothes that we probably wouldn't buy.

My phone pinged with a message while I was trying on some ripped jeans in a Hollister store. It was Nathan, he'd arrived back at school and was asking if I wanted to go for dinner in town. Since I was already in town, I didn't have anything nice to wear so I thought I'd buy the jeans I was trying on. I didn't usually like to splash the cash since I didn't have too much of it but I'd earned enough working over the summer holidays before school to be able to afford a few things.

"I'm meeting Nathan for dinner," I told the girls as I was paying.

"*Emilyyy*," Bea whined. "As a date?"

"I guess it's a date… or it's just two friends hanging out," I joked after seeing the look on her face.

"Be careful, that idiot is going to really hurt you one of these days."

"It'll be fine," I said as I texted him back. Bea grumbled her assent but made it clear that she was Team Donnie. They left to go back up the road to school and I stayed in the high street waiting for Nathan.

He turned up with ever so slightly damp hair but smelling fresh as I hugged him. He'd probably got off the coach, jumped in the shower and come straight to see me. The thought made me feel all gooey inside that he was prioritising me like that.

"I just passed Bea on the road and she had some choice words to say about me taking you out so make sure you tell my baby sister what a great time you have."

I twirled my hair around my finger but stopped when I realised how cliché that was. It was ridiculous him calling

Bea his 'baby' sister anyway when he was only ten months older than her. He just likes to assert his dominance. This I'd learned by now.

Nathan took my hand in his and he led me past shops and restaurants until we came to Pizza Express. He gave me a cheeky smile as he opened the door for me.

"What? It's a classic first date place." I shook my head but I was cool with pizza. We got a table by the window and when he took off his jacket, I saw he'd actually dressed pretty nice in a light blue shirt rolled up at his elbows.

"Oh my god, Nate, did you actually do ironing?"

"Do you like?" He flexed his arm to show off his muscles.

"Amazing how you can change the subject to your vanity so quickly," I teased. I scanned the menu even though I already knew I'd have a simple margherita. He was still flexing his muscles in my peripheral vision so I pretended to fan myself with the menu. "Stop, don't seduce me right here in Pizza Express." When he didn't stop, I swatted him with the menu. A waitress came over to take our order and he stopped mucking around at last.

"How did your sports thingy go? Did the ball go and all that jazz?" This was a little joke that we had. I was completely clueless when it came to pretty much any sport but since they almost all include a ball, I'd taken to just asking 'did the ball go?' in relation to his sporting activities.

"The ball sure went. We have a home game in a couple of days, you should come support your favourite boyfriend."

"My favourite boyfriend," I repeated with my eyebrows raised and took a sip from my lemonade I'd just been served while we were talking. "Funny... I don't recall having a boyfriend."

"You've got two," he said. "Me and O'Donnie but you should definitely drop the latter because the former is way more handsome." I gave him a look. "Or so I've heard," he shrugged.

"Now you're here though," I said and he took my hands that were resting on the table in his large ones. "I do want to talk about what I was going to say on the phone last night."

Nathan frowned. "You're the one that hung up on me, you remember that don't you?"

"Whatever I got a little worked up but that's because there's this thing about Rosie that I wanted to bring up with you."

"Let me stop you right there," Nathan said. "This date is about us not Rosie. Let's not talk about her tonight. We'll talk about whatever issue it is another day." He rubbed his thumb along my knuckles. If I wasn't so (as Donnie likes to put it) 'charmed' by Nathan, I would have pressed it a bit more but he was right in that we probably shouldn't bring up something, or *someone*, who could cause a potentially argument on the first date. That didn't mean I wouldn't bring it up tomorrow or even this evening though.

"Fine."

"Good," he said and poured more water into his glass.

The date went by slowly but not in a 'get me out of here' sort of way. Every minute was very sweet, although I had to make fun of how Nathan ate his pizza from the crusts inwards rather than cutting slices.

"Room for dessert?" he asked when we were finished and the bulging waistband of my new jeans were saying no but my heart was saying yes. Normally I wouldn't care about how I looked stopping me from eating more but since I was actually on a date, I thought maybe I should care a bit more. "I wasn't really asking, we are having dessert," he said. "I want cake."

Although I protested that I was full, Nathan said he was paying and he wanted to spoil me so I had to have dessert. To try not to burst out of my new jeans before I'd even had them a day, I opted for just a sorbet. Hopefully that wouldn't fatten me up too much. What if Nathan was to get a little touchy-feely later on and I was all bloated?

He was a perfect gentleman though, and he paid for the whole bill after dessert. "No I'm not going to split it, this is my treat." Then we walked back to school hand in hand again. I didn't even think about Rosie. I wasn't sure whether Nathan would want to carry on anything that night in his room or mine and I wasn't quite sure whether we were ready yet for much more than kissing either, but he apologised and said something about how much homework he needed to get done before the morning that he'd neglected to do while he'd been away.

Somewhat disappointedly, I let him slip away to the boys' dorm as we got to it but not before he gave me a deep kiss, hand tangled in the hair behind my head and everything. "I had a really nice evening," he said.

"So did I. Thank you."

Chapter 8

I went to watch Nathan's rugby game even though it was pissing it down with rain and Hannah had tried to convince me to stay and revise Shakespeare with her. Since Nathan had spent time with me on our date a few days ago, I did owe it to him to support him. My 'favourite boyfriend' who isn't my boyfriend.

Unfortunately it didn't go very well for the Darwin team but as the rain was so hard, I could barely even tell which boy was Nathan in their uniforms. Plus I didn't know the rules of rugby either so even if I could see properly, I wasn't sure it would have made much difference to me. I went straight back to my room afterwards to change into some dry clothes before going to meet Nathan in his room.

"That was a spectacular loss," Nathan groaned, picking up a pillow and flinging it angrily across the room. "I'm mortified."

"It wasn't that bad," I said, grabbing the pillow and putting it back on the bed.

"I can't ever show my face in front of coach and the boys," he said dramatically.

Nathan sat at his desk chair but I pulled him by the arm and we sank onto the bed, him falling lazily on top of me.

"Move," I said, pushing him to the side before he could

crush me. "Look at all the mud you're treading into your carpet," I said, having noticed how dirty his shoes were. He was still acting ridiculously mopey so I unlaced them for him and took them off, taking them into the bathroom. I took mine off too when I came back and Nathan was making 'come here' motions with his hands while he still lay staring at the ceiling.

"What. Do. You. Want?" I said as I climbed on top of him and smoothed his floppy hair back so I could see him properly. "You better get this cut or I'll have to start putting it in a man bun to see your face."

"Gay."

I smacked his shoulder. "Don't throw that around. Some of my best friends are gay."

"No one you know is gay."

"Steven's gay."

"Is he?" he said. I'd been surprised myself when I found out since he wasn't open about it but he also said he wasn't hiding it and most people already knew. He just never seemed to talk about boys like I did. But then he never talked about girls either. It made sense, then, why Donnie had always had a problem with me and Nathan being close but not me and Steven.

"Mmhmm." I threw a leg over his to straddle him and bent down to kiss him. His clothes were soaked through but he didn't care and neither did I.

"Losing the game is almost worth it when I have you," he said.

"Speaking of..." I started to speak. Nathan groaned again and covered my mouth with his hand before I could say any more. I raised my eyebrows at him.

"Can we not argue right now? Just for a minute." I rolled my eyes and he pulled me down beside him into a hug.

"You don't even know what I was going to say."

"Something about Ayres probably." He smushed me into him and I felt like he would crush my ribs. It was nice to be so intimate but it would be nicer if he could not break any bones. Why was he trying to keep me from talking about Rosie? It was either A, he's too busy sulking to focus on anything but himself right now or B, he knows there's something he could get in trouble for and he doesn't want me to ask about it.

If I wasn't allowed to talk about it, I decided to deploy my most pathetic female tactics: the puppy eyes. He tried to keep a straight face while he shook his head condescendingly at my antics but he couldn't help a small smile. I had to know though. At least - I had to ask even if he wouldn't give me an answer, maybe I could read his face.

"Did you go over to Rosie's dorm on Friday night?" I asked, dropping my expression into something I hoped conveyed how seriously I was asking. "Tell me that and tell me honestly because I keep hearing all these different rumours flying around that you've been seeing her again, that you're hooking up, that she's using you to get at me. I don't even know what to believe."

"Emmy the thing is, we're not even dating so I don't see how you can take it so personally if I see my ex-girlfriend when she wants me to. You know I would date you in a heartbeat if you said you wanted to but you're the one that said you're confused about your feelings and that you need more time so I don't see how you can hold me to those kinds of double standards."

"So you did go see her." I squirmed out of his hold and leaned my head against the wall, facing my back to him, ignoring the very valid points he had just made. It didn't matter that I need to sort my head out about what, or rather *who*, I want, at least I'm open with him about it instead of going behind his back and letting all kinds of rumours start. I wasn't screwing Donnie but for all I knew, Nathan could have been getting it on with Rosie on Friday night. "She wants to see you, so you just go running to her," I stated grumpily. "Am I allowed to ask what exactly you two were getting up to?"

"Emmy…" Nathan stroked my arm gently. "I hope you can trust me but what happened between me and Rosie the other night was private and she wouldn't want you or anyone to know."

I scratched his wrist, only partially by accident as I pushed away the hand he'd been stroking my arm with. "Isn't that nice of her!" I hated how choked up I sounded. "Usually she'd love to gloat that she can steal you back at any time for a quick shag but now she wants to keep it on the down low that you two are mucking around at night doing things you can't tell anyone about. Very considerate of her to not want me to know this time so I can't get jealous."

"For fuck's sake Emily, I'm not having sex with Rosie. You've got it entirely wrong but I simply can't tell you why she needed me. It's none of your business."

"So you've never shagged Rosie?"

"Well, we've shagged before but not any time since the first week of sixth form."

'Why can't you tell me? I've always told you everything you wanted to know about Donnie but you can't do the same back just this one time?"

I wiped my eyes on the sleeve of the hoodie I was wearing.

"Because I can't."

"Fuck you Nate," I said under my breath. Not wanting to be near him but not wanting to leave until I'd got the reason out of him, I went into his bathroom and locked the door, kicking his boots angrily and leaning against the wall. If it wasn't something bad he would tell me but he's keeping it all secret because clearly it is and he doesn't want me to be through with him because he chose Rosie one or two times. I locked the door so I could have some privacy for as long as I wanted.

I inspected my eyes in the on the cabinet mirror above the sink to make sure they weren't getting too red and puffy. When I confronted him the second time around, I didn't want him to see me looking sad. Pissed off, yes, but not like that bitch is worth my tears. Just out of curiosity, maybe more out of boredom - having nothing to do in here, I opened the cabinet above his sink.

There were sticks of deodorant, sprays that I had smelled on him many times, spare toothpaste and something hiding at the back of the highest shelf in the cabinet. A small plastic bag which I tried to take out carefully because it was rustling and I didn't want Nathan to know I was prying into his stuff.

"What are you doing in there?" he asked from outside.

"Just give me a minute."

I looked into the bag and was surprised to see several syringes and an unlabelled bottle. Correction - judging by the sticky residue on the bottle, it did used to have a label but it had been scratched off. There were loose pills in the bag as well. What could he be taking?

"Nathan," I said in an unsteady voice. The door unlocked from the outside, which I knew you could do if you were able to turn the little knob of the lock on the outside but I thought he would at least respect my space and let me unlock it. He opened the door, saw me holding the bag, and looked more panicked than anyone I'd seen in my life. "What's this?" I asked. Whatever wild suspicions I'd had were now feeling one hundred times worse.

"Emmy…"

"Don't 'Emmy' me, just answer the question."

"Fine, put that down and let's talk."

"Oh now you want to talk?" I put the bag back into the

cabinet nonetheless, staring him down as I closed it. "Lucky you, now we have two things to talk about. So spill." I barged past him and sat at his desk chair, spinning it to face him. Nathan couldn't look any guiltier as he worried his lip between his teeth and reluctantly sat on the edge of his bed, resting his elbows on his knees and refusing to look at me.

"I still can't tell you about Rosie because it isn't my place to." I scoffed at that, about to get angry. "Please don't tell anyone what you just found." I didn't know what I'd found, I just knew it was bad.

"What even is it? What are you taking?"

Nathan finally looked at me with worried eyes. "Please Emily, you seriously can't tell anyone if I tell you."

"Hurry up and tell me then or I might have to tell Dr Hilton that the school's star athlete is keeping some dodgy looking shit in his bathroom. How do you even get away with room inspections, Nathan? What the hell?"

"Promise you won't tell?"

I was ready to explode if he made me wait any longer. "For the love of god Nate, tell me what's in the bag."

"Steroids."

I blinked at him.

He looked away. Maybe ashamed. He should be.

"And where do you get them from?'

"A friend."

"This school?"

"I can't tell you any more than that Emily, I can get in so much trouble for this. If you tell anyone and it gets out, I'll never stand a chance of getting a scholarship anywhere. Not to mention it's -"

"Illegal," I finished for him. "You could actually be expelled for this. You should be. I don't like to make threats but I think now would be a good time to tell me once and for all *why you were at Rosie's on Friday night*. Since, I don't know, I think I have some pretty good leverage over you now."

Nathan looked like he wanted to hit something. He did seem like the type of stupid teenage boy who would stick a hole in a wall with their fist. He reached towards me and I flinched for a second but he just put his hands on me shoulders and spoke very clearly. "It doesn't matter that you can threaten me with this, I won't ever tell you because it's nothing to do with you and if that doesn't impress upon you how much this is a private thing to do with Rosie that I am literally ready to be expelled over it, I don't know what will."

It must be so bad, whatever it is.

"She's not… pregnant?" I guessed.

"No," said Nathan, putting his hands over his face like he did earlier. "It's nothing like that. It's not sexual at all, can't you understand that?"

"Is she the 'friend' who's supplying you?"

"NO!"

"Are you going to tell me anything else or should I just go to the principal right now?" I stood up, ready to leave to prove my point.

"Wait," he said, grabbing both of my hands. "Please don't do this. I'll stop taking them I promise. You can take them right now, just please don't go to Dr. Hilton or *anyone*."

I shook him off me. "I'm not going to take them from you. If you want to take them, go ahead and fucking take them, I won't stop you. You're lucky I liked you so much before all this shit went down because if I didn't I'd report you. Just don't talk to me again. At all, and I mean that."

I fumbled for the door handle behind me.

"Ok," he said. "That's fair… Thank you."

"Goodbye Nathan."

"One more thing."

He cupped my face with his hands and kissed me deeply and sorrowfully. I didn't reciprocate. Until I did.

Fuck it, one last time. But I didn't hang around to hear any more excuses when he pulled away. I opened the door and I was gone.

Chapter 9

When I told Nathan I didn't want to talk to him again, I didn't expect him to actually abide by it but he did. He must have been scared of me getting him into trouble. What I didn't expect from him, although maybe I should have, was for him to be seen hanging with Rosie almost instantly afterwards. Of course it was natural for popular to attract popular and little miss Ayres and graces was the pinnacle of being socially vogue.

It did absolutely nothing but confirm my suspicions about the two of them having whatever they had behind my back and I wondered how long it had been going on before the rumours even started. Certainly they had been seeing each other when Nathan had been acting all lovey-dovey with me. Why did he bother taking me on a date if it was so easy to go into the arms of another girl though? I know I'm a massive hypocrite because I never committed to him because of just a little spark that I had with Donnie but even though Donnie would undoubtedly treat me better than he would, Nathan knew damn well I was still leaning towards him.

But I guess it's acceptable to go straight into the arms of another when the chips are down. By chips, I mean illegal fucking drug use which I still can't get my head around. Nathan had natural sporting talent, he didn't need them at all.

I didn't go running into Donnie's arms after this all blew up did I, Nathan? I hope you're noticing that while you're eating lunch with *her* and practising on the fields while *she* watches. I'm sure she's giving you something else I never gave you either. But I won't speculate. I sound very bitter. It isn't fair because it feels like it's my fault, like I pushed him away, which... I *did* but that was me trying to do the right thing. Of course the real right thing to do would be to turn him in but I couldn't do that to him.

I'm not saying the situation with Nathan didn't push me in Donnie's direction a bit more because that would be a lie. It was like before there was some awkward triangle with me, Donnie and Nathan and now Nathan was out of the equation, I'd found that it was actually just a line now between Donnie and I. It was inevitable but it felt too soon to walk that line. We'd already skipped the whole friendship thing in one night and it has been an awkward distancing dance ever since.

There weren't too many days left to go until the October half term and I'd have to go back home so at least I wouldn't have to put up with boys distracting me from my A-levels for a week at least. My portraiture project was drawing to a close and I needed to submit my portfolio by the half term so I had a lot of work to do. I'd made plenty of portraits of my friends but when Mrs. Hayes suggested I do some more male drawings and I looked straight to Steven, she said "*other* male faces". I took this to mean I'd used Steven's face too much in my work. Who else could I use though? Nathan was out of the question and I didn't really have any guy friends besides Steven. That only left one person.

"Does this mean I get to look at your sketches now?" Donnie said as he tried to hold the pose I was making him do while I drew him. That seemed to be a thing he and Nathan shared: both always wanting to look at the art I created. I didn't think they were that good. It was only the upcoming deadline that made me desperately ask him to model for me.

"Since you've done me such a favour… I guess." Donnie hadn't been in the art studios since he did GCSE art so all of the paintings, drawings and sculptures around us were new to him and he kept moving to look at them all, causing me to yell at him that he was messing up my reference. I wanted to get a good few base drawings done in the time we had so I could develop them with paint later.

"I hear," Donnie drawled, while being careful not to move his face too much, "that I was right about a certain Nathan Horne and Rosie Ayres."

I gave him a dead look. I thought gloating was beneath him. "There certainly seems there was something between them that Nathan didn't want me to know about," was all I said.

"Is that why the two of you can barely stand to be in the same room as each other?"

It wasn't that I couldn't stand to be in the same room as him. There was no problem with that. The problem was that *she* always followed him like a lost puppy like she had the first week of school and catching her eye and seeing the smug look on her face only ever served to make me feel like shit. Does she know his dirty little secret too?

"You don't know what you're talking about. Something happened that's just between us and I decided I don't want to be concerned with him anymore."

"Did he do something to you?" Donnie jumped off the stool he was perched on. "Because if he hurt you I swear to god I'll-"

"He hasn't hurt me," I said. "Why would you assume that?"

"Why wouldn't I? It's Horne we're talking about. He only thinks of himself."

I was going to protest that he treated me pretty well most of the time like on our little date but then I A, didn't want Donnie to know we'd been on a date and B, thought about how he couldn't find it in himself to own up to what he'd been doing with Rosie even when he knew we wouldn't speak to each other again.

"Hmm, I'm starting to think you might be right."

Right that he didn't care about me, not that he only cared about himself, because he's shown he can care about someone else very easily. How could he be such a prick, knowing how much of a bitch she was to me and then do a complete about-face.

"I've hated watching you get closer to him, knowing it was going to end this way," Donnie said, tucking my hair behind my ear. "But I also knew you wouldn't listen to me if I tried to warn you."

I laughed. "I probably wouldn't have."

"I knew from the moment you came out of the memorial hall crying that day that I would never have a real shot with you. Nathan Horne always gets his way with girls even when he's treated them like shit."

"If that's what you thought then why did you kiss me?" I said in a small voice. We weren't going to get any more sketching done and I wanted to distract myself from the awkward question I'd just asked so I swept up the sheets of paper I'd been outlining on and stuffed them into a folder.

"You kissed *me*," he said.

"Um… no I didn't, you kissed me first."

"Um… no I didn't," he mimicked… like Nathan always does. I blushed against my will. "Would you look at me?" he said.

"Huh?"

"You're always getting nervous and looking away. I like it when you're embarrassed; you get the cutest look on your face."

Could he not point that out? It wasn't a cute look, it was a lobster complexion with a matching heat rash on my chest but he couldn't see that.

"I need to go. Thanks for doing this but I'm on a tight deadline and I need to get these painted by the end of the week."

"Go where? Surely the best place to paint is in the art studios?"

"Yeah but…" But what? I couldn't even think of an excuse. It couldn't be more obvious that I was trying to avoid him because I'd just made things so uncomfortable. For me it was uncomfortable, for Donnie, he was grabbing this cloud of awkwardness floating in the air around us and wrapping it around himself like he was enjoying it. "I just want to do it in my room, less distractions."

"Ok. I'll help." He took the folder right out of my hands and left the room. I was just left there dumbfounded for a minute and then I hurried after him after quickly collecting the pencils I'd been using.

He was waiting outside my dorm room when I got there, as I'd hoped he would be - because he had all my art pieces, not for any other reason. "How are you going to *help*. You're only going to slow me down." I let us in and he pulled out the drawings of him from the folder.

"I actually got an A in GCSE art, you know?"

"Swot."

"Not as swotty as you, Miss I got all A*s."

"I didn't get all A*s, shut up. I got two As."

Donnie spread the four drawings out on my desk. "Was one of them maths?" he asked.

"Fuck off," I retorted instead of telling him he'd guessed accurately.

He chuckled and then said, "these are actually really

good."

"They're just guidelines. Stop it!" He was tracing his fingertip along the edge of the line of his two-dimensional jaw line and smudging it. I seized his fingers and before I knew it, Donnie interlaced them with mine. "What are you doing? You said you wouldn't distract me and I mean it Donnie, these need to be done in time."

"Alright," he said and dropped his hand from mine. "Let me work on some of them to save you time."

"That's against the rules, I don't want to get in trouble."

"I won't tell if you don't tell."

"Ugh, fine but if you ruin them, you have to pose for them again."

"As tempting an offer as that is, here's what I'll do: I'll run down to the photocopier and photocopy them so if you don't like my beautiful masterpieces, you'll still have another copy and no harm done."

That wasn't a bad plan. As long as his art is as good as he claims it is or this will all be a waste of time. I let him take two (my least favourite two) of the drawings and go down to the photocopier in the common room. He was back before long and I'd got out my paintbrushes and acrylics paints. I had wanted to do them in oil but I worried they would take too long to dry and I wasn't sure I wanted to spend more time with Donnie than I had to. He was acting like everything was perfectly fine between us but I felt a bit at odds with spending time with him. I felt guilty.

Donnie was pleased that I finally allowed him to look through my sketchbook and research notes to gauge the sort of style I was going for in these pieces.

"Do you think you can do that?"

"Can't be that hard," he said, taking a few brushes and marking some thin lines of paint over one of the photocopies.

"Don't make me regret this," I said as I let him get to it.

While I worked on my own drawings, I cast several glances at his paintings and they were surprisingly good. He was standing hunched over the desk, having refused the desk chair in favour of me using it because, "we all know who the real artist is, I don't want to upstage you."

"Now I may be biased," he held up his painting to examine it at arms length. "But Picasso, Van Gogh and all that lot would probably be quaking if they saw this."

"I don't think you have anything on the Old Masters but it's not bad."

"Picasso and Van Gogh aren't Old Masters."

"I didn't say they were. Stop trying to lord your extensive knowledge over me. All I care about is that I can pass this off as my own."

Donnie scratched his chin. "You're right, Mrs. Hayes might see through this. My work is *so* much better than yours."

"Thanks for doing this. You really didn't have to."

"Ah well, when a pretty girl who's been ghosting you for the last few weeks asks you for a favour, you've got to go full out."

Did he think I was ghosting him? How could I have been ghosting him when I'd been seeing him all the time in maths lessons *and* in his tutoring sessions. Sure, I wasn't as communicative when he messaged me as I was with Nathan before the fall out but I still made the effort.

"I haven't been ghosting you, I see you all the time." There was still a bit of clutter on my desk so I moved things out of the way so I could spread the paintings out to dry.

"You see me but it's different. You don't see me the way I see you." He looked down at his shoes.

"It's not that I don't like you in that way; I do but it's not that simple. I had feelings for you and Nathan, you know that, but I didn't stop talking to Nathan because of anything to do with our feelings or whatever. It was something entirely unrelated and I'm just expected to not feel anything for him anymore just because we aren't talking but I do."

"Do you want to talk about what happened?"

"I can't."

"You can, you can trust me."

"I do trust you Donnie and I *do* want to talk about it but I promised I wouldn't and I still owe him that."

"Ok, keep your secrets." He didn't say it bitterly, which was a pleasant surprise because I certainly would have if I were standing in his shoes. "Do you want to forget this and go for a walk?"

Since he had been unexpectedly helpful, it wouldn't hurt to kill some time. I agreed to his walk idea but he wanted to go up the hill in the opposite direction to the town centre and into the countryside by the woods. "It's going to be windy," I complained but I'd already said I'd go.

Donnie went to go get a coat while I got ready and I went to meet him outside the boys boarding house. A throng of the sixth form athletes came up behind me to go inside and one of them knocked into me. My hands were dug into my coat pockets and I tripped while trying to keep my balance. I couldn't get my hands out of my pockets in time to break my fall and I was only inches from smacking my head on the stone path when someone's strong grip clenched around my arm and hauled me back upright.

"Thanks-"

It was Nathan who had caught me and his hand was still holding my arm. He looked at me emotionlessly and I wondered whether he was actually going to say anything but he just let go and turned away to follow the other boys. Donnie came out, sidling past the athletes and Nathan clocked that I must have been waiting for him.

"Be careful," Nathan said before he went through the door. It didn't take a genius to work out what the double meaning was there.

Donnie swung his head back and forth between me and the door Nathan just went through with a frown on his face, as if silently asking for an explanation. I decided he didn't need one.

"Are you ready?" I asked, rubbing my hands together. Donnie couldn't look like any more of a typical private school boy if he'd tried. He was wearing a schoffel gilet and a Burberry scarf. I thought his signature curtain hairstyle was already private school enough but now this.

"It's bloody cold, I can't believe I let you talk me into this. What an awful idea."

We were sat on a grassy field where the top of the hill flattened out and you could see for miles. The school was closest and easiest to see and the whole town was stretched out before us. My legs burned from walking up the steep hill for so long.

Donnie was already sat right up against my side because of my complaining about how cold it was but he gave a sigh and untied his scarf to wrap around me. Ever the gentleman.

"If this was a date, it would be an awful one," I mused. "I'm literally freezing my fingers off. I'm going to get frostbite because you wanted to look at the view."

I rubbed my hands together but having them out of my pockets just made them colder.

"Who says it's not a date?" he said.

"I do. If we ever went on a proper date it would be far better than this."

"That's presumptuous."

"No, the bar is just on the floor when I can't think about anything other than getting back indoors."

"Can we at least wait until the sunset?"

I looked at the sun, still with so far to drop and Donnie's

hopeful face but I had work to do and this was uncomfortable.

"Maybe another day."

Chapter 10

I always said my education comes first. And it does. My art work was all submitted on time, with help from Donnie, although I could have managed on my own. So if I was academically doing well in art, doing great in English and getting better at maths, would it be a crime if I perhaps, maybe, just a little bit wasn't pushing Donnie away anywhere near as much as I had been and was perhaps, maybe, just a little bit doing the complete opposite?

Hear me out, he's a nice boy, very patient, gives it to me straight even when I don't want to hear it (usually when talking about Nathan), an absolute looker, *and* a great maths tutor.

"*And* he's not my brother," said Bea over lunch on the last day before half term. Donnie had been making a few advances and I thought I should inform the gal pals before we all split for the week. They all were under the impression that Nathan and I had stopped talking because of the same rumours they'd heard about him and Rosie and I couldn't exactly correct them. Especially to Bea. Who knew how she would react if I told her?

"So you approve?" I swirled my spoon through a bowl of tomato soup that was getting cold.

"If you don't shag him, I will," Hannah said.

"Back off bitch." It was no secret that Hannah thought Donnie was cute but she wouldn't make a move and there were plenty of other boys she also thought were 'shaggable' and regularly did. "And I'm not talking about shagging him, I'm just thinking about opening up to the possibility of…" I gestured with my hands while I tried to think how to word what I meant.

"Getting dicked down?" Megan said unhelpfully.

"Shut up!" I said. The last thing I wanted to get overheard saying in the dining hall is that I've gone from one boy who I now don't even talk to, straight to 'getting dicked down' by another. "What's the plan for the hols then?" I asked about their half terms.

"Mum's gone mental and decided to book me and her on a flight somewhere and won't tell me where," Bea said. "How am I supposed to know what to pack? She's picking me up tomorrow from school so I don't even get to actually even go home for the week but fuck what I want, apparently."

"At least you have plans, I'm doing fuck all," Hannah said. "No need to ask what you're doing, Meg?"

"Skiing," all three of them harmonised in a stupid voice. It wasn't hard to infer that it must be an inside joke about how often Megan's family likes to ski.

"You up to much, Em?" Megan asked.

"No, I don't think so. I'll get the train home this afternoon and miss you guys for a week."

"Aww, I'm so touched," Megan said and then, looking past me over my shoulder, said, "I think someone else will miss you too."

I twisted around to see what she was looking at and I saw Donnie pointing at me, as though he'd caught Megan's attention and was trying to tell her who he was really after. He made a beckoning motion.

"Fuck's sake Peter O'Donoghue, what about my poor

soup?" I said as I started to get up from the table. The girls had started chanting, "shag, shag, shag" at me while I retreated and I flipped them off behind my back.

"What?" I asked Donnie who was leaving the dining hall but checking that I was following.

"Are you leaving today or tomorrow?" he asked and we sat down onto a bench. The same bench that I'd cried to Nathan on weeks ago, now that I thought about it.

"Today, in a few hours, why?"

"I wanted to ask you something. Two things, actually."

Those are the words, aren't they? Those are *those* words.

"What did you want to ask?" I said over the quickening beat of my heart which I could suddenly hear in my ears after he said that sentence.

Donnie combed his fingers through his hair and his curtains flopped back over his forehead. "Ahh this is more awkward to ask than I thought but I wanted to do it in person… and before half term. Shouldn't have left it this late really."

"Spit it out," I said and laughed just to clarify I was joking when I realised that might come across a bit harsh.

"Ok, I wanted to ask you… if you want to be my girlfriend?" He almost trailed off at the end. I stared at him for a second too long. "If you don't want to that's totally cool, I don't want to make things awkward between us. I shouldn't have asked at all; I don't know what I was thinking-"

"Yes."

"What?"

"Yes, I'll be your girlfriend."

I didn't actually think about it before I answered. It was just a gut feeling to say yes and in my experience, gut feelings were never wrong. Donnie's face split into a smile.

"That's great, thank you! I mean, oh my god, thank you? Sorry, I'm so nervous, I thought you were going to say no."

"Just stop talking," I said and put my hand on the back of his neck, pulling him in for a kiss. "What was the other thing you were going to ask me?"

"Yeah, so this is really short notice and I don't want to come across as rude but I was wondering if you wanted to stay with me over half term? Or just for a few days, I'll just miss you and you can stay in a spare room. I don't know if maybe you'd prefer it to staying at home?"

There was so much to process. Firstly, wasn't it a bit soon to be staying with him when he'd asked me to be his girlfriend all but a minute ago? Secondly, is he only saying this because I'm... how should I say... financially disadvantaged compared to him and *thirdly* who the heck lives in a house so big that it's not even 'the' spare room that I can stay in but 'a' spare room?

"Donnie that's really nice of you to offer but I've already made arrangements to go home and I need to be with my mum, she'll have missed me too, probably a lot more than you. She's been all on her own and I've barely contacted her since school started. It just isn't the right time, any other time, I would."

"No worries, it was just a thought," he said. "I'll call you every day though. I need to finish packing my things but maybe I'll be able to catch you before you go." We hugged goodbye and he hurried off. Well, that was a surreal moment.

I went back into the dining hall hoping to find the girls still there and they were. They squealed with excitement when I told them what just happened and I had to clamp my hand over Bea's mouth when she screamed, "so you *are* going to shag Donoghue!"

"Why would you not want to go to his house," Hannah asked. "I don't understand, if a fit boy asked me to spend a week with him I'd be on his dick faster than you could say - why is Nathan arguing with Rosie?"

I was about to ask why she'd say such a weird thing but then I realised everyone was looking out the window. Not just our table, either - other sixth formers who cared enough about upper school drama were watching too. Nathan was apparently in a tiff with Rosie who I think was crying.

"Whatever," I said. "Not my concern." And I finally believed it wasn't.

Unfortunately I hadn't had the chance to say goodbye to Donnie before I had to go down to the town train station. Most people just got picked up from the school, usually in posh cars but I couldn't imagine mum turning up in a Land Rover any time soon. It hit me suddenly how lonely I was going to be without the company of a few hundred people after living with so many, even if some of them were first form kids who just get under your feet and make you want to kick them.

At least I had Donnie to talk to. Wouldn't Mum be proud? I'd aced two of my three A-levels and was getting better at the other, including having a tutor for it who, did I mention, is also my boyfriend, mother? Yes that's right, I, Emily Greene, have finally got great prospects.

Donnie had messaged me while I was on my train so the time didn't drag by as much as it could have, although I wished I'd bought a snack in town. After abandoning my soup earlier, I hadn't eaten and hunger was gnawing at my insides. It would be nice to have dinner with mum again when I got home.

It was nearing six o'clock by the time the train pulled into the station nearest to home, another town over from which I needed to get the bus. I wrestled my suitcase and two bags off the train and started towards the bus stop on the opposite side of the road, aware of the loud trundling of the suitcase wheels over the pavement.

For a moment as I came out of the station, I felt like something was wrong. There was no plausible reason whatsoever besides a strong, sour gut feeling. I thought maybe it was because I'm a girl on my own but I was nearly home, why would I feel unsafe now? Through the hustle and bustle of passengers leaving around me, I heard a distinct voice.

For some reason, I didn't place it for a second, it was only vaguely recognisable. It was only when they said my name that my heart dropped and everything went upside down.

"Hold up a second Emily," they shouted. The hairs on the back of my neck and along my arms stood on end, even under my warm jacket. I didn't want to turn around. It couldn't be. Wishing very much that I was imagining things and that I'd only gotten confused, I turned to see who was calling my name.

There was my mum. But that wasn't all. Hand in hand with her was a man I almost didn't recognise after not seeing him since I was ten years old. Yet I'd still know him anywhere. He was my dad.

I was frozen to the spot, trying to take it in. He walked out on us years ago and we'd barely heard a peep from him since. It had been hassle enough trying to get child support money out of him. Here he was now like nothing had changed. And he and Mum were looking thrilled.

"Surprise!" Mum said, waving, and something glinted on her finger that I hadn't seen in a long time: her wedding ring. What was going on?

"What?" I almost shook my head in confusion.

"There's my little girl," Dad said, coming in for a hug. My arms were still laden with my bags so I didn't hug him back but I was so in shock, I don't think I would have moved if I could. "Look how big you are! How was school? I'm so proud of you for getting in."

I flicked my eyes to Mum, as if she might make sense of why we were all playing happy families with no explanation but she just kept smiling.

"What are you doing here?" I asked. It seemed like the easiest thing to say without coming across too rude. Strange how although I knew full well he'd treated me and Mum with no consideration when he fucked off with that woman from his work one day, seeing him after all this time made him feel like a stranger I had to be nice to. Especially since Mum was going along with it.

"You're my family, kiddo. We thought we'd surprise you and pick you up and then we can go for a family meal and catch up."

"I'm not a kid," I grumbled. You don't just turn up out of the blue for a catch up. Mum doesn't just start wearing her ring again for fun. They never divorced, Mum and Dad, partly because neither of them wanted to talk to each other. Dad took my bags and I followed him and Mum to the station car park. Mum doesn't have a car, so I knew it had to be Dad's.

She was still looking happier than I'd ever remembered seeing her as we loaded into the car. I couldn't help myself asking, "what about that other woman you were with?" Mum spun in her seat to glare at me in the back. Apparently it was obvious I wasn't supposed to ask that but considering no one had deigned to fill me in on the reason for all this, I hardly had a choice.

Dad cleared his throat, mumbled, "we're long over" and started the engine. After I'd killed the happy mood, the short ten minute journey home was painfully quiet. Mum only gave me a few minutes to put my stuff back into my bedroom before we were going out again to whatever fancy restaurant Dad had booked.

"What's going on?" I said in a hushed voice when she was helping me put my stuff into my room while Dad was still downstairs. Evidently, this wasn't a one off visit. He'd moved in as I could tell from the coffee mugs on the kitchen table - mum doesn't drink coffee - and other tell-tale signs such as the newspaper which Mum never reads.

"Please don't make a fuss Emily, I know this is a big change but this is good for us. Things have been so much better since he came back. He made a mistake and now he's making up for it."

"What, after six years?" I seethed and then stopped myself before I could say anymore because I heard Dad coming up the stairs. How could she forgive him so easily, when I'd spent the first few years of their separation hearing her cry herself to sleep almost every night? It was always just the two of us. We'd made it work without him.

"What's the hold up? Table's booked for six thirty."

I took the time to look at him properly for the first time. His hair was greying now, not completely, but there weren't any greys before he left. There were wrinkles etched into his skin that were deeper than before and they were exaggerated when he smiled. No one seemed to be noticing that I wasn't smiling.

"Tell me about your school then," Dad said. I looked around the restaurant. It wasn't one that Mum and I ever ate at because it was far too expensive but I had a feeling of déjà vu when I walked in that gave me the impression maybe I'd been here before when I was little and forgotten about it.

"It's good," I said non-commitantly and spun my fork into my spaghetti.

Your mother tells me you're doing art? I remember you were always such a creative child, even if the drawings you brought home from primary school were a load of rubbish, you were always proud to stick them on the fridge."

"Mmm." I ate a mouthful of spaghetti so I had an excuse not to say anything.

"Making good friends there? Boyfriend?"

"Mmm."

He tried for a different tactic. "I wasn't surprised at all that you got that scholarship, Greene girls have always been intelligent, just look at Grandma." Grandma was a doctor. We hadn't spoken to her in six years either. "I wish I could have seen you get your GCSE results. Best the school had ever gotten, wasn't it?"

"No." (But only marginally.)

"Ah well, you still did brilliantly, and you looked so gorgeous at prom. Mummy showed me the photos." I couldn't believe he was still referring to Mum as 'Mummy'. I'm not ten anymore, Dad, or maybe you forgot?

"It was just a charity shop dress," I said, hoping that it would be him that would feel bad about that, not Mum because she's the one that saved for it. My phone started ringing in my bag and I took it out to decline the call but not before my parents saw the caller ID on the screen.

"Who's Donnie?" Dad said.

Chapter 11

"When do we get to meet your boyfriend?" Mum said when we were back home in the living room. The TV was on in the background but no one was paying any attention.

I shrugged. "I don't know. Can I go do some homework now?" Dad had insisted on us spending some time together but I desperately wanted to escape and call Donnie. I didn't even have any homework.

"You've got all week to do homework. You haven't seen your old man in six years, do it tomorrow."

"Well it's hardly my fault I haven't seen you, is it?" I shouted, my eyes filling with liquid rage. I stormed up the stairs despite their protests. If that wasn't a statement enough, I slammed my door behind me and heard the house rattle.

I called Donnie and he answered on the second ring.

"Hey, what's up, I tried calling you earlier but I guess you were busy."

"Donnie, things are so fucked up," I said in a quiet, tearful voice, punctuating my sentence with a sniff. I was so angry but I didn't want to talk loudly in case my parents overheard.

"Emmy are you crying? What's wrong?"

"My Dad has come home, he picked me up from he train station and I haven't seen him in forever and everyone's acting all weird like it's normal and it's not, my whole life has just been pulled from under me like a bloody rug," I said all in one breath.

"Didn't he walk out on you? Why is he back now?"

"I don't know," I wailed.

"Are you sure you don't want to stay at my house. I can come get you immediately if you want."

"No, I want to be with my mum but it's just shit. He's treating me like a child and I have to act like I don't hate him for what he did and be nice for no reason. I wish I was still at school."

"Well if you change your mind let me know, but you can call me any time to talk."

Mum knocked on my door. "I need to go," I said and hung up.

She came in and sat on the end of my bed. "Emily, me and Dad both knew this would be a big shock to you but you didn't call much while you were at school and there never seemed like a good time to tell you so we thought it would be a good idea to surprise you at the station. I realise now that it wasn't but all I'm asking is for us all to be civil."

"Was it civil when he left us out of nowhere? Why would you let him come back, you hated him as much as I did?"

"I know." She tried to rub my back but I pushed her hand away. "But he's trying his best to redeem himself so you should really give him a chance." I couldn't believe she was so easily swayed, probably by his money.

"I just want to be alone right now. You can't honestly expect me to be fine with this. We can't just be a perfect family. You can do your wifey stuff and whatever but he's not my Dad, he can't make up at all for six years."

"Honey-"

"I don't want to talk to you!"

"Fine," Mum said and left in as bad a mood as me as if I

was being the unreasonable one.

I spent the rest of the night crying into my pillow, not even bothering to unpack my bags and when I'd finally got myself together, I messaged the girls' group chat and fresh floods of tears spilled down my cheeks. In the morning, I lay in bed for hours after waking up, wishing that it had all been a bad dream.

Eventually, hunger forced me to my feet to shower and go downstairs for breakfast. I ignored Dad as I opened the fridge which was fuller than it had been when it was just Mum buying food. There was loads of fresh and organic nonsense which I ignored and took out the bottle of milk for cereal. Dad tried to make conversation but I wasn't having it and I shovelled my breakfast down quickly so I could go back to my room. I unpacked the bags that had been lying on the floor and checked my messages again, responding to the pity messages from the girls.

With Dad in the house, I couldn't stand to stay home all day but I didn't know where I could go. I didn't have any friends in town that I still talked to. After checking that my bike was fit to ride, I decided to go on a bike ride in no particular direction until I came to a lake a few towns over. Mum messaged, asking where I was and I told her. Did she think I was going to run away from home? The idea was tempting.

The blue ripples of the lake were soothing to watch as I sat on a grassy bank with my bike besides me. I called Donnie and had a rather meaningless conversation. There wasn't much more to say about Dad and all we talked about was wanting to go back to school. I didn't bother with lunch and I didn't even start my ride back home until five o'clock.

"Where've you been?" Dad said when I came inside. "Went for a ride, I did tell Mum."

"Oh, ok. Hey, here's an idea: how about after dinner I take

you out and start teaching you how to drive."

"I wouldn't want to wreck your nice car," I said flatly. Although I would like to wreck it, just not with me inside it.

"No, we'll take it to a quiet road and I'll show you the basics."

"I'd rather learn with Mum."

"Why?"

I stared at him like he was stupid which I seriously think he is.

"Because I always planned to learn with Mum 'cos I didn't really have a choice and I don't have to do anything with you just so you can feel like you're making up for lost time."

"I'm not perfect, Emily, but I'm trying to do you a favour."

"Not perfect? Yeah, I think you're right that cheating on your wife counts as 'not perfect' but you have no right to be here anymore. I don't care what Mum thinks. You haven't done *any* favours for us. You've missed all my teen years, we barely know each other anymore and that's the way I wish it could stay. After I finish school, I'm going to uni and I won't see you again." I stormed out of the room.

"You don't mean that," his voice followed.

It was my birthday tomorrow and I doubted he'd even remember. Mum seemed so wrapped up in her cloud nine that I wasn't positive she would remember either. No one bothered to check on me and I was too pissed off to show my face, since I would be the one that gets in trouble even though I've done nothing wrong to ruin the family dynamic but that doesn't matter, apparently.

All I'd eaten all day was my cereal in the morning and I wished I'd waited until after dinner to have a go at Dad. Actually, I wished he wasn't here at all so me and Mum could go about our lives as we were, doing just fine without him. In my bad mood, I couldn't even be bothered to call Donnie so I just slipped into bed, hoping to sleep off the hunger, not even bothering to get undressed.

At first I didn't realise that something had woken me up, I just happened to be awake now at 2:53AM. It took me a good few seconds to process that my phone was ringing. There was no good reason to call me at such a stupid time. I fumbled blindly for it on my bedside table.

Nathan's face was beaming from his caller ID photo on the screen. So much for agreeing not to speak to me. I didn't care what sort of late night thoughts had prompted him to want to call but I wasn't having it, especially not at this time of night. I declined the call.

He called back. So persistent. Only to tell him to leave me alone, I answered this time.

"Which house is yours?" His voice said. No 'hello', no 'I've been thinking…' as an explanation for the call.

"What do you mean?" My voice sounded groggy from sleep.

"I'm outside but I don't know which house is yours."

Did he mean he was outside my house, somewhere on my road right now? I shot out of bed and pulled my curtain aside. Yes. Evidently he did. There he was standing in the middle of the street, eyes turned to me when he saw my flash of movement.

"Happy birthday, Em."

"What the fuck are you doing here?"

"Can you let me in?"

"It's nearly three in the morning!"

"Yes. Can I come in?"

"We aren't even talking. You can't just turn up to say happy birthday."

"Emmy it's cold, please let me in."

"Jeez alright."

I hung up the phone and trod lightly downstairs, careful

not to wake my parents.

"What are you doing here?" I whispered as I opened the front door as quietly as I could to let him in.

"I had to surprise you on your birthday didn't I?" Nathan said as he pulled me in for a hug.

"In case it isn't obvious, it is the middle of the night. What were you thinking?"

"Well since Bea said you were having a hard time with your dad being home, I thought you could use some cheering up and you need to celebrate your birthday so here I am."

"How did you even get here?"

"Um… well Bea and Mum are in Italy so it was just me and Dad home and then he had to go to Germany for business last night so I waited until he left and then…" He scratched the back of his neck in that way he does when he's about to admit something.

"Then what, Nate?"

"Then I stole Mum's car and drove here."

"Are you joking?" I said, forgetting to lower my voice. "How did you even know my address plus it must have taken hours for you to get here."

"You have your location on on your phone and it only took a few hours."

"A few illegal hours," I mumbled. "So you've come here for what?"

"To make your birthday memorable."

"How…?"

"I'll take you back to my place and then we can think about what you wanna do for the day in the morning."

He couldn't seriously be suggesting that I sneak out of my house at three in the morning to go for an illegal drive to a boy's house who isn't even my boyfriend. I would have to be completely mental. On the other hand, I did want to get out of here at least for my birthday and he'd already came all this way.

"Fine," I relented and started shoving a pair of shoes on and unhooked a jacket from the wall. "Let's get out of here."

Luckily Mum's room (Mum *and Dad's room*) was at the back of the house so they wouldn't have been able to see anything out of the window as Nathan noisily started the car. I wondered if that was what had woken me up in the first place.

"How come you're talking to me now? I thought we agreed not to."

Nathan shrugged. "You're letting me aren't you?"

I rolled my eyes but it was too dark for him to notice. It had been hours since I last ate and I was so hungry that my stomach was actually hurting. Even if I wanted to, I don't think I would have been able to go back to sleep.

"Are you sure you're alright to drive?" I asked once we hit the motorway. "You must have been going for hours and we've still got ages to go. Oh my god, why did I agree to this? It's so dangerous."

My stomach growled loudly as I complained.

"Are you sure you're eating?" Nathan joked.

"I haven't actually. I've been trying to avoid Dad for ages so I only had breakfast."

Nathan tried to convince me that we needed to stop so I could eat something but I just wanted to get to his place.

"Don't be stupid," he said and flicked the indicator when we got to the next service station. "There's a McDonalds. We're getting you a burger or something." Although I felt bad that he was doing so much for me, a burger was sounding really, really good right now. He bought two large meals and we sat under lights that felt particularly fluorescent at night and ate.

"What's Bea doing in Italy?" I asked as Nathan yawned widely.

"Fuck knows. Fashion shows or whatever they do over there. Whatever mum's decided on." He was still yawning.

"Nate, we need to sleep after this. There's a Travelodge right there, I'll pay."

He exhaled and looked like he was contemplating it. "I'll pay," he said. Just as well, I hadn't brought any money with me.

"One bed or two?" the receptionist asked.

"Two," I said.

"One," Nathan said.

The receptionist flicked her eyes between us.

"Two," sighed Nathan, taking his wallet out of his pocket.

"Why did you say two?" he asked as we climbed the stairs to the second level.

"Because it wouldn't be appropriate to sleep in the same bed."

Nathan found the right room and inserted the key card. "We could always push them together if you change your mind," he said. I fumbled for the light switches in the dark.

"I'm not going to change my mind Nate, I'm with Donnie." I found the light switch and for a second saw his face looking like a child who had just been told Christmas was going to be cancelled before he recovered.

"Oh. Good for you… and him."

"Don't make it weird."

"I'm not going to make it weird. We're friends and that's fine. It's my fault anyway." He kicked his shoes off and flopped down on one of the beds. "I haven't been using by the way."

"Using what?" I sat on the other bed.

"… the steroids."

"Oh, right… let's talk about something else."

"Or we could just go to sleep. I'm ready to pass out."

"Me too."

"Ok, night."

"Night."

I couldn't remember where I was at first when I woke up. The bed opposite me was empty and the shower was running. My phone said the time was 8:43. The TV remote rested on the little table between our beds and I turned the TV on which was set to a kids channel playing the Mr. Bean animated series.

"Didn't realise that was your thing."

The shower had turned off and I hadn't noticed. Nathan was naked but for a towel wrapped around his waist. I rolled my eyes.

"Should we get breakfast here or at McDonalds?" he asked.

"We can't have McDonalds again." I said. "It's so unhealthy."

"Since when were you a health freak?"

"Says you, you're the athlete, with all those horrible protein shakes. I'm gonna shower."

I washed my face in the sink first, wiping away the crust at my eyes and checking my swollen eyelids from being awake for too long last night. I took a brisk shower and unlike Nathan, dried off in the bathroom. It felt a bit gross getting back into the same clothes again but Nathan had said I could change into some of Bea's when we got to his house. The hairdryer the hotel provided was extremely gutless as I attempted to dry and comb out my knotted hair with my fingers.

"Can you be quieter, I can't hear Mr. Bean," Nathan teased.

"Shut up. He doesn't talk, you prick."

When I finished drying my hair, I turned to see Nathan holding my phone. I was surprised it still had any battery.

"Someone's been trying to call you," he said. It must be my Mum, I was going to text her and let her know I was going to be away for the day but I'd forgot. "Now they're texting."

I took the phone from him and read the message.

Where are you?!

I'd assumed it would be from my Mum but this was a different number that I didn't recognise. Dad, presumably.

Gone out with a friend for my birthday. Not that he would have remembered.

You selfish bitch. This is the first of your birthdays I've been here for in ages and you fuck off before we can even surprise you with anything. I've been up since six so I don't know how early you went out today but this is ridiculous, come home right now.

Nathan read the message over my shoulder. Annoyingly my eyes filled with tears.

"Sorry, I didn't mean to make things awkward between you and your dad."

"You didn't! It's him, it's his fault." My voice was sounding so choked up and the tears slid down my cheeks. "It's always his-"

Nathan pulled me into a hug and my face smushed against his bare chest which he still hadn't bothered to clothe. I cried against him for a bit but it was kind of gross because I was getting snotty so I went to the bathroom to blow my nose.

"That was… sorry. Can you get dressed for heaven's sake so we can go to breakfast?" He mock saluted and I turned away quickly as he started to undo his towel. A call came in on my phone and for a second I was worried it was Dad but it was Donnie.

"Hey?"

"Happy birthday Em!" I held the phone away from my ear, not expecting him to be so loud. Nathan (now dressed) mouthed 'Donnie?' and I nodded.

"Thank you Donnie." I was still quite in shock from the message from Dad and I didn't know what to say on the phone. My head was just reeling.

"Are you doing much to celebrate?" Donnie asked. I looked to Nathan who was stood with his arms folded over his chest. For a moment I felt guilty that I was here with him when I could be with Donnie, my actual boyfriend.

"Um… I don't know really."

"Well I've got you a birthday present for when I see you at school. I should have got you something to give you before we left for half term but I didn't know if you'd agree to date me by then," he laughed.

"Don't be silly. You didn't need to get me anything anyway."

"You're my girlfriend you goose. I love being able to say that."

Nathan was yawning and making motions with his head towards the door, clearly ready for us to leave.

"I need to go Donnie. Thanks for calling, can't wait to see you."

"Ok, have a great day. Bye Emmy."

"Bye."

"Breakfast time," Nathan said as if that phone call hadn't even happened. Maybe he didn't care but for me it felt so weird to be spending my birthday with the wrong boy. But he went to all the effort to come get me, it's not like I could say no and it's not like I'm cheating on Donnie. I'm not going to jump into bed with Nathan.

We went downstairs and Nathan dropped the keycard in the drop off slot and we went to get breakfast.

Chapter 12

"Fuck off, that is *not* your house," I said as Nathan drove us along a very long drive. "That is huge."

"Yeah, it's pretty big." He shrugged it off and parked in the driveway. I looked at the expanse of the building and couldn't get over how posh it was. Then I noticed something on the wall.

"Oh my God, Nathan you have cameras on your house. We're going to get caught!"

"No we're not. No one ever checks them."

I wasn't reassured much. The last thing I needed after getting in trouble with my parents was getting in trouble with anyone else's. "Come on," he said, getting out of the car. He gave me the 'grand tour' of the house and showed me into Bea's room so I could raid her wardrobe for some clothes to change into.

Nathan had already given me the Wi-Fi password so I sent a snap of myself in Bea's room to the girls group chat.

WHAT is happening???? Bea replied. I told them all about what had happened.

What is Donnie going to think? Megan messaged.

I bit my lip in worry; I was feeling worse and worse about how Donnie would react. Before he could hear from anyone else, I decided to message him. All I said was that I was out with Nathan for my birthday and that it was his surprise. I didn't know anything about it.

That wasn't really the whole truth, was it? Why wasn't I just honest with him earlier? My phone needed charging, I noticed. Donnie didn't reply until I'd got dressed and gone back downstairs to see Nathan playing with his boisterous labrador.

"This is Max," he explained as he went bounding over to me, jumping up and setting his paws on my thighs. My phone rang in my jeans pocket.

"Hello?" I said after seeing it was Donnie.

"I'm confused. How long have you been with Nathan? I thought you couldn't stand him?" The call volume was loud enough for Nathan to be able to hear.

"Just since this morning and yeah, I know, but I needed to get out of the house after everything with my parents. I can see... what it might look like to you but it isn't like that, I promise."

Nathan turned away to fill a glass with water but I still caught the small grin on his face.

"Ok... it would have been nice if we could have spent the day together since I said I would come and get you if you wanted but... ok."

"Please don't be angry."

"I'm not angry. I trust you. Just make sure-"

"Make sure what?" I asked after he went quiet for a few moments. "Hello?"

The phone had died.

"I need to charge my phone," I told Nathan.

"So what do you want to do today?" He asked after finding me a charger.

"I don't know... you really shouldn't risk driving anywhere again. Is there anywhere we could walk or something?"

"We could always chill here. I'm still really tired from last night."

"Oh fuck OFF!" I screamed after Nathan hit me with yet another banana skin on Mario Kart. Max was curled up with his head against my crossed legs and I was sitting on the floor in front of the sofa Nathan was sitting on. He'd just sent me from second to sixth place. I'll give you one guess as to who was coming first.

My phone was still in the kitchen charging and we'd been playing a Wii game for a couple of hours. The flatscreen TV was ridiculously big. "What can you chef up for lunch?" I asked.

"Uhh, I can order Dominos. That's probably better than me trying to cook."

"If it saves me from food poisoning, fine," I teased. Nathan gently whacked me on the top of the head with his remote. After I passed the finish line in what was now fourth place, he turned the game off and started ordering the pizza on his phone.

"Which pizza do you want?" he asked.

I sat on the sofa and looked over his shoulder at the menu on his phone. "The chicken feast one but take the mushrooms off and put onions on."

"I'll order it for… half an hour?"

I nodded, not fussed but he suddenly jumped up. "I know what we're missing," he said. "We need to make a cake."

I followed him into the kitchen. "If you can't even do pizza, what makes you think you'll be able to bake a cake?"

"Because," Nathan said, rifling through cupboards. "You can't go wrong with pre-made mix." He finally found what he was looking for and pulled out a sachet of devil's food cake mix. "Bea loves them."

Nathan got out a bowl and started getting the extra

ingredients he needed. "Seventeen now, you're catching up to me," he said even though it was barely a month since his birthday.

"I didn't know you could read," I joked as he squinted at the tiny instructions.

"Shut up, do you want cake or not?"

"I think it's you who wants it more than me."

"I never pass up a good reason for cake. Sweet tooth, me." When he'd mixed it all together and put it into a tin and then into the oven, I went back into the living room where Max was waiting for me to sit down so he could lay his head on my lap again.

"Hey, how come you and Rosie were arguing yesterday at school?" I suddenly remembered. "I thought you two were super close now."

I couldn't see Nathan since he was around the corner still in the kitchen but when he came back with a can of beer, I wasn't sure if I was going to get an answer or not, but then he said, "she seemed to think she and I are in a relationship." He cracked the can open. "And I don't. She wasn't so happy about it."

Where have we seen this situation before? It's always Nathan and Rosie. It's always going to happen isn't it? It's like Twilight with team Edward and team Jacob. And I'm Jacob.

I don't know, I haven't actually seen Twilight.

"Have you two been shagging then?" I hated how crude that sounded.

He ran his hand over his stubbly chin and pierced me with his brown-eyed gaze.

"Do you want a beer too?"

"Depends on your answer."

I found myself with a beer in my hands and assumed that was my answer. As much as I'd tried to convince myself it was all in my head and he really did care about me more, he'd finally as well as confessed all this secrecy about her was exactly as I'd suspected.

"It was only since you stopped talking to me."

A likely story, I was sure. I took a swig from my beer and went to go get my phone from where it was charging in the kitchen just for an excuse to get away from him a bit. It hadn't reconnected to the Wi-Fi so I had no notifications. When I got back to the sofa, I sat at the end furthest from Nathan, making it pretty clear I was in a mood with him and pretended to be interested in something on my phone.

"You mad at me?" he asked.

I made a facial expression that made it obvious.

He groaned. "It didn't *mean* anything and why do you care anyway? You're with Donnie."

"I don't care," I said, crossing my arms. "I just think it's rude that you strung me along saying how you only wanted to be with me for ages and then get with her anyway."

"It was just rebounding. I was pissed off because I blew my chance with you and you know what Ayres is like. She wants me and everyone knows it so I just went along with it. It sure didn't make me feel any better. It's *you* that I love."

I actually laughed. "If you *loved* me, Nathan, you wouldn't sleep with anyone else!"

At this sentence he flinched and downed the rest of his drink.

"Emmy I just think we see sex differently. It probably means more to you because you're a virgin whereas for me it doesn't mean anything - especially with Rosie."

"What makes you think I'm a virgin?"

He just raised his eyebrows.

"Ok, fine, maybe."

Max seemed to sense the tension between us as he sat up staring at us and whined. Nathan stroked behind the dog's ears.

"It's ok Maxy. Want to get some dinner?" Max instantly stood up and started wagging his tail. While Nathan went to go feed the dog, I texted Donnie. I told him about how Dad had turned hostile towards me and I just needed to get away since things had turned so ugly.

The TV was still playing some news channel since it hadn't been turned off after playing Mario Kart and I stared at it after I sent the text, just zoning out.

"Are you crying? Emily?"

I snapped out of my haze and realised my cheeks were wet. I hadn't even noticed I was crying. How embarrassing. With a concerned look on his face, Nathan pulled me into a hug and I sniffled, careful not to ugly cry into his clothes.

"I'm sorry I slept with Rosie. If I could take it back I would."

"It's not about Rosie," I said pulling away and wiping my eyes again. "It's just my Dad and everything. It's ruined everything. It's ruining what I have with Mum as well and I don't want to go home again. It completely *sucks* and I don't know what to do."

The doorbell rang and I jumped before realising it would just be the pizza arriving.

"I'll be right back." Nathan disappeared to the front door and came back with two pizza boxes and a large bottle of coke he must have thrown in as well. He put them down on a low table by the sofa and sat next to me. "It's gonna be ok, you can stay here all week until we go back to school."

I relaxed into his shoulder. "I can't stay all week, it'll look really dodgy," I protested. "I have to go home."

"Just stay the night and deal with it tomorrow." He played with strands of my hair and the feeling gave me goosebumps.

"Fine."

* * *

"I still can't decide whether I hate you or not," I said several hours and drinks later.

"Bummer," Nathan said. "And here I thought you really liked me."

"You can be…" I searched for the right words. "So *mean*."

Nathan made a puppy dog face to match Max's. He was showing me his bedroom and I sat on his unmade bed. It was already dark outside and it had started to get darker sooner in the day this late in October.

"I'm cold," I said, wrapping his football themed duvet around me. You can bet I made fun of him for it first. Nathan went to turn the heating on and my phone pinged with a text from Donnie.

Sorry I didn't have my phone on me for a while. Are you home now? Everything ok? You have to stay at mine for the rest of the week now. I'm not asking.

What was I meant to say? I had to go along with it or else look like the worst girlfriend in the world.

Yeah just got home. Ok you win. Send me your address and I'll get a train to yours tomorrow. I'm not staying here.

I quickly checked that my SnapMaps location was turned off just in case.

"Alright?" Nathan asked when he came back in.

I held up my phone. "Yeah just Donnie. He thinks I'm back home and I have to stay at his from tomorrow."

"Oh come on," he said, grabbing my phone and looking at the text. "You can just stay here."

"*Donnie* is my boyfriend. I will stay with him."

Nathan sat on the bed and I grabbed the phone back from him, setting it on the bedside table.

"Donnie doesn't even realise how lucky he is." He laced his fingers between mine and I found myself searching his face, trying to reveal his intentions. I had to get a grip.

"Stop it. You're always saying things you know you

shouldn't and it's not fair. I'm going to bed."

I made to leave but Nathan stopped me, holding my hand tighter and I stumbled, falling back on top of him.

"Don't be silly, it's only just past ten o'clock." We were an awkward tangle of myself, Nathan and duvet. I moved my hands so I could support myself a bit better in case I was squishing him. He was probably too strong to be crushed by someone as small as me but nevertheless.

He smiled when he noticed and he tucked a fallen strand of hair behind my ear. His smile was contagious. "There we go," he said.

"You're so annoying," I stated.

"So annoying," he agreed. "But so charming, I hear."

"Who said that?"

One of his hands was sneaking around my waist and he was stupid if he thought I didn't notice.

"Everyone."

With a tug of the arm he had looped behind my back, he pressed me flush against him and I gasped. Our faces were so close to each other I could feel his breath caress my cheek. He rolled us over so I was under him.

"What are you doing?" I whispered.

"I won't do anything you don't want."

My heart had started thumping loudly after he flipped us over and all I could think about was how wrong this was but also how much I still wanted it. For just a moment, I hesitated while I still had the chance to do the right thing.

I didn't want to do the right thing.

I pressed my lips against Nathan's and he kissed back instantly, deepening it with his tongue and bringing the hand he wasn't leaning on up my waist. His warm fingers touched the skin of my stomach as he started to lift my top.

"Are you sure, Em?"

"Fuck, I'm sure. Take it off," I said. He single-handedly

pulled it off me and I started to take his shirt off but couldn't reach all the way so he helped me. It wasn't like I hadn't seen his bare chest plenty of times before but this was different. Normally he was on a playing field not in bed with me, our breaths heavy and our chests heaving together. As I arched my back into him, his fingers deftly unclipped my bra and I tried not to think about how easy it was for him and how much practise he must have with other girls.

He kissed down my neck and I tangled my fingers in his floppy brown locks as he pulled my loose bra from my body. Suddenly embarrassed and feeling much more vulnerable, I covered my chest with my arms but he pulled them gently away, planting more kisses.

"I'm going to ask you one more time. This is definitely what you want to do?"

"Yes."

Chapter 13

I could smell Nathan's familiar scent when I woke up before I even opened my eyes. For a moment, the thrill of last night washed over me but then I remembered Donnie and it was replaced with regret. Actually, was it even regret, or just shame? I wasn't sure I regretted it and that was the worst part.

Nathan stirred next to me. His soft eyelashes fluttered open and he took me in as he woke.

"How're you feeling?" He asked. I was feeling awful in all honesty. I'd really just cheated on Donnie and I was supposed to see him today. There was no way I could look that poor sweet boy in the eyes and tell him what I'd done. It would crush him. Also physically, it wasn't feeling amazing down there either.

"Shit." I rubbed my eyes with the heels of my hands. "It wasn't meant to go like this. I've gone and ruined everything."

Nathan looked like he'd been slapped.

"Ro- Em! It's fine..." He grimaced.

"Did you seriously nearly call me Rosie just then?" I didn't even wait for his answer. I knew what I heard. Our clothes were scattered on the floor which I grabbed quickly without letting him see too much of my body before running to the bathroom. With the door locked, I broke down. Donnie was too good for me and Nathan was an arse. Always had been.

I gripped the sides of the sink until I finished crying. I needed to wash, there was a bit of dried blood on my legs so I turned on the shower. Faintly, Nathan's voice came from outside but with the water pressure, I couldn't make out what he was saying.

"Take me home," I said when I came out the bathroom find Nathan outside the door in just his boxers. "Or I'm getting a train. Either way."

Nathan hurried to catch up with me as I went back to his room to grab my phone so I could leave.

"Can't we talk about this? I only accidentally said Rosie because I'm used to arguing with her and we were arguing. I wasn't thinking you were her or anything. It's just habit."

"I really don't care. This is so fucked up. I don't even know what I'm meant to do now but you are so bad for me." He only served to show me time and time again why I should have just picked Donnie from the start and now, because of him, I've screwed my chance with Donnie. It wasn't all him, last night was on me too. I wasn't even sure I regretted it before he mentioned Rosie.

Then it occurred to me. What if I was jealous of Rosie? What if I really did want Nathan at heart? Why is it so fucking hard to know what I want? How can my own brain not know what my own heart wants? Nathan shut the door behind him and leaned against it after he followed me into the room.

"I'll take you home but not before we talk about this."

"We can talk in the car."

"We're talking now," he said, blocking me from reaching the door handle. "You're confused because you like Donnie. He is your boyfriend, but you also like me, yes?"

"I slept with you, I think it's obvious I like you," I sulked, giving up on battling him for exit.

"So the obvious thing to do is break up with him if you choose me over him. Stay here. There's no need to make a fuss when we're just letting what we both want happen."

"I don't know what I choose! I just want to go home now." When he didn't move, I added. "Or I'll tell Bea." That was a lie, I absolutely would not tell Bea.

It was a very, very quiet journey home. Nathan had agreed to drive me and I let him only so I wouldn't have to pay for a train. We made just one stop at a petrol station when he talked to me only once to ask what sandwich I wanted from it after filling up the car.

"Do you want me to come in with you?" he asked as he pulled up outside my house.

"You'd better not. Would probably make things worse. Thanks for caring about my birthday." (And then ruining it). "Just go."

An extra car I didn't recognise was on the drive as I walked up to the house, so naturally I wondered who else was home. I knocked on the door, praying that it would be Mum who answered and luckily it was.

"Emily, we've been so worried." She hugged me and I let her but then I saw Dad come into the hallway from the living room.

"Are you trying to scare us to death?" He said. "Finding out our daughter has disappeared in the night and didn't bother to tell us. You *completely* ruined your birthday surprise."

If Mum had said it I'd have felt guiltier but since it was Dad and I couldn't stand him, it really didn't have an effect on me. "We'd planned to have all your old friends over and we had to cancel them."

"What friends?" I scoffed.

"Georgia, Freya and Jen."

"I'm not friends with any of them anymore. You hardly know my life. I don't speak to anyone from that school; all of my friends are at Darwin. Besides, you never cared where I was the last few years did you?"

"WOULD YOU STOP BRINGING THAT UP?" he roared and I flinched.

"I'm not staying," I said as I slid past him so I could go upstairs. Mum and Dad followed me into my room as I started grabbing all of my stuff. I ignored Dad while he continued his tirade about how ungrateful I was until everything was packed and ready to go.

"Did you see that car out there?" he asked, leaning down so he was in my face. This was not the Dad I remembered as a kid at all. The lines on his face were not kind but cruel. "I bought that for you! For your birthday. If you leave this house young lady, I will take it away."

"I don't want it," I deadpanned, trying to pull my suitcase past him to the door but he pushed me back. I lost my footing and tripped over some bags, managing to bash my head onto the corner of my dresser. Stunned, I put my fingers to my forehead where I hit it and my fingers came away with blood.

"Carl, she's bleeding!" Mum shrieked. I regained my balance and dragged my stuff downstairs, the both of them letting me past this time. Outside, I barely glanced at what stupid new car could have been mine as I registered Nathan still waiting in his car. That idiot, I told him to go.

"Christ!" He said, bowling out of the car and coming to look at my head. For a moment, he looked like he was going to storm into my house but after I said, "just get us out of here," he put my stuff in the back, made sure I was ok in the front, and drove us away.

"Go to the train station," I said. He'd handed me some tissues and I was using them to dab at my forehead in the car's sunshade mirror.

"What happened?" he asked frantically, glancing at me out of the corner of his eye. "Are you sure you don't need to go to a minor injuries unit?"

"It was an accident. Head injuries always look worse than they are, don't you know that? It's basically stopped bleeding now," I snapped.

Nathan's driving was reflecting his anger and I rested a hand on his shoulder, trying to calm him. He was already driving illegally, he did not need to attract any unwanted attention.

"It wasn't a fucking accident, was it Emily? It's your Dad, don't defend him."

"Well I'm not going back so it's fine. Donnie's sent me his address, told me which trains to take. His family want to meet me and they're being kind enough to let me stay with them so I won't need to see my Dad again until Christmas at earliest. That's if he's even still around by then."

The views in the window rushed past in a blur and it was definitely more than thirty miles per hour that Nathan was doing through the town but he wasn't going to listen to me. As much as I may have been jealous earlier, he was now too. As well as being angry. At me, Donnie, my Dad, take your pick.

"Last chance to change your mind and come back to mine," Nathan said as he parked at the station. "It's all going to go to shit when Donnie finds out anyway." My stomach churned uncomfortably. It would be the easier thing to do. If I tell Donnie about Nathan, I'd have to go home and I can't do that so that does only leave Nathan. Unless I could go back to school early or maybe beg Hannah for a place to stay since she was the only one out of her, Megan and Bea that was still in the country.

"I'm going to Donnie's." I reached for the bags I had in the back seat then got out my suitcase, pulling up the extendable handle. I had to do the hard thing.

"Do I at least get a kiss goodbye?" he smirked.

"No," I said firmly and wheeled my case away towards the station entrance. According to my phone I still had an hour to wait until my train. Donnie had been kind enough to pay for my ticket despite my protests.

"We'll pick you up from the station," he said on the phone when I was about half an hour away from my stop.

"You don't need to do that, I can find my way," I said but he insisted. It seemed he'd been telling his family all about me and they were eager to meet his girlfriend. My guilt levels were at an all time high.

"Ok, I'll see you in a bit," I said and we hung up.

When I arrived at the station and I made my way through the exit, I couldn't see Donnie anywhere so I texted him.

Nearly there! He replied.

In the train toilets, I'd cleaned up my forehead but the split skin still showed the bloody cut quite clearly. It wasn't too big but it was noticeable. True to his word, a 4x4 rolled into the nearby car park just ten minutes later and I spotted Donnie in the back.

He and his parents came out of the car and Donnie led them over to me. They looked like nice people. Well, they looked like Donnie: all blonde and strong cheekbones. We shook hands and they introduced themselves as Paul and Anne.

"We're so glad to meet you. Peter's been going on about you for so long. It's clear he adores you."

"Oh really?" I raised my eyebrows at him. He hung back with me a bit as we started walking to their car.

"What happened to your head?" he asked, gesturing to the cut.

"My Dad happened," I said sullenly.

Donnie's eyes widened. "Emily! Why didn't you say something? We would have got you sooner. I didn't realise it was that bad." I assured him it was fine and that I hadn't spent too much time at home, especially as Nathan got me out for my birthday.

"Thank god for Nathan," Donnie said, opening the boot to help me put my stuff in. He wouldn't be saying that if he knew...

On the way to their house, his parents asked me all about how I was finding Darwin and I cottoned on pretty quick that Donnie had definitely told them about the bursary from the way in which they were asking questions. Not condescendingly but definitely knowingly. They probably wondered about the ugly cut on my face too but they were polite enough not to ask.

Donnie and his dad helped me with my bags while his mum got the door. They showed me upstairs to the spare room they were putting me in which was much bigger than my room at home. I couldn't stop thanking them. Two younger children, a boy and a girl, appeared in the doorway looking at Donnie and I bashfully while we were putting my stuff away. He told me they were twins, Lily and Hugo, five years old."

"You're Donnie's girlfriend," Hugo said matter-of-factly.

"That's right," I said, folding my clothes and putting them into the dresser while Donnie put my tops onto hangers.

"Does that mean you're going to get married?" Lily asked innocently.

I paused and laughed before pushing a drawer I'd finished filling shut. "We could do," I said. "But normally boys and girls get to know each other for a bit more than two months before they decide on getting married."

"Damn, there go my plans," Donnie joked, and herded Lily

and Hugo out from the room. With the door shut and the two of us finally alone, he smiled at me and pulled me in for a hug. "I've missed you," he said and we sank onto the bed.

"I've missed you too," I said, resting my head against his chest and feeling his heartbeat. He played with my hair, making my scalp feel all nice and tingly.

We lay like that and kissed for a while until he said he was going to get the first aid kit from the bathroom.

"Stop making such a fuss over it," I said but he wouldn't listen.

"You don't want it to scar do you?" he asked once he'd got back and had a look through the kit. "We should probably clean it."

I winced, knowing it would sting and it had finally just about stopped twinging. With a cotton pad and an alcohol cleanser he dabbed at my cut while I hissed through my teeth.

"Stop making such a fuss," he teased back at me and held my face still so he could apply some adhesive butterfly stitches.

When he was done I went over to the mirror on the desk in the room. "Very nice," I said, bending over the desk to look at my reflection closely. "Very Frankenstein's monster."

Donnie came up behind me and kissed me on the cheek. "I still think you look beautiful." He wrapped his arms around my waist and tucked his chin in the crook of my neck. It tickled and I squirmed out of his embrace. He reached for me and I thought he was going for the hips but he accidentally or not, grabbed me somewhere else.

"Woah... don't... what are you doing?"

"Sorry," he said, backing off. "I don't know why I-"

"It's ok!" I protested. "I don't know why *I*..."

I didn't really know what to say. Was I surprised because Donnie had never been so forward since that first night at his dorm room or was I just pushing him away because I was feeling guilty about Nathan?

"No." He shook his head. "I can't just touch you like that without asking."

I shook mine back fervently. "No, honestly. Donnie you're my boyfriend, you can touch me however you like. I just had a funny moment, that's all."

I sprawled back onto the bed.

"Emily, noooo, I respect you. I don't want you thinking I just want to fuck you or anything. I was just messing around and not thinking about your feelings. I know you aren't ready for any of that yet."

I cringed and felt my face flush red with shame.

"Donnie…" My nose started tingling and before I could stop them, the tears came. "We need to talk… about…"

"No, no, no," Donnie shushed me and perched on the side of the bed, leaning an arm over me and wiping my tears with his other hand. "I'm so sorry. I don't want to pressure you into anything you don't want to do. Your first time should be special."

I choked on a sob at that. How could I tell him? I had to tell him. I had to break his heart.

"And Emily?…"

"Yeah?"

"I love you."

Chapter 14

"You don't have to say it back," Donnie said. "I just wanted you to know"

An awkward silence hung in the air. He probably thought I was too stunned for words with his declaration of love.

"Oh." I laughed tentatively but it came out high pitched and strange.

"Sorry if I just made things weird."

I leaned forward and pressed a kiss on his cheek. "Can you stop apologising for everything?" I rolled over to the other side of the bed so he could get on properly.

"I really, really didn't mean to be upset you."

Fighting the urge to roll my eyes at his persistence and accidentally end up looking annoyed at him, I placed my hand over his mouth.

"Shut up," I said. It should be me apologising but now he'd read everything wrong and made it the complete wrong moment to owning up about Nathan.

The ringtone of my phone made me jump in the quiet. "God, I really hope that isn't my Dad again." Donnie took my phone out of my back jeans pocket since his hand was already in the vicinity.

"It's Beatrice," he said. She was making a FaceTime call and Donnie was already pressing the answer button.

Her face pixelated and froze instantly but the audio was unaffected.

"Is that you Donnie?" she asked. I moved closer to him so my face was in the camera frame too. "Oh there you are." I sincerely hoped this was just meant as a girls' chatty call and she wasn't calling because her brother had mentioned anything.

"How's Italy?" I asked.

"Full of pizza, pasta and carbs. The usual. Anyway my life is boring, tell me all about you two. Look at you! Lovebirds. What on earth is on your forehead?"

"If you could let me get a word in edgeways…" I started and then Bea's face finally unfroze and I could see her in her Italian hotel room, putting mascara on her eyelashes, going about her 'boring' life I'd kill for.

"I went home last night and my Dad went crazy. He'd tried to bribe me to get along with him with a car for my birthday and then I tripped and hit my head. He's taking the car away. Whatever. Now I'm at Donnie's," I said, side-eyeing him.

"What a psycho… and good, didn't want you spending all week with Nathan the manwhore."

Donnie laughed and I smiled, though my heart pounded. "Guess that probably gives him a few days free to go shag Rosie," she said, screwing the lid of her mascara back on. I felt a twinge of irritation at that and then anger at myself for feeling anything towards him at all.

"Probably…" I mumbled.

"YEAH, COMING," Bea yelled suddenly, presumably to someone outside her room. "I've gotta goooo."

"Ok bye," I said.

"You two have fun. Do *everything* I would do." She winked and hung up the call.

Donnie put my phone on the bedside table.

"Maybe not everything Bea would do," he said. "But I am

looking forward to spending time with you."

When we were nearly finished putting all of my stuff away, Donnie out of nowhere asked, "you *do* like Mexican food don't you?"

"Um. Yeah?"

"Mum's making fajitas. I should have asked."

"Fajitas are fine. I'm not going to complain after everything you've all done for me."

"I nearly forgot!" Donnie said after dinner. We were in his room and he took a small box out from under his bed. It was grey and tied with blue ribbon. Before I could open it, his door opened and his mum popped her head around.

"I'm sure you're not up to anything, but if you could just keep the door open when you're together, please."

"*Mum*," Donnie complained, clearly embarrassed. Once that awkward encounter was over, I tugged the ribbon off and opened the box.

"Donnie!"

Inside was a *very* expensive looking bracelet. I didn't even want to know how much it would have cost. Well, I would, but it would be rude to ask wouldn't it? It had a little heart pendant and it was studded with what I guessed were crystals.

"This is too much," I exclaimed but he was already helping me fasten it around my wrist.

"Nothing's too much for you." He kissed the top of my head and I melted.

"I can't thank you enough. Not just for this, but for everything."

For the rest of the evening, we ended up looking through old picture books of Donnie as a child that I'd managed to find in his room. I was in fits of laughter looking at some of him as a toddler, so much so that I could almost completely forget the bad knotted feeling in my stomach and I was just there in that moment with him.

"Tell me about your childhood," he said when we reached the end of the last book.

"Um… I don't know." I played with the bracelet on my wrist. "I lived in the same town my whole life. Had the same three friends all through school. Fell out with them halfway through year eleven though. I was a bit of a loner for a while."

"Boyfriends?"

"Nothing like this."

We linked our fingers together and I kissed him.

"Why don't you ever talk to me about your life before you came to school?" He asked. Both of us ignored his hand that was resting on my skin under my top. Easy enough to hide if someone walked past his open door.

"I don't know… it's not you though! I don't really talk to anyone about it. I'm not in contact with anyone from my old school and I was quite boring so no one misses me. I just studied really hard and didn't socialise much. I guess I was working so hard on getting into Darwin and making a better life for myself that I didn't bother to live in the moment and be a proper teenager."

Donnie nodded as if he understood and continued to brush his thumb over my stomach, causing goosebumps to rise. It hadn't occurred to me that my past before I came to Darwin was quite a mystery to everyone. Of course, it was up to me to tell them but it just never seemed important. I'd definitely been a different person since I'd left my old life behind. The old Emily Greene would never have dreamed about having moral dilemmas such as the one I was stuck in now.

"There's still plenty of time left for you to be a 'proper teenager' if that's what you want," he said and I smiled. "I'm just glad it's me that gets to hold you like this and kiss your pretty face. I couldn't stand it if Nathan Horny had managed to sway you like he does every other girl. What is it that made you guys fall out, anyway? You must have forgiven him for it if you were happy to be with him yesterday."

I thought I detected more than just a hint of jealousy in his voice and I stifled a laugh at his word play regarding Nathan.

"I promised him I wouldn't tell anyone about it…"

That couldn't have came out sounding any more dodgy. Donnie leaned up on his elbow, hair flopping over his forehead as he leaned over me, his eyes searching mine.

"Something happen between you guys?"

"No." And there it was. The denial. Sure, I was talking about a different occasion but I'd had the opportunity (twice now) to admit it to him and I hadn't. "He had his own issues and I didn't want anything to do with them." I thought it was safe to settle with that.

"Issues as in he can't stop putting his dick in Rosie Ayres even when he's got a shot with the world's most beautiful girl." He tucked my hair behind my ear and kissed my nose. "Not that I'm complaining."

"Are you?"… I stroked my finger along his arm awkwardly. "Can I ask you something?"

"Of course; anything you want."

"Are you… a virgin?"

The corner of his lips twitched momentarily and I couldn't work out if it was in a smile or a grimace.

"Uhh…" He removed the hand that had been up my top and started scratching the back of his neck instead. If he was, he would have admitted it by now, surely? I couldn't stand him stretching out the discomfort any longer so I cut in.

"Never mind," I laughed. I should have known a boy as good looking as Donnie would have lost it already.

"No, it was just one person," he said quickly.

"Is it… someone from school? Someone I know?" I

regretted asking immediately, already wondering whether Donnie and Rosie used to be more than just friends. "No don't tell me."

"Sure?" he asked.

I waved my hands in front of me and shook my head. "Absolutely. I don't want to think about it. Forget I said anything."

"Really?"

"Really."

The following morning I was half asleep when I realised I was scratching my forehead in the spot where the skin had split and I was close to messing up the adhesive stitches Donnie had so carefully applied. Now properly conscious, I checked my phone to see a text from him ten minutes ago telling me to wake up despite both my phone being on silent *and* him only being in the room next to mine.

I'm awake I texted back. His reply came instantly.

Good we're going on our first date today so get ready then we're going for breakfast

Where?

Surprise!

Being our first date, I'd better make an effort, I thought as I stepped into the ensuite bathroom and started to get ready. I was already hungry because I'd slept in a while, making it almost ten a.m.

After showering and brushing my teeth, I pulled on some my nicest jeans and a corded jumper. Being near the end of October, it wasn't the sunniest day outside. I thought about the hill we'd climbed the day he'd modelled for my art. It could be worse: at least it wasn't as windy.

A knock at the door and Donnie opened the door cautiously with his hand over his eyes. "You decent?" he asked.

"Well you would know if you'd waited for me to answer your knocking instead of barging in." I pulled his fingers away from his eyes. "But yes. I am, evidently."

Donnie smiled, showing his perfectly straight shiny teeth and his gaze fell on the bracelet he'd bought me that was still secured around my wrist.

"You look so beautiful," he said and I rolled my eyes.

He still wouldn't tell me where we were going while we made the walk into town. It wasn't too far away from Darwin but I was still completely lost, so far from home. In the town centre, he suddenly grabbed my hand to stop me walking as I went past a Pret A Manger. "In here."

"Oh *this* is breakfast is it?"

"You like croissants?" he smiled so widely I could almost lie and eat a dozen just for him.

"No, I hate them," I said. "They smell funny."

We joined the back of the queue and I looked at the other options available for breakfast. "Scones will do me."

Donnie had a mock flabbergasted expression plastered on his face. "No, too late. You don't like croissants? We're going to have to break up immediately," he joked.

"They do smell gross," I said, wrinkling my nose while he buttered his croissants at our little table in the corner.

"Whatever. Which way do you do your scones? The Cornish way or Devon?"

I shrugged. I didn't know and frankly didn't care which way around the cream and jam went. It all gets mixed up when you eat it anyway.

"Cornish," he noted as I put jam then cream. "I used to live in Cornwall until I was eleven."

"Really?" I asked ungracefully with bite of scone in my mouth.

"Newquay. By the beach, near Gordon Ramsay's house."

"He has a house there?"

"Yeah."

When I'd finished eating and Donnie had finished directing me to wipe off a bit of jam I'd managed to get stuck on the corner of my mouth, I asked what we were doing for the rest of the day.

I didn't mind what it was, as long as it was with him. Although, a niggling fear was bugging me that Nathan might tell Donnie about us if I didn't but I hadn't heard from him at all since he dropped me off at the train station.

"I have a few ideas," he said, which gave absolutely nothing away at all.

"Can we get started then?"

He held out his hand like he was about to ask me to dance and I suppressed a grin, seeing the twinkle in his eye.

He walked me all the way down the high street, hand in hand with mine until he took me off down a side road.

"Here," he said, gesturing to a shop we'd ended up just in front of. It was a bookshop, independently owned by the looks of it. Inside it smelled dusty like only my grandmother would shop here but it was cosy nonetheless. "This is one of my favourite places ever."

"Hello Peter," an old man behind the counter said. "Haven't seen you in a while. What have you been up to?"

"I've been at school! You know I'd be here otherwise." He threw him a cheeky wink. "Isn't Amy here?"

"She's upstairs," the old man said. "I'll go get her."

Donnie looked from the man to me and back again. "Oh there's no need to disturb her. I'm just browsing with Emily. My girlfriend."

The old man shook my hand but didn't introduce himself, he was already bustling off out the back, leaving the shop entirely unattended.

"What are we doing here then?" I asked. "And who's Amy?"

Donnie was deep in thought and I wasn't sure he'd even listened to what I said until he'd pulled some books off the shelves and pushed them into my hands.

"Getting some books, obviously. Amy's an old friend."

I looked at the books he'd passed to me. Walt Whitman's *Leaves of Grass* and Sylvia Plath's *The Bell Jar*, among others. None of them I had read before. Donnie was still picking books when a girl our age came running out from the back of the shop towards Donnie, knocking into me as she wrapped her arms around his neck.

He hugged her back and smiled at me over her shoulder, ignoring my frown. Oh, I wasn't hiding my sudden jealousy.

"I've missed you!" Amy said, arms still dangling around his neck when she broke away from the hug. She pecked him on the cheek and I raised an eyebrow at Donnie.

He seemed to understand my expression and took her hands away from him. "Amy, this is Emily. My girlfriend from school."

She finally turned around and surveyed me up and down, smiling but not offering an apology for bumping into me in her haste to throw herself at my boyfriend.

"Hmmm. So this is the famous Emily. I've heard so much about you," she said in a way that didn't do much to convince me this was necessarily a good thing.

"Oh?" I said unsteadily, unsure if she was about to try to hug me or not with her bouncy body language. "Donnie's never mentioned you. What's he been telling you about me?" I eyed him over her shoulder.

"*Peter*," she exaggerated his proper name, "has been going on about you ever since he saw you walk into his maths class. I can even show you the text he sent me when he first saw you!"

"I don't think she needs to see that," Donnie said, pushing her hand away as she reached for her phone in her pocket.

"Why?" I asked accusingly. "Weren't you saying nice things about me?" I wasn't sure if I was teasing him or genuinely asking.

Amy gave me a disappointed look. "Peter has told me about you screwing him over for some jock boy."

I blinked in surprise. Excuse me? How was any of this her business? She continued, "if you know Peter you'd know he prefers brains over beauty. Being his girlfriend, I assumed you'd be the same but... guess you can't judge a book." She took a book from Donnie's hand. "Speaking of! Good choice, I *love* Chaucer."

"Sorry," I said, hardly able to believe my ears. "Are you saying Nathan is stupid or something?" Donnie was obviously far more academic than Nathan but he wasn't an idiot. Nathan isn't *just* a pretty face and Donnie wouldn't stand a chance against him in a sporting event.

Amy shrugged. "I haven't met him or anything. I'm just going off what Peter's said."

"You don't think he might be a bit biased?" I shot back. I'd quickly decided I didn't like this girl. Not as much as I hated Ayres, but definitely second to her.

"Why are you defending him?" She crossed her arms. Donnie hadn't said anything and was just watching this unfold before him.

"You don't even know him!" My voice rose unintentionally. "I'm only saying he isn't some brainless 'jock' as you implied. That doesn't mean I like him more than Donnie or want to... I don't know... be with him or anything." I avoided Donnie's eyes.

"Okaaay," Donnie said, physically stepping between Amy and I. "I think we're just going to buy these books and then we'll be on our way."

He took the Chaucer book she'd snatched and the ones he'd piled into my arms over to the counter and Amy went behind it to serve him. I pretended to be interested in some of the books stacked on the table nearby while he paid.

"What was all that about?" he asked once we were out the door. I wheeled around to face him.

"You tell me. She looked like your other girlfriend or something."

We were walking further along the side road the book shop was situated on but he didn't tell me where we were headed.

"She's a friend, she's just very... friendly."

"Didn't seem to like me much."

"She's just protective."

I wrapped my coat tighter around my body, sulking in the cold.

"What was the point of all that anyway?" I asked.

"These are some of my favourite books and you're a literature student so you like books don't you?"

"It looked more like an excuse to see that girl."

Donnie shrugged off my moaning and by the time we'd got to a grassy park fifteen or so minutes later, I'd almost forgotten about Amy.

We were lounging in the grass by a pond even though there were benches dotted around. Donnie leafed through the pages of the books he'd bought for me and skipped to the 'good parts' which he read aloud to me.

"That all sounds really pretty but I have no idea what's going on when you're reading a passage from halfway through the book." My head was on his lap and I was reading along with the book held in front of my face.

"When you've got the time, you can read them all the way through then." He smacked me with the book, now closed.

"That girl... Amy. She's not the one you slept with is she?"

I closed my eyes, pretending it was because of the sun shining in my face but it was really because I didn't want to see his face when he told me.

"What? Amy?" He laughed. "No, I've never liked her like that."

"I think she does," I moped. "I'm sure wishes she was the one."

"Do you *want* to know who it was?" he asked. "If you're going to go on about it so much."

"Nope." I scrunched up my nose. "Have a bad feeling if you tell me I'll wish I didn't know."

"Maybe," he said, which did not help at all. It would probably be Rosie wouldn't it? It's always her. Every boy falls for the pretty blonde mean girl. Nathan and Donnie both like me, I wouldn't be surprised if Nathan and Donnie both liked her.

When lunch rolled around, Donnie took me to what he said was his favourite place to eat in town. Hopefully there wouldn't be another pretty waitress in this place.

"Noooo, what are you doing?"

I cringed as he dipped the chips that came with his burger into his strawberry milkshake. He'd taken me to a classic American diner, complete with a jukebox and all.

"It's good!" he attested.

"I'm more perturbed by your eating habits than I anticipated," I said. "First croissants and now this."

"Try it," he teased. He stabbed another chip onto his fork, dipped it in his drink and held it out towards me. Reluctantly I leaned forward and tentatively nibbled the end of the chip.

I scrunched up my nose at first but then took another bite. "You don't know what to make of it do you?"

I shook my head.

Chapter 15

Once we were back at school, it felt like everything was back to normal. After a few weeks, the night I spent at Nathan's and the altercation with my dad felt like nothing more than a fever dream. It wasn't like Nathan hadn't tried to talk to me since: cornering me in hallways between classes, trying to call me in the evenings and even managing to slip me a note at one point, but with how happy I was with Donnie, there was no way I could give Nathan the time of day.

I'd filled my friends in on my week at Donnie's house as soon as we were settled in Bea's room on the first night back at school because obviously they needed to know all the details ("what do you *mean* you don't want to fuck him yet?") and had tried to avoid discussing anything remotely to do with Nathan at all, which turned out be quite difficult when one of your best friends is his sister. Somehow I'd managed to convince them all that it was just a little friendly gesture that he'd taken me away from home for my birthday.

Schoolwork was really hitting me in full swing now though and I was swamped with literature essays and pieces to turn in for art. Dean Smith had been discussing with me whether I wanted to do an EPQ this year or next, or even both and it was all so much to handle. I felt like I could break down and cry sometimes but I quite frankly didn't have the time. Besides, Donnie was always there to help me through the maths work we were set. That's one of the perks of having a genius boyfriend studying the same subject as you.

I wasn't sure if I was imagining it until Bea mentioned it to me but Hannah seemed to be getting more and more short with me, like I'd done something to annoy her. Gen, a girl in Bea's classics class who had just started boarding with us only after the half term due to family arrangements, agreed after Hannah left us in the common room one afternoon that she had been snippy at me for absolutely no reason.

"Are you sure I haven't done or said something to offend her?" I asked. Gen looked at Bea who made a *don't-ask-me* face, then gave her input.

"From an outsiders perspective - and feel free to tell me to shut up if I'm reading it all wrong - it doesn't look like she's treating you as a friend."

I took a bite of the apple I was eating. "I don't know what I've done to put her off me," I said. A bit of the apple's skin got stuck between my teeth and I worried it with my tongue.

"Maybe try talking to her?" Gen suggested as if it was obvious, which it was. It would just be awkward to have to do it. Especially if I was reading it wrong and there wasn't anything going on at all.

"Ok, yeah. I'll ask her when I see her again."

I didn't see her again until the following day. She wasn't at breakfast but she was in English. We'd finished studying Shakespeare and had been on Christopher Marlowe's *Doctor Faustus* for a while now so I wasn't expecting Mr. Groves to spring a revision lesson for King Lear on us.

"I thought we'd try to recap what we can from memory," he said after we complained we hadn't brought our books with us. "It'll be good to commit some scenes to memory. We could do a sort of role play."

We groaned and that was the first time Hannah paid any

attention to me since I'd walked into the classroom as she caught my eye to make a face.

"It doesn't have to be Shakespearean English," he said.

Mr. Groves and Cameron, the one boy in the class, suffered through juggling the male roles at first since all the girls had protested at playing the male parts. Once Lear's daughters were introduced to the scene though, he insisted that the rest of picked some roles.

Against my will, I ended up as Lear's eldest daughter Goneril, with Hannah as Regan, my younger sister, and another girl as Cordelia. We were participating in the love test scene, vying for land from the king.

"My love for you is boundless, father," I said in a monotone voice, wishing this could be over. "More than I can ever say."

"Well *I* am just as worthy as my sister," Hannah said. "But more than that, *all* my love is for *you*. I could never love anyone else as much." The way she looked at me was as if she was talking about more than just the play.

"What?" I asked, breaking character.

"I'm saying although you had his love first - as the eldest sister - I am just as deserving when I reciprocate that love even more than you do. You take it for granted."

"That's an interesting take, Hannah," Mr .Groves said, seeming to forget the roleplay all together. "Would you like to explain why you think Regan feels that way. Is her jealousy of Goneril greater than her jealousy of Cordelia?"

Hannah sighed dramatically like we weren't getting it at all. "Never mind, forget it."

"No, go on," I prompted, also keen to see where she was going with this. Why was she in such a strange mood?

"Of course you wouldn't get it," Hannah said and rolled her eyes. She sulked for the rest of the lesson but didn't make any more remarks. She tried to hurry out of the room when the bell rang for the end of the period but I ran after her and caught up with her on the stairs.

"You alright?" I asked.

"Yeah?"

"Can we talk?"

"About what?"

"Why you're acting all funny. What was that about?"

Hannah was still hurrying away once we left the building and I couldn't work out where she was heading.

"How am I acting funny? Maybe you're just imagining things."

Was she really out here trying to make me feel crazy when she's the one that everyone's noticed is being off with me?

"I'm not imagining things, you're literally avoiding me!" I stepped in front of her but she side stepped me and kept walking.

"What have I done?" I gave up following her and let her walk away. She didn't respond.

"At least you tried," Donnie said that evening. Hannah had avoided Megan and Bea too and none of us had any idea where she was. "Stop it," he said, taking his calculator back from me. I was lying on his bed spelling rude words on it and he was sat at his desk trying to fix the errors I'd made in my maths homework.

He passed me my exercise book back and I looked at his squiggly writing, annotating how I was *supposed* to have answered the questions. I squinted at it for a second.

"Don't get it," I said and let the book drop onto my face as I was lying on my back. Donnie swiped it off and pushed me out of the way so he could squeeze onto the bed next to me.

"You're not even looking at it." I sat up and he pushed the book under my nose.

"Ok," I said, taking it. "I didn't do *that* bad."

"Yeah you did. You're factorising things, thinking you're making it easier for yourself but you're just confusing yourself instead."

"Looks tidier though."

I studied the notes he'd made but it was still French to me. His book was resting open on his bedside table so I grabbed that and started studying his response to the homework questions side by side with mine. Seeing how easy Donnie made it really made me feel in over my head. He was getting A's already in practice exams on the topics we'd covered and I was lucky to scrape a C in the last one we did.

For half an hour I tried to understand what Donnie was showing me in his work but my brain was fried. A-level was so much harder than the GCSE. For English literature it was only a little harder than GCSE and art was pretty much the same so why did maths have to be so god damn *hard*?

It was past nine o'clock, meaning I shouldn't be allowed in Donnie's room right now because we aren't supposed to be in the opposite genders' rooms after that time but it wasn't like anyone actually checked on the sixth formers so we'd long since stopped heeding that rule. I put my book in my bag and Donnie's back on his table. He swung his legs up onto the bed and we cuddled.

"Have you spoken to Nathan lately?" he asked.

"No, not since my birthday, why?"

It threw me for him to ask about Nathan so out of the blue and I hoped he couldn't feel me involuntarily tensing up. I was almost telling the truth. It wasn't as if I had had a conversation with him, it was just him trying to get me on my own to talk to me and I wasn't going to let him do that. I didn't want to hear anything he had to say. If he called my name, I'd be off in the other direction before you could blink.

"Oh, just I had a funny chat with him yesterday."

"About what?" He knew didn't he? Didn't he? Would he

still have invited me over for a late night study session if he'd thought I'd cheated on him? I hated myself so much for that stupid slip up. The phrasing sounds like an understatement, which it is, I know, but it was evidently such a mistake and I haven't wavered in my fidelity to Donnie a single time since... but I couldn't tell him.

"He was asking about you, actually. Told me to tell you to speak to him. Do you know what that's about?"

"No?" I said unconvincingly. "We don't talk at all and I don't see why we'd need to."

"Yeah and why would you, when you've got me?"

I smiled and kissed him to shut him up, hoping he would forget about it and it worked. When ten o'clock rolled around I said I should probably go back to the girls' boarding house and get ready for bed. On the way down the hallway towards the stairs, I noticed a door propped open with a slice of light from within the room hitting the wall opposite. As I came up to pass it, I looked to see if I could glimpse who was in there to make sure I wasn't going to get snitched on for breaking curfew.

A hand shot out, clenched on my arm, and pulled me inside.

"What are you doing, Nathan?" I asked as he closed the door behind me. I should have realised it was his room but I'd somehow just forgotten which was his after it being so long since I'd been in here.

He shushed me as I'd raised my voice in annoyance as if I didn't have the right to be a little pissed off when he manhandles me. "Were you waiting for me to go past like some creepy stalker?" I accused.

Nathan ran his hands through his floppy hair then picked up his TV remote to pause whatever he was watching on his TV in the corner of the room. His walls were so bare compared to how girls decorate every inch and even Donnie's room had his awards and notes of algorithms and such tacked to his wall. It was a bit depressing now that I thought about it.

"It's not like you gave me a choice," he said in a low voice. "You've been avoiding me for weeks and you spend every other night in *his* room… so yeah I thought I'd take matters into my own hands."

"In case you've forgotten Horne," I said icily, "I'm not yours to shove about however you want."

"You were for one night," he teased. If that was supposed to be funny, it did not hit its mark at all. The last thing I wanted was him bringing that up ever again. I reached for the door handle but he took me by the wrist and dragged me away, further into the room.

"Don't fucking touch me," I said, wrenching my arm out of his grip. "And don't talk about that shit. If anyone finds out I'll kill you. I'm happy with Donnie."

Nathan looked like he wanted to laugh in disbelief but it was only his fear of being overheard that stopped him. It was the quietest I've ever seen him be whilst angry; it almost made him scary, actually.

"You're gonna just act like it didn't happen then? That it didn't mean anything that you *lost your fucking virginity* to me?"

"It didn't mean anything!" I seethed. "It was a mistake. A stupid mistake and if I could take it back, I would in an *instant*, Nathan."

"Why are you lying to yourself? Just because you've shagged Peter fucking O'Donoghue a hundred times since me, doesn't diminish that you had to have some feelings for me to do it with me first." Maybe there was a little bit of truth in that statement but there was no way in hell I was ever going to admit that to him after he'd pulled me into his bedroom at night and started to blow holes in my relationship.

"I haven't 'shagged' him, as you put it so eloquently, at all actually." Unfortunately this had the opposite effect to what I'd hoped it would. I thought saying that would show him that what Donnie and I had was more serious than physical desire but Nathan's face lighting up at this admission was full of nothing but relief.

"Really? Why?" His face had fallen into a look of scepticism like I had any reason to lie to him. I crossed my arms and considered whether I even needed to justify my own relationship to a boy I wanted nothing to do with anymore. The answer was of course I didn't, but if I threw him a bone maybe he'd leave me alone and stop trying to get my attention so desperately.

"We're taking it slow, not that it's any of your business."

"Why do you need to take anything slow? You some kind of prude now?"

"What the *fuck* is wrong with you?" I yelled, not caring if anyone could hear us. "You're such a dick! Not everything is about you and I don't quite understand why you're suddenly so obsessed with me out of nowhere?" I was on a tirade now and there was no stopping me from keeping in all the things I'd bottled up. "You think just because of what happened on my birthday, I'd forget all about Donnie and come running back to you when you're still not over Rosie. You don't even want me anyway. You've already got that bitch, you don't need me too."

"Are you done?" he said. Surprisingly he hadn't interrupted me. Usually I wouldn't be so lucky to rant without being interrupted by his denials. "I haven't been seeing Rosie. Not since before half term."

"Am I supposed to care?" By the look of hurt on his face, apparently I was supposed to care. Oh, poor Nathan hasn't been trying to put his dick in another girl (so he claims, anyway). He must only want me. How sweet.

"I thought it might mean *something* to you, yeah but with the attitude you've got tonight, I guess not."

"Ok, I'm going now." I was sick of listening to him trying to manipulate me into throwing away everything I'd worked so hard to rebuild. I didn't want him like he wanted me and he'd have to realise that soon.

"Fine Emily, go but just remember, you can pretend you're little miss perfect to your heart's content but you've still done what you've done and Donnie doesn't deserve that. It'll all blow up eventually. These things always do."

"No it won't. You're the only person that knows. Unless you're threatening me?" I raised an eyebrow in challenge, hoping he wouldn't actually rise to it.

"I care about you too much to do that to you. You know I just want you to be happy. I only… don't want you to get hurt."

Chapter 16

Bea had eventually talked Hannah around to spending some time with us by the weekend and the following Monday everything seemed back to normal with her. Or so I thought. We were at lunch, twirling forks of pasta and chatting, although Hannah was still a little quieter than usual. The conversation topic fell onto Donnie and I, as it naturally did every now and then but Bea was talking about how I'd dodged a bullet with her brother since he's so Rosie-oriented lately as we could see from just looking at them. I quickly agreed and hoped someone would change the subject soon.

Hannah put her knife and fork down with a clang against her plate and huffed haughtily. We looked to her expectantly. Did she have something she finally wished to share with the group?

"Donnie doesn't deserve the shit he has to put up with from you," she said, fixing me with a stony look. I felt my mouth fall open and Bea and Megan's faces were in similar states of shock.

"What?" I asked. I knew she had talked a couple of times about liking Donnie herself but she'd never acted as though she thought he and I weren't a good couple.

"You heard me," she said, placing her palms on the table top. "He's a really great guy and only has eyes for you yet you're still all caught up about Nathan and Rosie's business."

"I don't care about their business! I was just saying. *Jesus*. Get a grip. Sounds like you're just jealous," I proposed.

Hannah started laughing in my face as if it was the most far-fetched idea. Bea eyed me curiously.

"Me?" Hannah pressed her splayed hand over her chest. "Jealous? Are you hearing yourself? I have no need to be jealous over you dating a boy you're too scared to even fuck when I've already been there, done him."

My heart clenched. She had to be lying. The uncomfortable look on Bea's face said otherwise.

"What?" I whispered weakly. "When?"

"Oh ages ago. Don't worry I'm not the type of person to step on anyone's toes when it comes to relationships unlike you."

"Why?"

"Because we wanted to. Simple as that. I'm surprised he never told you. I don't see why he had to keep it a secret from you. Maybe he didn't want you to compare yourself to me because let's face it..."

She eyed me up and down animatedly.

Before I could hear what she would continue on to say, I picked up my glass of orange squash and splashed it into her face.

"I'm *so* sorry!" I said once I'd come to my senses after a second. "I just got mad."

Hannah pushed her chair back from the table as she stood up. She shook her damp hair out of her eyes which were fixing me with a scathing look. An apology definitely wasn't going to be enough on this occasion.

"What the fuck, you freak!"

"I'm sorry!" I repeated. Megan looked like I felt whereas Bea was trying to hide her smirk in her sleeve.

"You can't get pissy at me for something that happened

before we even knew each other." She looked from me, down to her half eaten pasta and back to me. I knew what she was about to do half a second before she did it. She was going to get me back.

I didn't have time to dodge the handful of spaghetti she flung at me. It hit me in the chest and dropped down my skirt then onto the floor. A few strands of spaghetti and the stains of the sauce cling to my uniform. Megan gasped and so did some other people at neighbouring tables. Over Hannah's shoulder I spotted Rosie Ayers nudging Nathan.

"Hey!" Donnie appeared behind me out of nowhere and offered a napkin to wipe myself off with. "What's going on?" He looked from me to Hannah for an explanation.

While I scrubbed at my blouse, probably only making the stain worse, Hannah filled him in. "Emily got a little surprise finding out that she's not as special that she thinks she is and since you didn't deign to tell her about me being your first body, I did."

"*That's* what this is about?" he asked, eyes widening. "Really Emily? I told you I don't have any secrets. You're the one who didn't want to know. It was so long ago, it's hardly relevant."

"You're taking her side then?" I said, hardly believing it but before it could escalate beyond that, Dean Smith came marching purposefully over to us. She took in Hannah's wet face, my orange stained clothes and the spaghetti on the floor as well as the piercing look I was giving Donnie. Behind her I could see Rosie. It looked like she'd been the one to waste no time telling tales on me.

"Girls!" She said. "You are supposed to be young adults setting an example to the rest of the school." This was not a great statement when there was no one below the ages of fifteen in the dining hall at this time and they're all old enough to think for themselves despite how much Dean

Smith likes to go on about our influence. "I expected better from you especially, Mr. O'Donoghue."

"I had nothing to do with it!" he said quickly but she didn't seem to care.

"At this age, I shouldn't have to do this but you can all join me at four o'clock for a detention." It was pretty clear she counted Bea and Megan in this too. I tried to explain that they were innocent too but like with Donnie, it fell on deaf ears. It was so unfair, sixth formers aren't even supposed to be given detentions.

When she walked away, Hannah was still glaring daggers at me but Donnie was tugging on my arm.

"Come on, let's get you a clean shirt before maths." The class wouldn't start for another couple of hours yet but I was happy with any excuse to get away from that table.

In my room, I pulled my blazer off and started unbuttoning my blouse.

"Wow, let me at least close the door before you start seducing me," Donnie said but I was not in the mood.

"It's not funny!" I said. Before I knew it, I had tears in my eyes. "I had no idea you and Hannah were a thing."

"We weren't a thing," he reassured, enveloping me in his arms. "It was a one time hookup. Nothing like what we have, I promise. You know I would have told you if you wanted to know." He held me by the upper arms to be able to look into my eyes, even though I was stood there in just a skirt and a bra and I know he wanted to be looking other places. "You know that?"

"Yeah," I admitted. I hadn't meant to but I'd brought it on myself. But that still didn't explain why Hannah was bringing it up now unless she still had feelings. Which… judging by the way she'd been acting lately suddenly explained a lot. "Ok," I said and wiped my tears. Donnie let me go and I got another shirt out of my wardrobe. "I just wish it wasn't my friend."

"Me too."

That being said, I really wasn't so sure that Hannah and I would be friends anymore and then where did that leave Bea and Megan? Whose side would they take?

"Where do we go from here?" I said.

"We destress for a while and then we go to maths," he said calmly.

"Where I can restress?" I joked.

"Yeah, and then we can destress for another hour before we have to restress in that detention."

I'd almost forgotten about that. It would be so awkward, having to face Hannah again.

I didn't have a clue just how awkward things could get. First off, no one was particularly happy with me for landing us in an hour's worth of a detention by being the person who instigated what Dean Smith was calling a 'food fight' (which sounded like an overdramatic way of putting it to me). Hannah was definitely not forgiving me any time soon and she wouldn't even look at me when Donnie and I entered.

We were the last to do so and the others were talking with the Dean. I soon concluded that they had explained what had happened at lunch and, as we deserved, Hannah and I were getting the brunt of the blame. Dean Smith had decided that Megan and Bea's failure to step in had put them at fault too.

"I'm going to call both of your parents," she said. "In the meantime, you can do lines." She left the room to make the calls after giving us all paper. I'd never been made to do lines in my life. Then, I'd never actually gotten a detention before.

"You two sorted your lovers' tiff?" Hannah asked as soon as the door closed behind her.

Deciding it would be best if we tried to resolve this, I said, "Yeah, I guess I overreacted because I was surprised. I'm not mad at anyone." I tried a smile. "And I'm sorry," I added.

"Oh!" Hannah said. "This is awkward, I didn't mean about *that*."

I frowned and watched Hannah's eyes flick to Donnie. I turned at my desk just in time to see him mouth 'don't' at her.

"What?" I said shakily.

"I think Donnie has something he wants to ask you about," Hannah said then put the end of her pen between her teeth in a Cheshire Cat grin. Confused, I turned back to Donnie but he just rolled his eyes.

"Am I the only one here who has no idea what's going on?" Megan asked but judging by Bea's quietness and the tension between Hannah and Donnie, they were the only two that were in on whatever this was.

"Donnie?"

"Ignore her, everything's fine," he said and he took the lid off his pen and began writing his lines.

"Is it fine though?" Hannah said in an annoyingly high pitched voice and her scrunched up nose indicating she knew something was up only made me want to wipe that grin off her face.

Donnie didn't look up but kept writing as he spoke. "It's something I'd like to discuss privately, if I'm honest," he said.

Hannah clicked her teeth and fake grimaced.

"If you don't tell her, I will."

I stared at the clock ticking behind Hannah, not wanting to meet her eyes. What did Donnie have that he would want to tell me but only in private? Something between him and Hannah. She was probably going to use this as an opportunity to rub more salt in the wound while it was still raw about those two sleeping together.

"Hannah," he warned.

"What?" I asked Hannah with conviction. If she wanted to bait me, I'd rise to it.

"Donnie knows you cheated on him," she said quickly. My ears started ringing and I felt like I was going to be sick. Here it was: the confrontation. I didn't know how he knew but he did. How long had it been?

"Emily?..." Megan was trying to snap me out of my daze. I looked to her guiltily and the surprise on Bea's face. I didn't want to look at Hannah but I could see Donnie stroking his jaw out of the corner of my eye. "Is it true?"

I opened my mouth to reply but I didn't know what to say. In the end, it came out as a feeble *"how?"*. Whether I'd directed it at Hannah or Donnie, I wasn't quite sure but it was Donnie who answered.

"Suspected as much. You spend a whole day with Nathan when everyone knows he wants you. He always gets what he wants. Connect the dots, it's not hard."

He sounded so calm. I'd expected him to be angry if he ever found out but he just sounded so detached. Maybe he'd known for so long that he'd come to terms with it. Thinking about what he'd just said though, it only sounded like speculation. No one actually had any proof.

"I didn't want to believe it. Amy was putting all these thoughts in my head when I told her about it," he drawled.

"Why would you listen to her?" I said accusingly. Amy has it in for me for some reason despite not bothering to actually know me.

"Well, she was right, wasn't she?" he said, raising his voice and finally sounding angry at me. I flinched.

"You fucked my brother... and didn't bother to tell me?" Bea said. While I tried to find my voice, Hannah raised an eyebrow, waiting for me to confess.

"No, it wasn't like that."

"You *didn't* fuck Nathan Horne?" Donnie said, clasping his hands together. Well, I'd already gone and denied it now.

"No," I said softly. "You can't just assume I'd give in to

him."

I tried to gauge whether everyone believed me but Donnie buried his face in his arms on his desk and laughed.

"I was actually going to forgive you for it. But you denying it… now I'm not so sure."

"What *proof* is there?" I asked. My heart was racing and I regretted asking immediately.

Hannah jumped in. "Donnie heard you in Nathan's room the other day." Everyone's face swung back to me and I felt the blood rise in my cheeks. So I hadn't been snitched on. I'd just been caught red handed.

"I went out to follow you because you forgot your maths book he said." I remembered I'd forgotten my maths book because he'd returned it the next morning instead. "Went into the hallway just in time to see you disappear into his room."

I put my shaking hand over my mouth. I was too numb to cry. "I wouldn't have eavesdropped but I heard you yelling at him and I wanted to be there to make sure you were ok. Then I heard him say what happened. It was bittersweet - finally knowing for sure. In that moment, I thought we were over. There you were again going straight from me to Nathan behind my back… but then I heard you calling him a dick and saying it was a mistake, that you still cared about me, et cetera."

"So… you forgive me?" I ventured.

"I don't know." He frowned and my heart wrenched at the sad look in his eyes.

"Spoiler alert." Hannah cupped her hands around her mouth and staged whispered, "if Emily still cared about you, she wouldn't have just lied to you when you called her out."

"I'm sorry," I said. My face fell into a frown to match Donnie's. "I never meant to hurt you, that's why I kept it from you. I'm sorry it happened and I'm sorry I lied. You have to believe me," I implored.

"I believe you," Donnie said sullenly. "I just wish you could be honest with me."

"I wanted to!" Everyone else in the room except Donnie and I faded away and it felt like just us, everything finally out in the open. "But I didn't want to lose you and I thought that if I did tell you, I would for certain." Donnie and I locked eyes and I could sense the understanding lurking in them. He was listening to me and he was not as mad as he should have been at me. Perhaps there was still a chance?

"Trademark cheater's excuse," Hannah yawned.

"How are you even so involved in this?" I asked, changing the subject slightly.

"Because he came to me about it when he found out."

Donnie looked to me and shrugged.

"She's your friend and mine sort of so I thought she'd be a good person to confide in," he explained.

"Except she clearly has a crush on you!"

"So what if I do like him a bit?" She exclaimed. "*I* wouldn't cheat on him."

I stood up, ready to leave the situation but at that moment, Dean Smith walked back into the room.

"Sit down," she said, completely failing to read the energy in the room. The clock on the wall was reading twenty minutes past four and I couldn't understand how so much time had passed so quickly. I suppose there was a lot of awkward silent pauses. "All of you can go. Everyone except Emily."

It didn't make sense that she was letting everyone go so soon, especially when Donnie was the only one who had even wrote any lines.

"Why me?" I asked.

She said only that she'd explain when the other students had left and while all the girls eyed me with distaste, Donnie's expression was one that I simply couldn't read.

"When I called your mother, I found out that she'd been in an accident. She's in hospital."

"What?" I stood up. "How serious?"

"She's absolutely fine, she just took a tumble when she was at the top of the stairs. No need to get in a tizzy but there's good news she wants to share with you too."

"What's that?"

"She's pregnant."

Chapter 17

On the way back to the dorms, I got my phone out to send a text to Nathan. **Busted** I typed out. **Thanks a lot**. I knew it wasn't entirely his fault but if he hadn't pulled me into his room against my will, Donnie wouldn't have overheard us and I wouldn't be in this mess.

After hearing that my mum was pregnant as well as having fallen down the stairs, I wanted to be able to go and see her but Dean Smith said that Mum had said she was fine and wanted me to stay at school until the Christmas holidays which weren't too long away anyway. I won't pretend it isn't a relief to avoid my dad as well. I thought maybe I'd just give her a call at some point.

Deciding to give the girls a miss, I headed straight to my room, wanting to be on my own for a bit. I didn't know if or when they would forgive me, Bea in particular, for what I'd done. I changed out of my uniform into my pyjamas even though it was far too early for bed and turned my phone off. Nathan would love an excuse to call me or try to talk if he thought Donnie was out of the picture.

Since the whole fiasco, I took it to mean that my relationship with Donnie was over. Well, it had sounded to me as though he was going to bring it up with me in private at some point but Hannah had to interfere and he didn't sound like he was going to break up with me. He'd just sounded disappointed and almost like he'd expected it. Plus he sort of implied I'd redeemed myself with what he'd overheard between Nathan and when I basically told Nathan to fuck off. But then I'd lied and ruined everything.

I let out an involuntary sob and collapsed onto the bed. With the covers wrapped tightly around me, I stared blankly at the ceiling, tears filling my eyes but not falling until I rolled onto my side, fixing my gaze on the wall instead. Mr. Groves had given us poetry homework that was due tomorrow morning which I hadn't even made a start on and Mr. Barnes, the maths teacher, had set some exercises that I was supposed to have completed online by tonight but I had been relying on meeting with Donnie to get him to help me with them since I'd never manage them on my own.

For an hour or so I just lay there. Finally caving and turning my phone on, just to see if anything was going on, I left it on my pillow while I got up to sit at my desk and open the laptop I'd borrowed. Even if my answers were completely wrong, at least I could say I had attempted the maths questions which is better than nothing. Deliberately ignoring the pings that emitted from my phone while I started work, I did the best I could to get the set work over and done with.

It took a lot longer than I thought and all I could think about, to make things worse, was how much easier it would be if I had Donnie at my side. With a frustrated sigh, I closed the laptop and picked up my phone from the bed. Immediately I saw several things that were happening. Gen had been added to our group chat, she had messaged me and so had Megan. Nathan had texted back **How?!? It wasn't me I promise. Want to talk?** and then left a voicemail when his call didn't go through.

I opened Megan's message first.

Bea will come around just give her time x

Well, that didn't sound like she was angry at me. Megan, that is. Evidently Bea was not feeling so forgiving. Not that I could blame her.

I checked the group chat but nothing had been said despite Gen being added to it. With a sense of foreboding, I opened Gen's message. It was a snapchat and as soon as I opened it, her bitmoji popped up in the corner for a second then disappeared almost immediately. I'll pretend I didn't see her lurking.

The message was not a particularly friendly one. **Looks like Hannah was in the right. Hope Donnie gets rid. You can't have two cakes and eat them**. Punctuated with a winky face. Rolling my eyes, I closed the app and went to my missed calls so I could listen to Nathan's voicemail.

"I'm outside the girls' dorms but your lovely Dean won't let me in," his tinny phone voice said. "She thinks I'll only cause trouble. Anyway, come down and let's go to dinner." I checked the time it was sent and it was only around fifteen minutes ago. Against my better judgement, I opened my window and looked straight down to the entrance. I hadn't expected him to still be there but he was. It wasn't like it was the first time he'd waited outside my window before.

His head snapped up when he heard my window crack open. "Rapunzel, Rapunzel, let down your hair."

"What do you want, Nate?" I sighed even though I already knew the answer to that.

"Well, it's lasagne night and I know a girl who loves pasta who might need cheering up right now," he said earnestly.

I shook my head. "Do you have any concept of how fucked up things are right now? I can't sit with you of all people at dinner. Just think how that will look, won't you?"

Nathan looked up at me with his ridiculously pleading eyes for a moment and then suggested, "we could go into town to eat. Avoid everyone if you want?"

I opened my mouth to tell him that I didn't need to avoid anyone but him but then I thought of Bea and Hannah's current feelings towards me. They wouldn't be so pleased to eat dinner with me and the thought of seeing Donnie so soon was not a good one.

"Fine, but you're paying."

"I *am* a gentleman," he said and I raised my eyebrows sceptically but didn't respond, only closed the window.

Pulling an outfit out of my wardrobe, I changed out of my pyjamas and deftly ran a brush through my hair before shrugging a thick jacket on and grabbing a bag. Outside, my breath formed mist in the cold and it was already dark. Nathan was looking like he was trying to appear contrite but it wasn't a look he's familiar with.

"Come on," I grouched, starting our trudge into town. "Where are we eating then?"

"We could get Italian if you want," he said, digging his hands into his coat pockets. "I know you love lasagne night and I suppose it's partly my fault you're too scared to show your face in the dining hall."

"I'm not scared!" I shot. "Just guilty. An emotion *you* don't have the capability to feel."

Nathan grimaced and avoided my eyes. "I *am* sorry. I didn't mean for any of that to happen. I just had to talk to you."

How could he apologise and then continue to make excuses that completely invalidate everything? It was him simply wanting to talk that ruined Donnie's trust in me. He didn't even talk to me about it - he went to Hannah of all people. He'd already suspected all along but he never asked. He didn't think I'd really do that to him.

But I did.

"You couldn't just respect my boundaries could you?" I mumbled. "You never do."

"I can't stay away from you," he said.

"Maybe you should."

"At least let me buy you dinner first," he said flatly. I looked at him out the side of my eye and he was trying not to smile. I couldn't help myself.

"What kind of reverse flirting was that?" I laughed.

"I don't know," he admitted.

He showed me to an Italian restaurant off the high street that I never knew existed. It actually looked quite fancy and I really hoped it wouldn't cost too much for Nathan because I hadn't brought any money with me since he'd agreed to pay. But then, he was the one who suggested this place.

I wasn't so keen on the dim lighting and candles on our little table setting an atmosphere like we were on a date. His face changed constantly in the flickering light and it was impossible to read what he was thinking. After settling on the type of pasta I wanted, I felt eyes on me from across the room. I turned my head to see who was so blatantly staring at me.

Of course it had to be Rosie fucking Ayres. I narrowed my eyes and looked back at Nathan.

"What exactly made you want to take me here of all places?" I asked and sucked on the straw in my Diet Coke.

Nathan frowned. "I thought you'd like it and it's quiet... do you not like it?"

I shrugged. "Seems alright, I was just wondering whether Rosie being here had anything to do with it."

"What?" Nathan cast his gaze around until he saw her in the corner with the guy she was with. "Why is she here with *Ben*?"

"Who's Ben?"

"From a school we played rugby against a while ago. They absolutely smashed us."

"Jealous?" I asked, sipping my drink again. Nathan humphed but said, "no."

Our garlic bread starter arrived and as I tore a chunk off, a thought occurred to me. "Hold on… you're not using me to make her jealous, are you?"

Nathan gestured with a piece of bread. "How was I even supposed to know she was here?"

"Snap maps is a thing."

He assured me that he had no idea Rosie would have been here and I was inclined to believe him, although I wasn't fully convinced he wouldn't at least take advantage of my presence to try to make Rosie jealous. Even worse, what if Rosie got wind that I'd slept with Nathan? She'd hate me even more than she does *and* she might tell Donnie she saw me here. This was the last thing I needed. Part of me wanted to leave right now and go back to my dorm but the damage was already done.

"So…" Nathan dragged out as we were finishing our pasta. "I know it's not my place to ask but where are things standing with O'Donoghue right now?"

"Um." I swallowed wrong and started choking. Nathan poured a glass of water from the pitcher on the table and handed it to me. I gulped down the water and felt somewhat thankful for the excuse to have tears running down my cheeks. To be honest, that question had kind of set me off and the tears leaking from my cheeks right now had nothing to do with choking. "Thanks. Things aren't great. Obviously. I think he might give me another chance but he isn't going to trust me the same is he?"

"Well he shouldn't, really," Nathan laughed. "Look at what you did."

"Seriously?" I seethed. "Could you not take even a bit of responsibility too?" Not wanting to put up with him anymore, I stood up and headed to the toilets. If I just left to go back to school, he'd follow me and annoy me more. Staring back at my face in the mirror in the dingy toilets, I splashed some water over myself and wiped under my eyes where I'd been crying.

I'd only been in there a couple of minutes, wondering what I was going to do next when the door opened and who should walk in but Rosie herself.

"Hey," she said. "I brought your bag and your coat; I figured you didn't want to go back out there and I know someone that works here so I can get us through the back exit."

Rosie was actually being nice to me. There had to be an ulterior motive. It was only earlier today that she was snitching on me in the dining hall.

"Thanks. Why are - why are you suddenly being nice to me?"

"I know how it feels to get fucked over by Nathan Horne better than most."

"Oh…"

"And I suppose I'm sorry for being a bitch when I told everyone about your bursary."

"Oh, that's ok. Turned out it wasn't a big deal anyway so I guess you really did me a favour making it easier to tell everyone. But um… what about your date? Isn't he missing you in here?"

"I'm going with you," she asserted, raising her eyebrows. "Out the back. I'm walking out on him."

An uneasy feeling told me that she was only done with her date because she'd achieved what she wanted with regards to making an impression on Nathan but that was none of my business. So what if she was? I don't care about him and they'll end up together in the end.

"Ok. Let's go."

The two of us shuffled out of the toilets and around the corner into the kitchens before Nathan or Ben could spot us. I followed her as she waved to a girl a few years older than us working in the kitchen before she pushed out the back door into the black night. I wasn't sure if we were going to head back to school together or what but as we went out into the street I saw a play park and she asked if I wanted to go in there and talk for a while. Out of interest in what we might have to talk about, I agreed.

Rosie settled into one of the swings and I sat on the one next to her. The metal chains were numbingly cold as I lightly swung back and forth on my tiptoes.

"You and Nathan are a thing then?" she stated, looking a bit sad. "You and Donnie break up?"

"You could say that," I said. "About me and Donnie breaking up!" I hastened to add. "Not that me and Nathan are a thing because we're definitely not. It was his damn fault we broke up. Well, both of our faults."

Rosie seemed to light up a bit after this admission. "What's all this about though? You were telling on me to the Dean at lunch only hours ago and now you're being all friendly? Sorry if I sort of don't buy it."

Rosie shrugged. "You'd been avoiding Nathan for ages and then I see you all cozy with him on a date. I can't keep up either."

I laughed. "So you only hate me when I'm a threat?"

She laughed too and tossed her hair back as she leaned back on the swing. "Something like that. I like Nathan, I really, really like him and there's no point pretending I don't or I'd look like a complete idiot. Look at it this way though: say you and Donnie weren't broken up and there's this other girl that you know he's got eyes for. She's new, she's smart and she's pretty too. You wouldn't want a boy who wants someone else and also, wouldn't you hate her a little bit too?"

I had to agree with where she was coming from.

"Yeah, I see your point. I'm not exactly innocent either. I only didn't like you because Bea doesn't and she's my friend.

Supposed to be my friend, we might not be now. Plus I got jealous when he was sneaking behind my back to your room to fuck you when he was saying he wanted me. He's so full of shit," I sighed.

"What are you talking about?" Rosie laughed nervously. "He never…? Did he say we were fucking?"

"That's what he told me. Sorry, I don't mean to pry into your business."

"No, what did he say? We haven't fucked since like the first week of school."

"What?" My heart went a bit funny and I didn't understand. He'd said the other day that they hadn't been sleeping together since he did with me but before that he'd said he and Rosie had been at it. He said so on my birthday. One of them was lying. "He was seen going into your room at night, there were witnesses, you must have heard the rumours."

"Yeah that's true but it wasn't for sex."

"What about after I got with Donnie? He was around you all the time and then during half term he told me he'd been sleeping with you then."

Rosie's mouth fell open and she looked scathingly angry. "That's such a lie! Why would he go around saying that?"

"Why was he going to yours at night then?" I asked. I wanted to get to the bottom of this before it could get much more complicated. Oh my god, wait. "Do you have anything to do with him and his drugs?"

"You know about that too?" Rosie breathed. She sounded relieved. "I don't have anything to do with it besides trying to help him. Just trying to get him to stop taking them. He's probably addicted. Can you get addicted to steroids?" she asked.

"Don't ask me," I said. So that was it then. Everything was clicked into place. That's why he was sneaking over to Rosie's but still wouldn't tell me even when I found them in his bathroom.

"Did he say anything else?" Rosie asked quickly.

"About what?"

"Um. About… never mind." She smiled. "So he lied then," she said decisively. "Used me as a convenient scapegoat to make you jealous because he knows you would never ask me and everyone thinks we're friends with benefits or whatever anyway."

"If what you're saying is true, then yeah. He must have but… he told me the other day that he wasn't seeing you recently and I'm a bit confused why he'd say that if he wasn't before."

"It's obvious isn't it?" she asked. When she saw how clueless I still was, she continued. "He tried to make you jealous before by claiming to have me as an alternative but when that didn't work, he changed tactics and tried to say that he was crazy about you and only you. He couldn't take back what he'd already said about being with me because then he'd be outing himself as a liar and then how could you trust him?"

That was plausible. That was very plausible. Rosie didn't seem to be lying and if she was making this up on the spot, she was very quick. I had no choice but to believe her.

I "hmm"ed.

"He is crazy about you as well. All he talks about is you, I'm almost sick of hearing your name." She laughed. "And he's been trying to get me to apologise to you about sending the mass text around the school about you for months now. I think he is actually trying to do right by you."

Wow. So he really wasn't interested in Rosie like that but personally, after realising all his lies and manipulation, I couldn't see how he could possibly do me 'right' in any way. Before I could have too much time to dwell on it, my phone went off. I looked at Nathan's caller ID and rolled my eyes. Then Rosie's phone went off too and I saw 'Ben' on the screen. We shared a look and laughed.

"Should we entertain them or not?" she asked. I had a momentary vision of Nathan with Ben, whom he must dislike so much, confused together, wondering how it had turned out like this.

"I'm not answering mine," I said with a smile. At least tonight I didn't need to hear any more bullshit from him.

"Same then." She declined Ben's call.

"Back to the goss, how was you and Donnie breaking up Nathan's fault? That's what you said isn't it?" she frowned while she remembered.

I groaned. "Don't even get me started. It was all a stupid mistake. When me and Donnie had just started dating, Nathan had me over to stay at his during half term and like you said, he tried to make me jealous with you."

"You didn't?" She said breezily. I smiled guiltily. "Oh my god! You did! Why didn't he tell me? I've been waiting to hear that for so long. You two are like endgame."

"Rosie noooo," I whined. "I was with Donnie, I was drunk and I was actually really upset because it was my first time as well and I really owed it to Donnie and I was so guilty I still haven't slept with Donnie. It was the worst thing I've done in my life and I wish it never happened because I love Donnie!" It all came out in one big blurt and Rosie nodded slowly. I'd never even admitted to Donnie that I'd loved him yet either. "I think I need to go talk to him."

Rosie looked contemplative for a moment but then said, "from my point of view, I've seen how Nathan feels about you but in your eyes it's obviously Donnie. You'd better go."

"Thank you for everything you've told me," I said, doing up my coat, picking up my bag and getting ready to go.

"If you need a friend in the future, I promise I won't be an enemy."

"This has been a *crazy* night."

"The course of true love never did run smooth did it?"

Chapter 18

I almost ran back to the school. My phone rang again but I ignored it. It was cold and dark but only just past seven o'clock so I had ages before curfew. Once through the school gates, I had to guess whether Donnie was in his room or at the library. I thought I'd check his room first since it was closest.

Winding up the stairs to the top floor of the boys' boarding house, I tried to plan what I might say but I was coming up with nothing. I rapped on his door and half hoped he was in there but also half hoped he wasn't so I could have more time to think.

It swung open and I was met with Donnie's piercing blue eyes. "Emily? What happened, you're all flushed." I became aware of how heavily I was breathing.

"Can I come in?" I wasn't really asking and I stepped past him before he could process and close the door in my face.

"What's happened?" he repeated. I dropped my bag onto the floor and shrugged my coat off too. Donnie was in only his pyjama bottoms, bare chested.

"I just- I don't even know. So much has happened today, it's mad. I was just talking with Rosie-"

"You don't even like Rosie."

"I know, I told you, it's mad but I was talking with Rosie

166

about you and what happened and everything and I realised-"

"You realised what?"

"That I love you."

I bit my lip in anticipation. I couldn't take it back now. Donnie ran his fingers through his hair in the signature way that he so often does.

"That's the first time you've said that to me. It's very convenient for you."

I sat on his bed and rubbed my arms as goosebumps rose involuntarily. "I know."

Donnie groaned into his hands. "Em, this isn't fair."

He paced the room and as he came close enough for me to reach, I grabbed his hands and gently pulled him to the bed. I kicked off my shoes and swung my legs up onto the bed.

"I did you really, really wrong. I know that and I shouldn't have kept it from you and I shouldn't have lied. I was trying to protect you and I went about it the complete wrong way and I'm sorry."

Donnie couldn't meet my eyes but he spoke. "Would it be fair to say that you had stronger feelings for Nathan than you had for me during half term?"

I swallowed and considered it. "I suppose I must have done," I said in a small voice. His hands were still in mine and I gave them an apologetic squeeze.

"It's really shit but I think I understand that I perhaps pushed you for a relationship before you were ready to be invested in it," he said and I nodded. "You've been holding out on me for weeks but apart from that you've been a model girlfriend. I'm not happy with you for what you did but... I can't hold it against you."

"Donnie," I said, my voice breaking pathetically and my eyes tearing up. "I was only holding out on you because I wanted my first time with you to be special and I wanted to definitely be in love with you. I feel like an idiot because I wanted you to be my first and I'd already *wasted it*."

He sighed. "You made a mistake. We've all made mistakes."

"What mistakes have you made?" I asked, eyeing all the trophies and awards lining his shelves. Donnie was beyond perfect. He was too good to be true. Too good for me.

"You think I'm proud of my first time being with Hannah?" He laughed. "We were both drunk and it was very disappointing." Despite Hannah's boasting about it, that did make me feel a little better.

I lay back on Donnie's bed and he relaxed down next to me, one of our hands still intertwined between our bodies. "I don't think the girls will want to be friends with me anymore," I said. "They probably won't talk to me."

"You've got other friends," Donnie said speculatively. "You still have me, you know. You have Steven and Rosie Ayres apparently. What's all that about?"

I played with a loose thread on my sleeve. It wouldn't be the brightest idea to mention going for dinner with Nathan when things were falling into place in the remains of my relationship but considering how I'd lied to him earlier, I at least owed him some semblance of the truth.

"Turns out she's not really who I thought she was. She's not even into Nathan any more. You know when everyone thought they were shagging and he even said that to me himself? Well, it was all a lie. She wasn't close to him because she was hooking up with him; she was actually trying to help him with something. Then she said…" I rolled onto my side so I could look into his eyes. "She said Nathan would only go on about me to her. So, all this time, he was only trying to make me jealous. She told me this and I think she was hoping I would melt and realise how much Nathan cares about me."

Donnie let go of my hand and clenched it into a fist. He

turned his head from me and gazed blankly at the ceiling instead.

"But all I could think about was *you*," I emphasised. "I know I've never said I loved you but I realised it in that moment. I was suddenly sure. I might have royally fucked things up but I had to tell you."

"I love you too," he whispered. There was still hurt lurking in his eyes but he cupped my cheek with his palm and rubbed his thumb across my skin all the same. "And I'm kind of glad you didn't go from Nathan to me and tell me you loved me if it wasn't true and try to sleep with me if you weren't ready. I'm glad it *means* something to you."

I licked my dry lips that had cracked in the cold. "It does," I affirmed. "I'm sorry. No more secrets."

He leaned in, closing the space between us and planted a tentative kiss on the corner of my mouth but I moved and captured his lips in a proper kiss. My hand fell naturally into the curve of his neck as we pulled each other closer and his smooth chest pressed against mine. I'd put on a thick wool jumper for tonight's excursion and I was quickly overheating.

In a break between kissing, I pulled it off over my head. Donnie raised his eyebrows and seemed hesitant for a moment.

"Emily," he said, pulling us both out of the mood. "It's not that I don't want to sleep with you but tonight I'm just not in the right headspace."

My fingers slipped from his neck down to his collarbone. "I wasn't trying to," I mumbled.

"Ok, I was just checking. Don't get moody," he said when it was him that was killing the heat that had just built up between the two of us. Unexpectedly, he pulled me over his body to straddle him and tugged at the top I was wearing under my jumper. I let him pull it off me and discard it on the floor. He pressed his hands into my waist as I leaned down to kiss him again. Being so flush against him, I felt him hardened beneath me and without the boldness of alcohol in my system this time, being in bed with him suddenly became a lot scarier.

I sat back just as he unclasped my bra and my hands flew to hold the cups in place before they could go anywhere. "You're right, we should wait before we go much further."

Donnie sat up too. "Did I do something wrong?"

"No, of course not." I fumbled trying to do my bra up behind my back but Donnie courteously did it back up for me. "I just think I need a little more time and maybe we need to be a little more... stable before I'm comfortable showing myself to you like that."

Donnie pursed his lips but nodded slowly. "I don't want to rush you. Take all the time you need."

I climbed off him but didn't collect my clothes off the floor. I was comfortable enough as I was.

"Fuck, I was supposed to call my mum," I remembered out of nowhere.

"Right now?" Donnie laughed but stopped when he saw the expression on my face.

"She's in hospital, Donnie. That's why the Dean kept me behind earlier."

Donnie gently rested a hand on my stomach. "Is she ok?"

"She fell down the stairs, injured her ankle but she's fine apparently. That's not the worst part."

"What's the worst part?" He prompted.

"She's pregnant. I don't know if she went to the hospital and found out then or..."

"Or if she knew before?" Donnie said casually.

I finally voiced what I'd been pushing to the back of my mind and distracting myself from all evening. "Or if her falling down the stairs wasn't an accident and has something to do with my Dad finding out."

Chapter 19

In the morning, I woke up with enough time to notice an email from Mrs. Hayes about a meeting for all A-level art students at lunch. Refreshments would be provided (but I imagined they were only to persuade us to attend rather than go socialise with out friends in the dining hall). I'd already skipped breakfast as I was in the habit of doing and this was a welcome excuse to sort of skip lunch too.

I had no classes on until after lunch so I decided to text Steven to meet him early at the art studios and he replied that he was already there. There were texts from Nathan from last night, asking what was going on with me and Rosie but nothing from today. Presumably, Rosie would have filled him in by now.

"Look at you, Picasso!" I said to Steven as I walked in to the studio. He was working on some type of abstract portraits that were incorporating what I took to be the sun and moon into them.

"Hey miss thing," he said, putting his paintbrush into a dirty pot of water. "Have I been hearing some rumours about you lately."

"From Ayres?" I almost rolled my eyes out of pure habit.

"Why yes, and now I'm an awkward middle man between the two of you."

I took his dirty water pot and poured out the water to refill it so I could use it too. "Nothing needs to be awkward, we get along now."

Steven snorted. "And I'm the Queen of England," he said.

"No, really," I said and set up an easel so I could finish off one of my paintings. It was a self portrait and I'd looked at it too long and started to hate it. I needed to finish it before I despised it completely. "We had a talk last night and it seems I had the wrong end of the stick all along. Apart from right at the beginning of the year, she really isn't interested in Nathan."

"Ohhh, you mean like I told you all along?"

I gave an apologetic smile. "I thought you might be a bit biased."

Luckily, I managed to finish my painting before I could turn into Dorian Gray and rip up the horrible portrait. Students from upper and lower sixth form started to accumulate as the lunch hour started and, as promised, Mrs. Hayes had provided a buffet of food along one of the cleaner tables that we were less likely to get poisoned from the tubes of paint and jars of white spirit that littered this place.

When it seemed all who would bother to turn up were here, Mrs. Hayes started explaining whatever it was that she couldn't be bothered to put into a simple email.

"You're all going to be invited to participate in a young artists competition. If you choose to do it, it'll be alongside your studies and finalists will have their work exhibited in London galleries before they do a tour of the UK."

"Sounds kinda like the BP portrait awards," Steven said to me. If I had to do one more portrait, I might actually scream.

"It's a great opportunity for everyone," Mrs. Hayes continued, "and if you haven't yet started an EPQ, this would be acceptable to use as a project. Come speak to me afterwards about it if that's something you're interested in doing. The competition guidelines allow you to interpret the stimulus in any way you choose, be that painting, drawing, sculpture, film, photography, whatever you want."

She started handing out pieces of paper with the details to the students.

"That doesn't sound like a bad idea," I said. I had after all been wanting to find something substantial to use for an EPQ and with art as my best subject and the fact I'd probably do the competition whether I'd use it for an EPQ or not, it seemed a stupid idea not to go ahead with it. Mrs. Hayes handed me the guidelines and my eyes were instantly drawn to the single word written in red in the middle of the page. The stimulus: 'love'.

Steven received the guidelines next and he sniggered. "Oh, girl they made this for you. You should make something with loads of triangles."

"Triangles?"

"Like the love triangle you're always falling into."

I folded my paper into quarters and swatted him with it, then went off to distract myself with a slice of pizza before he could laugh at me any more. Of course the theme would have to be something so apt. My response would have to be somewhat personal to be meaningful enough to win and to be interesting enough to write a whole EPQ about. Maybe this wasn't the good idea it seemed to be five minutes ago. I barely knew how I felt about love as it was, let alone being able to organise my thoughts into something I could visually present.

Steven was already jotting down ideas in a spider diagram inside the notebook he always carried with him for when he gets struck by inspiration and I couldn't stand how easily it came to him. I skulked off to find Mrs. Hayes about signing up for the EPQ instead.

I found out I needed to get started on the paperwork

straight away so Mrs. Hayes could write her feedback on my initial ideas. She said she would email it so I made a mental note to start that this evening. Before I could do that, I had to go to my English lesson and there was a maths revision session but I'd probably skip that. Can't revise something if I never managed to nail it in the first place.

When I went into the English classroom, I first thought that Hannah wasn't here yet but I realised as I took my seat that she was here, but she'd moved to another seat across the room. Whatever, I didn't want to discuss semantic fields and metaphors with her anyway. I wondered if she knew Donnie and I were ok and how she felt about that. I'd have to keep a closer eye on her now I knew about her feelings towards him. I trusted Donnie though, so I didn't think I had anything to worry about.

Jess, who normally sat where Hannah was now, saw her seat occupied when she came in and came to sit by me.

"You two fall out?" she asked.

"Guess so," I said, setting out my books and opening my notebook to a new page. "It's her problem not mine."

Jess didn't probe for anything more about Hannah so I started a discussion about the books we were reading instead. Might as well do well in English if maths was going to grow to be a complete failure of an A-level for me.

Steven wanted to meet me in the library after last period so we could help each other fill in the EPQ forms. I hadn't looked at them yet but he had and he wanted to make sure he was filling it in correctly. He was sitting at a bay of computers and I made my way over to him. On the way I passed Donnie. He spent a lot of time hiding between the bookshelves of the library so it wasn't a surprise to see him here. I didn't think he'd noticed me but he gave me a little wave and went back to his work. I hoped he was just busy and not trying to be dismissive of me.

The first page of the EPQ log (it turned out to be a whole log that I'd fill out as I did the project) was relatively simple. We started by filling in our names and the school name. Then it was just a process of ticking boxes to acknowledge we wouldn't receive help from others on the project or plagiarise. I thought about the time Donnie helped me finish my portraiture work once. That wouldn't fly this time.

Then came the trickier part. We had to fill in a title for the project. I hadn't had time to think this far ahead in the space of only an afternoon and neither had Steven but I realised I'd be able to give it a working title and a final title further along. 'The Love Project' I entered into the working title space and cringed.

I still hadn't had any specific thoughts on how I was going to interpret the brief but I used all the information on it to fill in my log with my aims for the outcome of this project. Bit by bit I filled out the first sections of the form and let Steven read it over while I read his. We approved them and sent them off in emails to Mrs. Hayes. My mind started wondering as the computer shut down.

I'd called my Mum last night. She was home, albeit with a sprained ankle. She was thankful that Dad was there to look after her. I asked if she knew she was pregnant before she went to the hospital. Yes, she knew. And how did she fall? Oh, you know, just silly her, always been a bit clumsy and being pregnant only makes it worse. Was she happy that she is pregnant? What about Dad? Yes and yes. Of course, there's more risk being an older mother but it'll be fine. Was I still welcome home for Christmas? Yes, all that fuss from half term was forgotten about. How was school going? Fine. Ok. Ok. Bye.

"What are you up to?" It was Donnie, drawing up a chair next to me and looking at the art competition brief that was set on the desk before me. He picked it up and peered at it. "Wow, doesn't that sound interesting?"

His tone was slightly condescending but I ignored it. "I'm doing it for an EPQ," I said.

"Oh, yeah. That's not a bad idea," he said. "Might as well get an AS out of it if it's going to distract you from your other art work and maths isn't looking promising." Steven had already left so I couldn't look to him to help me psychoanalyse what Donnie had just said. To me, it came off as rude.

"What's your problem?" I asked, snatching the brief back. "Why are you being such a dick about me doing some extra work instead of just being supportive?" I wasn't sure exactly what Donnie was doing for his EPQ but I'm sure it was something far more complicated than a paltry little art project. "I might as well do something easy to do for an EPQ because I'm what? So shit at everything else?"

"No, Em, you know that's not what I meant."

I didn't care to hear whatever it was he did mean. I picked up my bag from under the table and swept out of the library. It was only 5 o'clock so it was a bit early for dinner and there wouldn't be anything hot available yet but I went into the dining hall anyway. Donnie followed me in even though I thought I'd lost him in the dark outside and I ignored him as I got a cold chicken salad to go. I'd eat it in my room.

Annoyingly, Donnie flagged what I was doing and got a pasta pot to go too. "Emily," he said meaningfully as I made my way outside. "I *was* trying to be supportive."

I quickened my pace but Donnie stepped in front of me, barring the door into the boarding house. Before he could say anything, the door opened behind him and out came Hannah, Bea and Gen. No Megan in sight. Their eyes flew between the two of us and I pushed past them inside before any uncomfortable confrontations could take place. I could hardly fathom that it was only yesterday that everything blew up.

"Fine, come on," I said to Donnie. Despite how he'd wound me up, I didn't want to leave him there to talk to the girls. I set my bag down in my room, kicked off my shoes, and opened my salad box at my desk while continuing to ignore Donnie. He sank onto my bed.

"Stop being moody," he said.

"Stop making me moody." I stabbed my salad with more force than was necessary for some leaves and vegetables. "You were being a twat."

"I said it was a good idea and it's good to get an AS!"

"Yeah but then you said it would distract me from my art A-level work and maths."

"Well it's true." He twirled his fork in his pasta but I was turned away at my desk, only able to see him through my desk mirror. I ate another mouthful.

"That's so nice of you," I said sarcastically. "So nice to have a boyfriend who gives it to me straight." My voice rose several octaves and I cursed myself, knowing I was on the verge of crying.

"Am I still your boyfriend?" he asked and froze. I'd assumed he was. Maybe now, after everything, he wanted to keep things casual.

I finally turned to look at him. "You tell me."

He returned to stirring his cheese and tomato pasta rather than eating it, long tendrils of melted cheese sticking to his plastic fork. "I guess, as long as we can work things out."

He guesses? "What's there left to work out? I thought we were on the same page now." I squeaked, getting out my desk chair to sit on the bed with him. His mouth twitched and I could see him trying to mentally work things through.

"Stop being so emotional," he said.

"Stop telling me what to be."

His eyes bored into mine. Neither of us said anything. I leaned in. He leaned in.

We both moved at the same time, closing the remaining space between us. We both forgot about the pasta. The pot crumpled between us as I fell onto him, our lips and legs tangling.

When we broke apart, I inspected my shirt. "This is the second shirt I've ruined with pasta in two days," I complained and took the pot and set it on the desk.

"You could always take it off," he suggested. I tried not to smile. I was supposed to still be annoyed at him but I pulled my blazer off anyway and sat back on the bed, a little further away, but Donnie pulled me onto his lap. Somehow he hadn't managed to get anything spilt on him. Only my luck. I fiddled with the top button of my shirt and took so long that Donnie began undoing them from the bottom, meeting me halfway.

He softly pushed it down my arms. "You too," I said, nodding at his blazer and shirt. I didn't want to be the only one stripping off. I helped him to take them off and then his hands came to the back of my bra just like last night.

"Is this ok?"

"Yeah," I breathed and kissed him, partly so he couldn't see me as he undid it. I wasn't embarrassed by my body but… I wasn't wholly comfortable.

"Are you sure?" he said, fingers resting on the clasp. "Yesterday you said you wanted to be more stable or something first."

"That was yesterday. Stop talking." A lot can change within a day as we both well knew. I felt the release of my bra's band constricting me and it fell down my arms and I pushed it off the bed onto the floor. He broke the kiss and his hands came to cup my breasts. I felt myself blush.

He was such a gentle boy and his touch made my bare skin

prickle. His thumb brushed over my nipple and I rested my palms against his chest and pushed us down to lie flat with me half on top of him. Not knowing what I was doing, I trailed a hand down to his belt and started tugging at the buckle.

"Someone's very eager," he said.

"Do you have a condom?" I asked, and managed to work the belt open.

"No, do you?"

I paused. "No."

Donnie was pulling his trousers off and I was trying not to look at the bulge in his boxers.

"So we can't do anything then?"

"Of course we can still do things. You didn't do any foreplay with Nathan?"

"Any what?"

"Are you really that innocent?" Apparently I was. "Handjob? Blow job? Did he do anything for you other than fuck you?"

I shook my head. I didn't want to think about Nathan. I hadn't bumped into him all day but it was only a matter of time and it would be so awkward with both of us knowing Rosie had told me of his infatuation. I almost felt a little sorry for him.

"Wow, the bar is on the floor. Trust Nathan to only think about himself."

"Stop talking about him," I said, getting annoyed. I didn't need the reminder.

Donnie rolled his eyes, thinking I wasn't looking but continued nonetheless. He flipped me over so I was underneath him. His hands came up under my skirt and I wasn't sure what he was doing until I felt my tights sliding down my legs.

"What are you doing?" I asked, sitting up.

"Just tell me if you want me to stop," he said and waited for me to lie back down. His fingers came up to my hips again, catching under my underwear and beginning to drag it off like he did with my tights. This was so much more intimate than anything I'd experienced. I could tell he actually cared about how he was making me feel.

I was lying there in just my skirt, feeling his soft hands on my thighs. He planted kisses from my jaw down my breasts and my stomach but stopping before going any lower. I felt one of his hands travel further up until I felt him against my heat. His finger dipped slowly inside me and I felt my breath hitch. He met my eyes, seeing how I was reacting but when I nodded slightly, he started to pump his finger in and out, extracting an "oh" of pleasure from me as he added a second finger and started to curl them.

"Do you like that?"

"Yes. Keep going," I breathed.

In answer, he started to rub slow circles on my clit with the thumb of his other hand, making me moan and arch my back, pressing myself into his hands. It was nothing like how it felt when I had occasionally tried to do it to myself. I never got any pleasure from it but this was so different. It was the unpredictability. Donnie sped up and I gritted my teeth, scrunched my eyes up as the tension built.

It shattered with a knocking at the door.

Donnie looked at me like it was my fault, like I planned to have someone come and interrupt us. What could I do? I was in only a skirt and Donnie in only his boxers, I could hardly answer whoever it was. With a devious smile, Donnie slid his fingers back in and at the gasp that emitted from my lips, he pressed his other hand over my mouth and continued to work me. How he could manage to rub circles on me while pumping his fingers with the same hand was beyond me, but the least of my concerns.

"Emily are you in there?"

Nathan's voice. My eyes widened but Donnie only got faster and we were both lucky his hand was muffling the sounds that would have come out my mouth if it was not.

"Emily?"

I was overwhelmed, the pleasure was spreading right up to my bouncing chest and my legs were beginning to shake uncontrollably. I was almost screaming into Donnie's hand when he removed it all of a sudden the sound came out loudly. So loudly there was no way Nathan wouldn't have heard it. I placed my own hand over my mouth in embarrassment.

My chest was heaving and Donnie was still grinning. "Did he ever make you feel like that?" He nodded his head towards the door. As the feeling melted away, I heard the tell-tale floorboard outside my room creak as Nathan walked away.

"Did you just do that with me because you want me or because you want to be able to say you did something that Nathan didn't?" I flared, drawing my legs away and curling them up.

"Why are you getting all angry and defensive again?" Donnie said, matching my anger.

"Why can't you answer my question?"

"Of course I want you. Why would I have done that if I didn't want you?"

"I don't know, why did you have to make sure he heard me when we could have pretended we weren't here?"

"Because I'm your boyfriend and he was outside your door like he didn't understand that."

"It's not a competition!"

"It feels like it!"

I opened my mouth to retaliate but I didn't know what to say. I felt used. "It's like we *share* you," he continued. "Who do you belong to most: mostly him or mostly me?"

"Mostly *me*!" He was talking about me like I was a doll to be passed around.

"God, you're just as bad as each other," I said. I was scooping up my scattered clothes and pulling them back on, ignoring the tights, knowing how undignified pulling them back on would look. "You can't trust me any more so you have to make a show of me and he… well, I don't know but at least he genuinely has good intentions even if he does go about them in a questionable way. He has always cared about me and I don't think he really did anything wrong."

Donnie now started to tug his clothes back on. "You don't think he did *anything* wrong? You think sleeping with someone in a relationship is *right*?"

"No! Obviously in principle it's wrong but, I mean, from his perspective, he had feelings for me and he knew I had some back so if I he made a move and I made one back, that's on *me* not him."

"Yeah, we sure know he made one. Everyone knows now that *my* girlfriend threw herself at someone else and then wouldn't even sleep with me."

"Maybe I *don't* want to be your girlfriend!" I shouted in the heat of the moment. Didn't I?

"It's very clear you don't," he said steely and made for the door.

"No, wait," I said but he was already gone.

My phone buzzed in the pocket of my blazer that I was holding but hadn't put back on. It was too soon to be Donnie. Please don't be Nathan.

It was Bea.

Wow, I never noticed how thin the wall between my room and yours is.

Chapter 20

It only got worse. Another message came through.

I guess it's some consolation. Nate goes to try to talk to you, you're with Donnie so he comes into my room and he gets to hear you two have a screaming match over him.

My heart dropped. Nathan heard all of that?

Bea would be seeing the notification that I'd read her messages. How was I meant to reply to that? I'd just fucked up so bad. I didn't know if I'd meant what I said to Donnie. A little voice in my head said that if I had to question it, I didn't love him as much as two people in a relationship should but I'd chosen Donnie, hadn't I? Through everything, I'd ignored Nathan, it was always Donnie, so why did I have to ruin it?

I wrapped my duvet around myself to shroud myself. It wasn't all my fault entirely. Donnie had been acting a dick. I'm not saying I didn't deserve it but he wasn't treating me fairly; it was like he was trying to get his own back. It was so unlike him. Jealousy had brought out the worst in him.

My phone vibrating another message snapped me out of my head.

He wants to see you, should I let him?

Well, that was a far friendlier tone than before. I was in such a state to be seen, though. My shirt was still on the floor with my tights so I was in just my underwear and skirt with the duvet covering me. The barely touched pasta pot sat crumpled on the side.

Nathan had seen me in worst states.

So far, I'd managed to keep the tears at bay, more confused than anything.

If he wants to I sent.

It took him probably only five seconds before he was in my room. I held my breath, unsure what to say, but he took one look at the clothes left on the floor, at me all wrapped up and my bottom lip that was starting to quiver and came over with his arms outstretched for a hug.

"I hate seeing you upset," he said and enveloped me and my duvet cocoon in his warm embrace. He smelled like those awful lynx scents that boys get given for Christmas by relatives who don't know what to actually get them, but it was comforting. "What happened?"

I swallowed thickly. "Was there anything you *didn't* hear?"

"Well, no, to be honest, I think I have a good idea of what went down but if you wanted to talk about it…"

I sniffed, willing myself to keep the horrible upset feeling in my throat rather than spilling down my cheeks. "I don't want to talk about it."

"That's ok," he said soothingly and sounding like he meant it even though I know Nathan and I know he likes to know the details of things. "Can I give you a proper hug or are you going to stay wrapped up like that forever?"

"I don't have a top on."

"I don't mind."

I rolled my eyes but couldn't resist a smile. "I know you don't."

He slid his hands between my skin and the duvet so it fell away as he drew me into his chest.

"Are you two over?" he asked.

"I don't really know," I said, feeling empty. "I'm not really sure what happened, it was all so quick. He's definitely not happy with me."

"From what I heard, it sounded like he was trying to prove something."

"Yeah, that's what I said... how mad at me is Bea?"

I needed to know if there was anything left of our friendship to be salvaged.

"She's not really mad at you. Hannah is upset because she liked Donnie or something so she feels like you stole him and then didn't appreciate him or some rubbish. Bea's known Hannah since they were both tiny so she has to side with her but they'll both get over it."

"I think she's more annoyed that I slept with, actually."

The corners of his mouth twitched momentarily. "Ah yes, that might take more time to get over."

Nathan finally let me go from his hug and I went to my wardrobe to get a top out. While I pulled it on, with my back to him, I said, "so Rosie told me a lot of things last night."

He groaned, seemingly from embarrassment and jokingly covered his face with his hands. "I knew I told her too much about you. I never thought the two of you would talk though! You hated each other, I thought, and then you bailed on me with her, of all people. How was I supposed to see that coming?"

"Yeah, I didn't either. She made me realise what a liar you are."

"What do you mean? What have I lied about?"

I picked up my abandoned salad from my desk and stabbed my fork back into it. "All that talk about how you had been hooking up with her?" I deadpanned.

"Ahhh." This seemed to be news to him that I knew about that. I guess Rosie had only told him about informing me about his feelings towards me. "That was stupid of me," he said. "I was trying to sort of make you jealous. I shouldn't have lied."

"No, you shouldn't," I said accusatorially. "Is there anything else you want to own up about?"

Nathan grimaced shiftily. "Is there something I should have?"

I didn't know, I was just punting to see if he would admit to anything else I should know about that I didn't. "How about your little steroid problem. How's that going? You told me you stopped taking them, was that true?"

He took a beat too long to think of an answer.

"Ok," I huffed. "I don't think I ever really believed you when you said you'd stop anyway."

"I was going to," he groaned. "I tried!" He started to gesticulate. "It's a lot easier said than done."

"And Rosie is helping you with it?" I bit into my salad and caught an unwelcome chunk of onion.

"Yeah we help each other?"

"Each other?" I raised my eyebrows. She hadn't told me anything about that.

"Like I've told you many times before, if she chose not to tell you about it, it isn't my place to say."

"She has a drug problem too?"

"No, she has problems. They aren't drugs. Can we talk about something else?"

What else did we have to talk about? Unless we were arguing something, we didn't have much in common to talk about. "You should probably go, actually. It doesn't look so good if every time I have an altercation with Donnie, I then see you."

Nathan got up, as if to go, but twisted his wristwatch, shifting his weight from foot to foot, stalling for time. "You going to try to work things out?"

"I think that *was* us trying to work things out. It doesn't look like it's going to work between us."

He finally went to the door, presumably he'd heard what he'd wanted and as we stood there, I noticed how his gaze dropped to my lips and I wondered if he would kiss me. I wondered if I would mind. In the end, he only kissed the top of my head.

"Bye Nathan."

I eventually made up with Bea with a box of her favourite liqueur chocolates. Hannah begrudgingly stopped ignoring me after a week or so, and things were almost back as they used to be. I was single again, I was focusing on my school work and I was doing just fine.

To bite the bullet, I'd also befriended a girl in upper sixth who was tutoring me in maths. The way she explained things was so much clearer than Donnie's methods and she was very patient. I wasn't worried I'd fail an A-level anymore. I *was* worried I'd have to go home in only a few days for Christmas.

Before that, though, was the highly anticipated drama department performance of Legally Blonde, four months in the making. Rosie was so excited about it. We'd drawn closer but it had earned me a fair few reproachful looks from Bea. Megan, who was usually the most chill, also didn't appreciate me being so friendly with the girl she saw as the competition for roles in the drama department, but when it came to Legally Blonde, I'd seen both of their auditions and Rosie won Elle fair and square.

The performance we'd all got tickets for were for Thursday night and we'd be going home on Friday or Saturday. I'd told my parents I would come home on Saturday. I didn't want to spend a single second longer than necessary stuck at that house playing happy families. The best part of the Christmas half term was it meant I got a break from that stupid art project.

Rosie, of all people, had given me the idea for the direction I took my project. I'd been whining about Donnie and Nathan and boys in general, then family and friendship and how love was so messy in all instances of my life. There was no way I could create something that would reflect genuine feelings of love, because I didn't have any.

"How about self love?"

"Self love?" I had snorted. "What do you mean?"

Rosie had shrugged and I thought we had both written off that idea but a few minutes later she had collected her thoughts and broached the subject again.

"You have to have loved yourself enough to cut yourself off from Nate and Donnie when you did. Nate said you cut him off when you found out about-" she lowered her voice because we were in the common room - "his *problem*, even though you still really liked him at that point, didn't you?"

"I mean yeah but-"

"And even after you dramatically declared your undying love for Donnie, it didn't take you long to recognise that he wasn't treating you right and you didn't let him hold a grudge against you in an unhappy relationship. You loved *yourself* more and walked away from it."

I frowned. "It wasn't quite like that Rose."

"It was though! This is like the perfect hot take on the theme if you ask me. Everyone's going to be doing odes to their boyfriends. This is something different."

"I'll think about it," I'd said, but I'd mentally ruled out doing any self portraits.

I sat with Nathan and Bea to watch Legally Blonde. Bea pretended to be thoroughly uninterested in it unless Megan was on stage and she wouldn't clap for any of Rosie's singing. It was a surprisingly good performance but I could see most of the students in the audience were just waiting for the afterparty that I'm sure a lot of the parents weren't so aware about. It would only be a reasonably small one compared to what was planned for the New Years Eve party that was going to take place at Rosie's house. The whole year was invited and her place was pretty big, with the added bonus of no parental figures about.

Donnie had managed to actively avoid me outside of maths lessons but even he would be at Rosie's on December 31st. He probably wouldn't be seen tonight. He'll be hiding in his room doing maths and physics equations and being better than everyone else.

Megan downed four successive shots as soon as she was out of costume and in the boys' common room. The teachers on duty turned a blind eye to these parties if they saw we had a reason to celebrate and no one asked where the alcohol came from. The answer was the upper sixth formers, of course. It was the last performance before everyone went home, the actors deserved a little fun (at least that's what Rosie said when she started mixing drinks). I tried not to drink too much since in true Emily fashion, I had still prolonged packing my bags and I'd have to do them tomorrow so I could be ready to be picked up the day after. Yeah, picked up. No more train for me. Dad was picking me up. Oh joy.

The night slipped smoothly into morning and the throbbing in my head reminded me that I may have drank a bit more than I'd planned. We were all sprawled over furniture and rugs in the common room still. I went into the adjoining mini kitchen to fetch a glass of water only to find several of the athletes, Nathan and Donnie sat around the table in there.

"Speak of the devil," one of them said.

"What?" I said, wincing as I found a glass and put it under

the tap.

"Nothing, ignore them," Donnie said. I hadn't realised he was friendly with any of these people.

"Donnie boy got a call from his mummy last night," Nathan said and Donnie glared at him.

"Shut up."

"She wanted to know if his lovely girlfriend would be visiting over Christmas."

I put the glass to my lips but a sour feeling was twisting in my stomach. He hadn't told his parents we broke up? I hadn't told my mum, I suppose, but I never told her anything about Donnie in the first place and he hadn't stayed at my place for a whole week. How awkward.

My stomach suddenly flipped and I lurched towards the sink just in time.

"Here." Someone held my hair back as I threw up.

"Time to go back to bed," Nathan, who had been pulling my hair back, said.

"No, I'm fine," I said, "just woozy."

I picked up my water from where I'd set it down on the side and went to go back into the common room.

"What you need is sleep on an actual bed, not half a sofa." Before I knew what was happening, Nathan had scooped me up from behind my knees and back and was carrying me out towards the stairs.

"Put me down, I don't want to be dropped down the stairs," I said, although I knew he wouldn't drop me. I righted my glass when I realised I was about to spill it on myself. He set me down once we got to his door.

I looked from the door and back to him. He must think I'm an idiot.

"I'm sure you have the purest of intentions," I joked as he opened it.

"I do," he said unconvincingly. "I thought you'd want

somewhere quieter to sleep."

"What time is it?"

"About half five."

"Wake me up for breakfast," I said. "I need to pack, I can't sleep in."

When I woke up again, I couldn't remember for a moment why I was in Nathan's room or why my dress was on the floor. Nathan was sitting in his desk chair, propped back with his legs resting on the desk. I thought he was sleeping but when I shifted to lean down and grab my dress, he looked down at me. I pulled the duvet up a bit.

"Hey," he said.

"Why is my dress on the floor?" I asked warily.

"You took it off because you got too hot last night. Drink some water." He nodded at the half full glass on the bedside table. I remembered now, tossing in the bed, getting all wrapped up and overheated in the folds of the dress and taking it off.

"Why was Donnie with you and your mates last night?" I asked and took a swig of the water. "I thought he wasn't going to the party. I don't remember seeing him."

"That's because you were off your head, and I can only guess, but I'd assume he wanted to keep an eye on you."

"And you," I laughed. Most likely, anyway. "That's so pervy though. I'm not his responsibility. I don't stalk him, do I?"

"He's still protective over you."

"He doesn't even speak a word to me."

I flung my arm across my eyes and groaned. I felt like shit. Not because of Donnie and his evident lingering feelings but from the sheer amount I must have imbibed last night. I'd not even managed to put my dress back on - the scoop to the floor to collect it had made my head swim. "I don't want to move… for like the rest of the year."

Nathan chuckled and picked up his phone. I saw the time 12:06 on the lock screen. "Nathan, I told you to wake me up for breakfast." I remembered that much at least.

"You looked like you needed the sleep," he said. "You'll have plenty of time to pack, don't worry your pretty little head." He was scrolling through instagram, liking pictures from the party. "Look, there's you." He showed me the picture from Megan's page of her, Bea and Hannah posing. In the background, Rosie and I had our heads titled back and arms linked, pouring shots down our throats.

"Lovely," I said at the unflattering picture. "I'm hungry."

"Want me to get you something?"

"Mhmm." I wanted nothing more than to go back to sleep and as hungry as I was, I didn't even know if I would be able to keep anything down.

I must have passed out before he left because the next thing I knew, I was smelling the soup in a styrofoam cup Nathan had brought up from the dining hall. He put it down along with a pink iced doughnut.

"Ooh," I said, reaching for the doughnut, suddenly wide awake. He slapped my hand away.

"You drink the soup first and if you manage that, you get the doughnut."

"How are *you* so sober?" I whined. In a swift motion, I pulled my dress over my head and down over my body.

He grinned, watching me push myself up in a sitting position. I took he lid off the cup and sniffed suspiciously at the soup. I'd been hoping for something tomatoey and smooth not creamy and lumpy.

"It's chicken just eat it."

It was still pretty warm and it wasn't too bad.

"I don't want to go home."

In all honesty I was dreading having to spend a few weeks

with my pregnant mum and a dad who I had to admit I was somewhat scared of. He'd manipulated me last time he'd seen me, he'd yelled at me, and he'd hurt me. He might have hurt Mum. I don't trust him one bit.

"Don't then."

"I don't really have a choice. I'll have to get used to it and I have to make sure my mum's ok."

"Stay with me and Bea. Please."

"If anything bad happens again, I promise I will leave. I'll see you at Rosie's for New Years if you're going?"

Nathan wasn't particularly content with me going home considering he'd seen my head split open last time he dropped me off there. I wasn't particularly content with pretending I was going to be fine when I knew I wasn't.

Chapter 21

I stood with Gen, Megan and Bea, with our bags at the car park, waiting for our parents to pull in. There was a very awkward moment when Donnie's mum had drove in and waved when she saw me and I thought she would try to dodge Donnie to speak to me but luckily at that moment, Rosie's aunt appeared and I hastened to help her load a couple of her bags.

When my Dad turned up, I didn't recognise him or his car for a moment. I'd forgotten what the car looked like, it was hardly something I'd made a note to remember and even my Dad himself would have to make much more of an impression on me before I could ingrain his face back into my memory. I looked to the passenger seat for my Mum but she wasn't there.

I picked up my bags.

"Stay safe," Nathan said, coming from nowhere and wrapping his arms around me.

"I will," I said and he kissed my forehead and let me go. I went to the back of the car to open the boot but couldn't work out how to.

"It's automatic," Dad said, climbing out of the front and pressing a button on his keys. I stepped back and it opened. As I loaded the bags in, he asked, "was that Donnie? Should we be introduced?"

I was surprised he remembered.

"No. He's not Donnie," I snapped slightly and went around to get in the passenger seat.

The girls and not-Donnie waved me off as Dad backed back out and started off down the road. "Where's Mum?" I asked bluntly. Was it such a chore to get in a car and pick your only child up when you haven't seen her for two months?

"She had to stay home."

"Why?"

"You'll see when we get home. It's a surprise."

I didn't tend to go much for Dad's surprises. His idea of a surprise was fucking off from us with a moment's notice, turning up out of nowhere and buying me a car I couldn't even drive. It was a stifling drive home.

"I thought you were getting rid of that," I said, when I saw said car still sitting on the driveway. Hadn't he told me I'd been too ungrateful for it?

"We decided to keep it for now."

Dad unlocked the door and I shouldered my way in, manoeuvering my bags into the hallway and dropped them where I stood.

"Who's that?" I asked, looking not at Mum but the small girl kneeling on the sofa next to her. I felt like I already knew. This was Dad's surprise.

"Let's sit down and put the kettle on first," Mum said, then to the girl, "do you want to go and say hello to Emily?"

She was blonde, around four or five and clutching two barbies, one of which had hair hacked off badly. We looked into each others' eyes and she shyly buried her face into Mum's side. She looked just like I did at that age. I didn't know how I felt. Somehow I knew what to say.

"When were you going to tell me I had a sister?"

Finding out Mum was pregnant was one thing. Finding out Dad had been hiding a sibling from me during his time away from us was another and what was she doing here, now?

I stepped into the living room while Dad went into the kitchen and started filling up the kettle. The noise of it let me and Mum talk without being overheard.

"She's Fran's daughter?" I asked. Fran: the secretary from Dad's work that he ran off with. Six years ago. He sure didn't waste much time did he? Mum nodded with her lips pursed. "And how long did you know about this?"

"Not long. We were going to tell you in October but you were already so overloaded we thought it would be best to wait for some other time. We have her on the weekends."

"What's her name?"

"My name's Pippa," she said, looking up at me with her big blue eyes. I felt slightly guilty, talking about her like she wasn't right there just because she was young and... unexpected. "It's actually Philippa but don't call me that."

I laughed. "Yes boss."

Dad came back in with three mugs of tea. I wasn't a tea drinker at all and neither was Mum but of all things to argue about right now, it shouldn't be beverages. It was too hot to drink but I didn't know what to say so I sipped at it instead to occupy myself.

"Isn't she the spit of you?" Dad asked.

Pippa and I looked at each other. "Yeah. I was thinking that."

"Wouldn't you like to look like Emily when you're older?" Dad asked her.

Pippa stroked the hair of her barbies back. "Yeah, we're both pretty."

I had to laugh again. The confidence of children.

Dad continued to make idle small talk and before I knew it,

196

I'd managed to finish my tea. I put the mug down on a coaster and stood up. "I'm going to put my stuff away."

Mum offered to help but it was a pretty silly gesture when her foot was propped up on the footstool, still in its cast. She assured me it would come off soon but I didn't want to trouble her. Dad didn't offer his help, nor did I want it. He likely knew that.

In my room, I put all my clothes away first and then got my books and things organised. I'd nabbed as many art materials as I could plausibly get away with to use over the break. My impulse was to hide in my room and call all my friends to update them on yet another fucked up situation with my parents but another part of me told me to just get a grip and be an adult about it. Poor Pippa didn't ask for this. She hadn't done anything to me to whinge about. I could only blame my dad, once again. If I'd bothered to stick around during the October half term I could have met her then. Alternatively, things could have escalated worse than they did and they could have decided not to have her visit and hid her away instead.

I wanted to hate her. What she stood for. She was Dad's perfect little second child, just like me. His chance for a do-over. He could be better for her.

He could be worse. He got her for weekends only. He wasn't on good terms with Fran, that's why he came back to Mum, not because he loved Mum, but because we're all he has left when you take Fran away. I wondered what he did for them to split up. I'd wondered this a hundred times over the last few months. I always assumed whatever it was was Dad's fault. And here was the proof: why else would he be the parent that only gets weekends? At least before he left me and Mum he was present all the time. I couldn't imagine only seeing him twice a week like Pippa was getting used to. It must be nicer than having him snatched away indefinitely, thinking you wouldn't ever get the chance to see him again.

I'd missed him when he left us. I hated him when Mum eventually explained what had happened and I hated seeing her sad but still, I missed him. He was my Dad and I loved him. Ugh. My thoughts had just gone back to my stupid love project.

There was going to be a third child on the way. I could hardly believe it, even after seeing the little bump. She was really going to keep it. If Dad stayed around for this one, he or she truly would be the absolute perfect child. The best parts of me and the best parts of Pippa all in one. I didn't want any siblings. I'd always been an only child. I liked it that way, I realised, as much as I'd fantasised about having a brother or sister growing up.

I was so much older than both of them, neither of them would ever feel like a brother or sister, really. I could tell this already. Would Mum's baby be a boy or a girl? It was only a few weeks along, we won't know yet. Three girls? Two girls and a boy? I'll pray he's not anything like his dad.

What a happy family. I thought it was pathetic that Mum took him back. I understand why she did but I hate it. We'd managed on our own.

"Are we going to get to meet Donnie at any point over the holidays?" Mum asked as chicken and vegetables sizzled in the frying pan that evening. I added seasoning to the mix.

"No, we broke up ages ago."

"You didn't tell me?" Mum said disappointedly. It's not like I owed her the low down on my relationship status when she never deigned to tell me anything about hers. She wasn't even upset that I'd broken up with my boyfriend, she only cared that I didn't tell her. "Why did you break up?"

I shrugged non-commitantly. Because I took a leaf out of Dad's book, that's why. "Are you sure Pippa is going to like this?" I asked, stirring the chicken and vegetable mix. "It looks really spicy."

"She has a much more refined palate than you had at that age."

If she noticed I was changing the subject, she didn't say anything.

"Got any plans for the weeks to come?" Dad asked while we ate. God, it was just question after question in this house. Well, I'm stuck home with none of my friends around, and a secret sister to get to know, so no, it didn't look like I'd be running out of the house every day with something to do.

"Lot of schoolwork," I said. Hopefully they'd leave me alone and let me get on with it. Tara (who was tutoring me in maths) and I had a schedule to keep up the maths sessions over FaceTime and I honestly did have a lot of work set. Especially for art. After Christmas I'd be starting my coursework so I needed to pick a theme to focus it on. I'll say for certain, it definitely won't have anything to do with love or relationships.

I needed to stay in Dad's good books long enough to make it to New Years Eve so he could drive me down to Devon for Rosie's party. It was awkward, pretending like I hadn't stormed out, saying I didn't ever want to see him again last time I was here. I didn't know if we were ignoring it for Pippa's sake or if Dad was trying to be more relaxed. I couldn't figure him out.

"Think you might want to learn how to drive?"

I thought of the little car parked on the driveway. He'd mentioned this last time. I still wanted to learn with Mum but with her pregnant, it wasn't fair to put her in a car with a complete novice. Hours at a time in a confined space with Dad couldn't end well. Maybe if we were getting along better after a few days I'd think about it. I'd have to learn at some point.

"Maybe."

After dinner I went back up to my room. I know my parents wanted me to spend time bonding with Pippa since they only had her for the weekend but I needed some time to myself. I texted Rosie and the girls about Pippa then opened a message from Nathan checking that I was ok. He'd sent it some time ago, I should have replied earlier. I messaged him back that I was fine but he should ask Bea about my new sister. I couldn't be bothered to type it out again when he could just read it off her phone.

Yeah Bea said he replied immediately. **How are you feeling about that?**

I didn't know at this point, how I felt. Surprised but not surprised at the same time.

It is what it is I replied and added an eye-rolling emoji. **As long as he doesn't throw her about.**

I really hoped he'd dote on her. I really hoped he hadn't done anything to give a good reason to restrict him to weekend visits. Later that night when I heard Dad coming up the stairs with Pippa in tow, I took my chance to find out. Pippa had been staying in my room, it turned out, while I was at school but while I was back we would have to share. She had her little sleeping bag to put on the floor.

"So don't stay up too late," Dad warned as he set things up for her. I stole downstairs while he tucked her in and found Mum resting on the sofa.

"Why did Dad and Fran split?" I asked quietly and in a hurry. I might as well be out with it.

"Why do you think?" she sighed resignedly. "A leopard doesn't change his spots"

As I'd suspected. Once a cheater, always a cheater.

"Does Pippa know?"

"No, don't tell her. She won't understand."

She said this like I planned on going up to bed and

interrogating the poor girl all about her mum and dad. This revelation irked me though. So she knew that Dad was never going to be loyal to her and she let him back into our home anyway. He hurt me, maybe hurt her, and she still welcomes his daughter here. I loved my mum but this angered me a bit. It was like she was getting back with Dad just for the practicality of it more than anything.

Well, isn't that great for her. If that's how we did things, I should just go crawling back to Donnie right now, knowing that neither of us would make each other happy.

"Ok. I'm going to bed," I said even though it was early for me. I had nothing to stay up for and I didn't want to disturb Pippa by going up to bed late.

She was settled in her sleeping bag with a worn looking purple stuffed rabbit. The light was turned off so I stepped carefully over her to my bed. My phone was plugged in charging at the wall down the side of my bed. I turned the brightness all the way down to reply to the girls' messages. I wished I could add Rosie to the group chat but I'd be murdered for it. Just because I was friends with her now, didn't mean they'd be following in my footsteps anytime soon.

Rosie started going on about how she'd always wanted a sibling but there wasn't any chance left for her. She lived with her aunt because, as she'd told me a little while ago, her mum and dad both died abroad after contracting some foreign disease when she was eight. Bea's claim about Rosie reeking of Daddy's money when I first saw her wasn't so true after all. At least my parents were alive, as much as I could hate them sometimes. After conversation died out, I put my phone under my pillow.

It felt weird to be sharing space with someone after getting used to being on my own for so long at school. I became more conscious of my breathing, every noise I made when I rolled over. Pippa was doing her fair share of fidgeting too. She wasn't getting that comfortable on the floor like that.

"Pippa?" I whispered.

"Yeah?"

"Do you want to come up here with me?"

"Is there room?" she asked innocently.

Of course there was room, she was only small and I was skinny enough.

I lifted a corner of my duvet. "Yeah, come on."

She unzipped the sleeping bag and climbed onto the bed with me. She turned so her back was to me. I was almost drifting off to sleep when she said, "it's hotter up here."

"You're more than welcome to go back on the floor," I teased, nudging her.

"No," she whined and clutched her frayed rabbit closer. "I like it here with you."

Chapter 22

After Pippa went home on Sunday night without incident between any of us, I caved in to Dad's driving lesson propositions, asking him to take me out on Monday. He had work during the day but he'd take me afterwards. Mum was working from home while she couldn't drive. She'd traded in the three jobs she'd had before Dad came back for something administrative.

It wasn't a bad little car. A Honda. I wasn't that interested in different cars but it was nice to drive. Dad even said if I wanted to take up driving lessons while I was at school, he'd pay for someone to teach me. I decided to take him up on that. Whether I liked him or not, I wanted my license.

"Is Pippa coming over for Christmas?" I asked one day.

Dad started. I didn't usually talk to him unless he talked to me.

"No," he said, eyeing me over the top of a newspaper. "Not a weekend."

I'd thought maybe there would have been cause for an exception on Christmas Day. Maybe there would be enough civility between everyone that Fran could come over with her but it was to be just the three of us. My mum was easy to shop for. We always got each other fuzzy warm clothes for Christmas like socks or jumpers and usually books too. We'd buy each other books, read them, then swap them back so we could read our own presents. I had no idea what to get my dad. I couldn't remember what I used to get him when I was younger. He didn't deserve anything if you asked me, anyway. My being here without complaining too much should be enough.

For the girls, I'd got matching jewellery from a shop down the road and sent them off at the post office. I hoped Nathan wouldn't get me anything because I didn't know what to get him either. We were closer now, sure, but I couldn't gauge if that was close enough for Christmas presents or not.

It turned out to be a quiet affair, Christmas. Normally we would have my nan and grandad over and back when Dad was still here, his parents too but none of them came this year. I had the sneaky suspicion that Mum's parents didn't approve of Dad either. Well, I knew they didn't for the last six years and I don't think him coming back made anything better on that front.

I got my books from Mum, as usual. Some candles that I wouldn't be allowed to light at school from Dad due to the fire alarms, but he tried. I'd settled on just a plain T-shirt for him. Second hand from a thrift store. No one could say I didn't get him anything. On the days I didn't see Pippa and go on days out as a 'family' with her, I surged through my homework and prep for the coursework I was due to start in art. I spent a bit of time brainstorming ideas for the stupid love project too. It was probably best I got it done and out of the way sooner rather than later once I got back to school.

The days rolled by until December 30th. Rosie invited me down a day early along with some of her other friends. I'd begged Dad to let me go for weeks but he said it was too far. Eventually I told him I was going whether he let me or not and Mum relented and said she'd take me. Her ankle was fine now.

I packed a bag of outfits and toiletries to take with me and we set off towards Devon. Rosie lived by the coast, or rather, her aunt did but she was away for a few days. She'd allowed Rosie to have some friends over but if she had heard how big an affair these things were like I had, I doubt she would have let it happen.

It took us a few hours to get there and I was the first to arrive. The house was sleekly modern: floor to ceiling windows, and a huge patio that wrapped all the way around the house. Rosie's friends were nice. I'd already met most of them at school but more and more people from the village that were local friends of hers kept turning up. There were soon so many of us, I could hardly believe there would be hundreds more by the next day.

What I thought would be a chilled day of having a bit of fun and maybe a few drinks ahead of New Years Eve turned out to be more work than I imagined. We had decorating to do, snacks to buy, music playlists to set up, and most importantly, we needed someone who looked old enough to buy alcohol without getting ID'd.

"I'm literally eighteen you mong," one of her guy friends said at this. I thought at first he must be a friend from Devon but it turned out he was a day student at Darwin in the upper sixth form.

"Ok, you can go get drinks then," Rosie said and rummaged in her purse for some notes and handed them to him. "Buy a lot of the cheapest shit you can find." She looked over at me and back to this guy, Sam. "Emily, you go with him and buy some food." She thrusted more money at me. As the two of us made to leave, Rosie wiggled her eyebrows suggestively when his back was turned.

I shot her a *calm down* look.

"You single then, I take it?" Sam said almost as soon as we were out the door.

"What? Yeah." That was very forward. He must have noticed the startled expression on my face because he quickly followed with, "I'm not trying to pull you! I meant that Rosie is trying to play the match maker, telling you to go with me. I can read her like a book."

I laughed. "Yeah, I know. She's a nightmare. Can't even let us go to the shops in peace."

We walked to where Sam knew the nearest Tesco was and on the way I found out Rosie had probably tried to put him onto me because he was still trying to get over someone. "Is it a similar story for you?" he asked.

The question flustered me. Donnie and I hadn't talked still for quite a while now and I hadn't even thought about him once in the past few days, yet I didn't know if I'd count myself as being over him.

"Yeah," I said as we went into the shop. "Something like that."

Sam headed over to the alcohol section while I wondered off to the crisps and sweets, piling them all into a basket. We paid with Rosie's money and I offered to take one of the bags of alcohol from Sam since they were a lot heavier than mine.

"I'm a big strong man, I can handle them myself."

He was quite tall. Short sandy blond hair, and, as he said, strong. I did end up taking a bag from him on the way back regardless because despite being double bagged, the sheer amount he'd bought was making the bag look like it was going to rip open at any second. Once we got back, we set everything on the big island in the kitchen and I saw red grooves in his fingers from the weight of it all. Men are so stubborn.

Rosie forbade us to open any of the bottles until tomorrow, which I agreed was a wise idea since the self control of teenagers was very predictable and we all knew there would be nothing left by the end of the night. She did, however, cave and let Sam open a case of beers after she'd hidden the bottles in various cabinets. We ordered a mass Chinese delivery for the twelve of us that were there and we munched our way happily through that in the kitchen before going into the spacious living room with our drinks.

Hanging out with Rosie without Bea and co. was the farthest thing I would have imagined at the start of September when she was throwing us dirty looks at parties, or even just a few weeks ago when she was snitching on mine and Hannah's fight in the dining hall. It really goes to show how you don't really know someone.

Also how much easier it is for girls to get along when there aren't stupid boys getting in the way and making us hate each other for no reason.

"To friendship," I toasted my beer can to Rosie.

"And new friends," said Sam, clinking his against mine. I didn't like beer much. It was ok when I was already drunk and not really tasting anything but I preferred the fruity drinks that Bea had got me into. Rosie's aunt's house was even bigger than it initially looked on the outside. It boasted way more bedrooms than I'm sure her aunt would ever need and upon inspection, the garden actually backed directly onto the beach. No wonder everyone was happy to have the New Year's Eve party here.

There was even a basement games room with a pool table and a long couch with the biggest flat screen TV I'd ever seen. I'd never played pool before but it wasn't long before Rosie had set Sam to teach me the ropes. When it started getting late, I went back upstairs to the living room where people were starting to settle down for the night. Blankets were thrown all over the place and it reminded me of the common rooms at school after a party.

In the morning I was woken up by Sam offering me a cookies and creme Pop Tart. I took it, barely awake and bit the corner off. "It's so early," I realised, immediately noticing the dark sky out of the windows.

"Wondered if you wanted to go for an early morning walk with me," Sam said. I was somewhat frustrated that I didn't get to lie in like everyone else would and probably wouldn't be able to get back to sleep.

"Well, since I'm already awake," I huffed, making sure to show him I wasn't entirely happy. I stepped over the sleeping bodies to go and find my shoes and coat. Sam was lucky it was a cookies and creme flavour Pop Tart. They were my favourite.

We went out the back door and through the garden down to the trail that led onto the beach. It was bit chilly and I shivered even with my coat on. I hadn't been to a beach in ages. I lived in the midlands and the last time we went to one was before Dad left.

"This is a stupid idea," I realised out loud and continued to eat.

Sam laughed. "It is a bit, isn't it? I don't really fancy a walk now."

The sun was just beginning to peek over the horizon. I guessed that meant it was about eight o'clock. My phone wasn't in any of my pockets and I couldn't remember the last time I had it. Hopefully I hadn't lost it anywhere. I sat down in the sand and rolled up the cuffs of my jeans before taking off my shoes and socks and sticking my feet in the cold sand.

"This would be so much nicer if it were France or somewhere not absolutely fucking freezing," Sam said. "Don't you think?"

"I guess so. I wouldn't know, I've never left the country."

Sam looked shocked. "What do you mean you haven't been abroad?"

"Bursary girl," I mockingly waved at him. I'd grown used to explaining this to people by now.

"Ohhhh," Sam said. "I know who you are now. Didn't Rosie hate you?"

"Yeah."

He frowned but sat down on the sand next to me. "Girls are so confusing."

"So are boys," I countered.

Sam leaned back on his elbows. "It should be my one year anniversary if I was still with my girl," he said, looking pained. "We got together at the party last year."

"When did you break up?" I asked softly.

"Couple of months ago."

"Oh… is she coming today?"

"No, she's older than me, she's at uni now, that's kind of why we broke up. We didn't end on bad terms or anything, it was just the distance and everything. Is what it is."

"If it makes you feel better, the guy I was dating and the guy I cheated on him with are both going to be here later, and obviously that didn't end on good terms."

"Damn," said Sam, sitting up and resting his elbows on his bent knees. "I thought you were a good girl!"

"I am! Usually." I picked at my nails. "I swear I was wholly innocent before I came to Darwin."

"Maybe in the light of the New Year, with lots of booze you can get him back."

"I don't want him back."

Sam grinned knowingly. "Ahh…you want the *other* guy."

"No," I said, but he didn't buy it.

Chapter 23

I'd forgotten Donnie only lived in Somerset, so it shouldn't have come as a surprise when he arrived with the first wave of people. I stuck to Sam like glue and it didn't take long for him to work out I was avoiding Donnie. I found my phone, eventually, between some sofa cushions after getting someone to call it and saw that Nathan and Bea were supposed to be arriving around mid-afternoon. It had only just gone lunch and I was already holding myself back from throwing myself out of a window if I accidentally bumped into Donnie one more time.

When they did turn up, just about everyone who was coming was here and there was barely room to move. I'm sure Bea wouldn't have came if I hadn't been friends with Rosie and I'm sure Nathan was glad I was, as an excuse to come. He could never resist a party, especially one this big. I introduced them to Sam but Nathan already knew him. Judging by their body language, they didn't like each other for some reason.

It didn't take long for it to get dark but the fairy lights that had been put up in the garden kept the patio illuminated. Rosie had unleashed the drinks at four o'clock and now everyone had had a few. I got separated from Bea and Nathan at some point while Sam and I were in the kitchen helping ourselves to slices of pizza and refilling our drinks.

At some point I ended up out on the patio and swept into a conversation with a group of people including Donnie. "Hi," I mumbled when he looked at me.

"Alright?" he asked, as if we hadn't been ignoring each other for near on a month.

"Yeah…" I was holding a bottle that I'd nicked from the kitchen and raised it in offering. He held out his empty cup and I refilled it. It was clear neither of us were invested in the group's conversation so he asked if I wanted to go talk in the house.

"How've you been?" he asked once we'd found a comfortable spot in the living room. By comfortable I meant closer than we would normally sit since there wasn't much room or vacant furniture. He'd found a cosy armchair and reluctantly I'd sat across his lap.

"Not too bad," I said. I knew I'd have to talk to him at some point but I didn't imagine it would be with me on top of him with an incredibly awkward silence between us despite the blaring music from the speakers. I took a swig directly from the bottle, giving up with wasting time pouring it into my cup. "How about you?"

"I've been better, what's happened lately, though?" he asked.

I crumpled my solo cup for something to do. "Got better at maths," I said and then wondered if that was a bitchy thing to say when he'd tried and failed to help me with it.

"I've noticed," he said. "But I meant at home. Everything all right at home?" He twisted a strand of my hair and I tracked my gaze along his arm up to his face.

"Mostly, yeah it's fine." I told him about Pippa but impressed upon him that, no, my dad wasn't treating me badly. "See, you don't have to worry about me," I joked and took another drink from the bottle.

"I always worry about you," he admitted, snatching the bottle from my grip and setting down on the floor where I couldn't reach it. I was feeling the heady effects of the alcohol and the confidence that accompanied it.

"That why you spend a night I know you'd rather spend studying watching over me at a party the other week?"

He didn't have a reply for this. As much as he could ignore me in lessons all he wanted, as soon as he thought I might put out when I'm drunk, he had to come along to supervise like I was his badly behaved child.

"You did go up to Nathan's room," he sulked.

His jealousy wasn't even remotely subtle.

"Not exactly obligingly though, was it? He picked me up and then he took me to bed- *not* like that," I said at the sceptical look on his face. "So I could sleep - not like *that*, either!"

Donnie looked as though he didn't know whether to believe me or not. "Honestly, you two," I said. "You're like a pair of peacocks trying to show off and outdo each other all the time."

"Because I can see how everyone else sees you!" he said, sounding annoyed.

"How's that?" I asked and folded my arms that were now empty but for the crumpled cup. "A whore?"

"No!" He pulled my arms apart. "You have no idea how much… how much male attention you attract. Boys talk about you *all* the time but none of them want to go anywhere near you because Nathan would probably knock them out."

"Now you're just being silly," I said.

"It's true!"

I rolled my eyes.

Sam appeared out of nowhere in front of us. He must have identified me as in need of his help because he asked if I was alright. Donnie wrapped his arms around my waist while I assured him I was more then fine.

"More than drunk is more like it," Sam said. "Look at you."

"I'm not that drunk," I protested though I knew this was far from the truth.

Sam held out his hand. "Come on, let's go down to the basement. It's a lot more chilled down there."

I swung my legs off the side of the armchair and stood up, stooping only for a moment to pick up the bottle that Donnie had tried in vain to hide by the side of it. He looked at me meaningfully. "What was I just saying?" he goaded. I ignored him and let Sam lead me off to the basement. There were people in there playing pool, beer pong, and what I think looked like ring of fire with cards. I made to join them but Sam steered me over the a couch in front of the TV instead.

"It looks like you've had enough for now," he said.

"I am so fed up with boys trying to tell me what to do," I moaned but didn't protest when he took my bottle for himself.

The TV was playing some eighties film even though there was no chance of hearing it. There were no speakers playing downstairs but the volume upstairs was enough to make you still need to shout to be heard. "So that boy?" Sam said. "He the one you cheated on or with?"

"On," I said. At that moment I spotted Nathan in the crowd of card players. "*With*," I said, pointing surreptitiously at him. It was like he knew when he was being talked about even though I knew he couldn't have heard me. He looked up at me, then darkly to Sam. I wondered if Donnie was right about boys being too scared to approach me because of Nathan. For a moment, in that look, I could see it.

We ended up spending most of the evening down there. I eventually shook Sam off after I'd rejected his attempts to come onto me the third time and he slunk off upstairs.

Nathan lightened up considerably at this point and told me to join in the card game they were playing. I didn't know what the game was and I was way too drunk to understand the rules. I just drank when they said to.

"I give up." I threw my cards down dramatically. "I'm bored of this, it's making my head hurt." I headed over to observe the pool game going on without any interest in it or the players. I didn't know most of the people in the basement anyway.

"You up for a game?" Nathan said from behind me, making me jump. Two boys had just finished playing and he took the cue sticks from them. I agreed and it actually made my head feel a lot clearer to be able to focus on hitting the balls into the pots, hearing the satisfying clinks of one ball against another. "You're actually better than I expected you to be," he said after we'd finished two games, winning one each.

I set up the triangle for the third game. "What can I say? I'm the master."

"Let's raise the stakes then," he said as he positioned the cue ball.

"What do you mean?"

"Want to make a bet?" He had that cheeky look in his eye. I didn't even want to know what he was up to this time.

"The last time I had a bet… not a bet… a what's it called? A *dare* with you, I ended up throwing up on the side of the science block in my underwear and a pair of your mates trainers." I wagged my finger at him. "You can't be trusted, Nathan Horne.

He caught my hand that was in his face. "All right, all right. A *simple* bet then."

"What?" I asked to hear him out.

"If you win," he said and paused. I nodded slowly for him to continue. "You get to kiss me."

I laughed. "What makes you think I would want to kiss

you?"

"Because I am oozing raw sex appeal and because you know you want to."

"Ok and what if I lose? Let me guess, *you* get to kiss *me*? I'm not an idiot, I know how you work, Nate."

He shook his head. "No. If you lose you have to kiss Donnie."

That made no sense and I knew it still wouldn't have even if I was sober. "How do I win in either of those situations?"

Nathan put a hand to his chest and pretended to choke. "Would kissing me be so bad? I thought you'd jump at the chance," he teased. "And so much more preferable to Diddy Donnie."

I tilted my head and fixed him with my best glare. "This is stupid."

"Yes." He smiled. "Come on it's only a bit of fun. I'll even let you break."

Reluctantly I set myself up to take the first shot. "Oh, wait, wait, wait," he said, stilling my hand. "Just for clarification, so you can't wiggle out of it, by a kiss I mean a proper kiss not just a peck."

"When I win, I'm not kissing you," I said. "I'm not making a deal with you."

"Yes you are," he said. "As soon as you hit that ball, that's what we're playing for."

"Shut up," I said and hit the cue ball into the triangle to start the game. It was a pretty rubbish break. I'd been distracted by Nathan's insistence on there being terms on this game. None of the balls found a pocket.

Nathan sucked his teeth. "Oh dear darling, that didn't set you up well. Unlucky." He hit a solid orange into a corner pocket across the other side of the table despite the fact it was sitting right next to another pocket. He just wanted to show off. He then potted his yellow, followed by his red. I twirled my cue stick between my fingers and Nathan bent over the table again and looked up at me out of the corner of his eyes. Something about the intensity of his look and his posture made me imagine myself underneath him, kissing him as I would be if he won this game.

"Don't get too cocky," I said more to snap myself out of my thoughts than anything. "Once it's my turn, you won't be so smug."

"I'm not going to give you a turn," he said confidently and threw his shot, sending one of his balls, one of mine and the cue ball into the pockets. "Ah, shit."

"What were you saying?" I asked as I lined up the cue ball for a good shot. Like Nathan, I potted a few of my balls fairly easily in a row. Then missed entirely. To be honest, I struggled more the less balls were left on the table as my aim wasn't as spectacular as I'd pretended after I won the last game and it was harder to just hit balls in by chance. We took a few more turns each until it was down to one ball each left. It was his turn. Things weren't looking good.

I swore I could feel my depth perception getting fucked up. The alcohol's fault. Who let me drink half a bottle on top of everything else I'd had? I swallowed uneasily. Nathan was concentrating hard now. He knew he needed to get his ball in or I'd have a good shot at winning. He was lining himself up, drawing back and before I could convince myself to hold onto my dignity, I leaned on the edge of the table opposite him exaggeratedly, knowing that the cowl neck of my red dress was revealing my cleavage.

Nathan's eyes flicked up at the last second. I knew he wouldn't be able to resist. He missed his ball and lined it up perfectly for my next shot. His nostrils flared. "I don't remember mentioning that you could try to seduce me in the terms," he said.

"Whatever do you mean?" I asked innocently and batted

my eyelashes. My shot was easy. The ball went in and all I needed was to get the eight ball in to win. "I'm not kissing you if I win." I said. He attested the opposite.

I was pretty sure if he was the one with the chance to pot the eight ball right now, he would throw his shot and let me win. As if he'd let want me to kiss Donnie over him. I stooped low over the ball, taking my time to make sure I'd get this in. If I missed, I would not be able to stand his jeering.

I took the shot. I watched the black roll and drop it into the hole. My face split into a grin at Nathan but he was still watching the table. I looked down and saw the white cue ball rebounding slowly, edging near to another pocket. "*No*," I warned as if it would listen to me. I felt my face fall as it got closer and closer until I barely dared breathe. It fell in.

"No," I repeated to Nathan. How could I have been so, so close to winning only for it to fall away so quickly? Nathan had the most shit-eating grin I'd ever seen.

I shook my head, putting the cue stick down on the table. I realised now, that I would much rather have to kiss Nathan than Donnie. "It's ok," he said. "I forgot to mention, if you forfeit, you can just kiss me." I couldn't believe him. We were both single, sure. I know. It wouldn't hurt to just kiss him but he needed to understand that I would never be all over him like he wanted me to be.

"No," I said. "I'll hold up my end. It's only a *bit of fun*, right?"

I started walking towards the side of the room with the stairs. "Ooh, what's that?" I asked, spotting a girl bringing down a load of shots to her friends? "Vodka?" I needed one for that I was about to do. She let me take one and I tipped it back, screwing my face up as I thrust the empty glass to Nathan who had followed me.

"Emily," he called but I was already climbing the stairs and scanning the crowds. I spotted him quickly. He was centre of attention in a group of people in the middle of the living room who were hanging on to his every word. I didn't care what he was talking about. I didn't care who was watching. I wanted them to watch. Especially Nathan who had come up behind me and was reaching for my wrist. He must have thought I would never really do it.

Well Nathan, I'm several drinks past giving a fuck. I strode over to Donnie, pushing my way between two of the people he was talking with and grabbed his chin firmly in my hand. I saw his eyes widen and closed my own before I could change my mind. The next second I stood up on my tip-toes a bit to reach him and with my other hand, hooked his neck and pulled him down towards me to kiss him.

God, please let him kiss back or this is going to be the most embarrassing experience of my life. Even with my eyes shut, I could feel all the other eyes on me. As much as I'd been purposeful, coming over to him and grabbing him like I had, I didn't want to force him if he didn't want to so I nipped playfully at his bottom lip and relaxed my hold on his neck now I had him. He didn't pull away so I went in again, fully taking his lip between mine and going from there. He kissed me back now, I could feel his mouth working against mine, felt him leaning over me, arching me back and tilting me down but his hands came to my lower back to steady me as he deepened the kiss even more.

We kissed for what could have been a few seconds but what felt to me like minutes. I could taste the alcohol we'd both consumed.

"W-wow," I stammered when he finally broke the kiss and I pulled up the strap of my dress that had fallen down my arm before I could flash anything. I don't know what I'd been expecting but it wasn't that. I almost shook my head to attempt to clear it. Nathan drew into my peripheral vision looking sulky. It was his own fault. He only had himself to blame. I looked back at Donnie.

"Where did *that* come from? Not that I'm complaining."

I giggled. "I don't know." People were still watching us and I didn't know what to do. I didn't know how to extricate myself from the situation but suddenly the music was turned down and Rosie was announcing that the countdown to midnight was going to start in around a minute and someone was getting ready to set off fireworks in the garden.

Everyone surged for the back doors and gathered around on the patio. As the countdown began, I felt myself swaying in the press of bodies and Donnie wrapped an arm around me and pulled me against his chest. People began to count and I joined in once we go to ten. The fireworks were lit and they exploded, lighting up the sky only a few seconds too early.

"Happy New Year," Donnie said into my ear.

Chapter 24

It was a relief to get back to school a week later. Although it was bearable now to be at home, I really missed everyone at Darwin and that was made only harder by spending all day texting, knowing I couldn't see them. Donnie had been back in contact since Rosie's party. I didn't know what to do about that. I felt guilty stringing him along when I knew my heart wasn't in it but on the other hand, it wasn't anything flirtatious - just friendly. So I wasn't doing anything wrong, really.

Regardless, it was nice to have classes to distract myself with. It was nice to be doing almost as well as Donnie in maths lessons after all the hard work I'd put in over the half term. I had to get a move on with my love project submission so that I could meet the deadline at the end of the month. After that, I could focus all of my art entirely on my coursework.

I enlisted both Rosie and Steven to help me with this. For what I wanted to do, I'd needed it. After all my research over Christmas I'd decided on creating a clay bust of my own torso. I'd already done far too many paintings and drawings over the last few months and working with clay was something different. Going with Rosie's 'self-love' idea, I'd thought I would make a cast of myself with my arms crossed over my chest, holding onto my opposite shoulders. The idea was that after I'd made a cast and put the clay over it, I'd be able to work the edges into something resembling a heart with the shape of my shoulders and my elbows meeting at the bottom.

"I think this would look better if you weren't clothed," Rosie said at the last second. We were in one of the little classrooms in the art block and I was wearing a spaghetti strap top.

"No one wants to see that," I said. Rosie made a face like she was going to make a joke (the direction of which, I could guess: almost certainly involving Nathan or Donnie) but she elaborated, "I think it would add to the message, like love is raw… like… naked."

I had to laugh but the points she made did sound good for when I'd have to write my reflection on it for my EPQ. Steven agreed and somehow I let them talk me into it.

"I don't care about seeing your boobs, girl I'm gay," he said. Rosie had run off to get some nipple pasties from her room because I wasn't about to cast my body in a room that couldn't be locked without something to hide my boobs with. With my luck, the fire alarm would go off or something. We put a sign on the door anyway, so hopefully no one else would come in and the pasties shouldn't be visible under my arms. I could always adjust how it turns out when I put the clay over the mold if it does look weird.

We had alginate prepared, courtesy of Mrs. Hayes. After Bea had helped me position myself, she and Steven set to pouring it over me. I'd wrapped plastic sheets over my jeans to protect them like I was wearing some funny transparent skirt. I shuddered at the coldness of it.

"Only ten minutes," Rosie reassured when I whined about how uncomfortable it was. "And it makes your boobs look really nice squished like that."

"Can the both of you stop talking about my boobs!" I laughed.

I finished the whole thing within the week. After I'd put clay over the cast and built it up until it could stand and balance unsupported, I rounded the edges into more of a heart shape and was quite satisfied with the effect surprisingly. I fired it and put it with all the other submissions. I still had plenty of time to write a little accompanying piece to explain its meaning.

Turning instead to my coursework, I'd finally settled on studying feminist art, despite Mrs. Hayes trying to push me in the direction of 'feminine' art. She argued it was nearly the same thing. I argued there was a fine line.

"Whatcha doing?" Nathan asked nosily, drawing up a seat besides me in the dining hall. Lunch finished a while ago but I still had a free period to continue my work in the quiet. I'd worked through lunch and couldn't be bothered to move to the library. There wasn't really anyone else in here. Donnie was over in his corner poring over maths work he'd been doing during lunch and Nathan had just walked in sweaty from sports. Donnie wasn't ignoring me, we just both respected each other's space while studying.

"It's an art thing," I said. I had one of the school's laptops out and was doing a bit of writing about my piece. I'd attached a picture but I felt self-conscious about it now that Nathan was actually looking at it.

"That's really cool!" he said excitedly. "You're so talented."

"Yeah, whatever," I said and closed the laptop. I'd finish it later. Lately I'd been working so much harder than I had been. For once I felt on top of things, like everything was on track. *This* is what I'd been aiming for back when I started in September. No silly boys, no falling out with friends or failing any subjects. I was powering through my three A-levels and my EPQ like it was nobody's business. Nobody's but my own.

"What are you doing about old lover boy over there?" He nodded his head over towards the corner.

"Nothing," I whispered, wishing he would keep his voice down. "I have to go." If he'd just come in from finishing the period after lunch that meant I needed to be heading off to maths. I made to leave and head off towards the maths and science block but he was following after me. He must have been more interested in bugging me than getting a post-exercise snack.

"Let me take you out for a proper date then," he said, jogging behind me to catch up after I'd departed so swiftly. "And don't walk out on me this time." From behind him emerged Donnie who had the air of someone pretending they didn't care about Nathan and me but also secretly wanted to overhear our conversation.

"No, I can't. I'm very busy at the moment, in case you haven't noticed. Did you not just see me doing my art project? That's got to be finished by the end of the month." He opened his mouth to argue so I quickly made it more black and white. "Leave me alone." He was trouble and I didn't need it.

"You can't or you don't want to?" Nathan challenged. "Don't want to because you'd rather sit in O'Donoghue's room and do nerdy little maths equations together. Is that what turns you on? Him?"

Upon hearing his name mentioned, Donnie stopped walking past us and turned, observing the two of us arguing. I thought he might say something to defend me but there was just a tense silence in which he came to stand beside me. "Is there something you'd like to say to me, Nathan? Because I have the feeling you have for a while. So let's get it out in the open." He was very cool about it and I blinked in surprise.

"She's using you," he said simply.

"I'm not using anyone," I said sharply.

He ignored me and addressed Donnie. "Do you think she'd have kissed you on New Years Eve if it hadn't been for a bet? If it wasn't you it would be me."

I gawped like a fish, trying to think of how to explain myself. I didn't want Donnie to find out about that. He must have looked as flabbergasted as me because Nathan continued cruelly, "yeah, don't kid yourself. It didn't mean a thing."

Donnie turned on me and took a step back with hurt in his eyes.

"I was drunk," I started.

"So was I," he said, "but I still thought you meant it. *I* still meant it."

"I'm sorry."

"See mate? You don't mean shit to her," Nathan said. I wanted to tell him to shut up, that neither of them meant anything to me anymore. We got drunk, we had our fun and now it's over.

"Neither do you, in case it escaped your notice," Donnie retaliated. "If she really wanted you so bad you would have had her by now."

"Hey!" I protested at the same time Nathan said, "I could have her whenever I want."

I didn't have time to react. Donnie swung his fist into Nathan's face and I heard a sickening crack. Blood spurted from his nose that I was sure must have been broken. I screamed without meaning to. For a moment nothing happened, then I saw Nathan collect himself and knew he was going to get him back, and so much worse.

He wouldn't hurt me, I was sure of it, so I threw myself in front of Nathan. "Stop it! Both of you!" I watched him wipe the back of his hand under his nose and it came away scarlet.

"*Don't*" I warned, trying to gauge his reaction.

I felt Donnie's fingers close around my wrist and wrench me out of the way. I looked around. We'd attracted a small crowd of younger students who were walking from one class to another but there were no teachers around. Nathan's chest was heaving with anger but he hadn't hit Donnie back yet.

"What's going on here?" A science teacher came around the corner and saw the confrontation. Finally someone else who could handle those idiots. Before he could realise I was involved, I turned around and sped off towards the maths classroom, knowing I may be a couple of minutes late.

I later heard that Nathan had tried to play his broken nose off as a sports injury but considering he was not in his kit and there was no one around to back up this claim, the truth came out relatively quickly. Possibly, it was his pride that was hurt more than his nose at having someone smaller than him catch him off guard like that. If they'd properly fought, I knew Donnie would suffer a lot worse than a broken nose.

I had to admit I felt kind of bad for Donnie. He had a perfect track record at school, as far as I knew, and it was because of me that he'd got himself in trouble. I only hoped he wouldn't get excluded.

That evening I was in the library with Tara for maths tutoring when I saw him walk in and settle at a desk. He looked thoroughly moody. There was a good chance me speaking to him would only make things worse but I couldn't just sit there and ignore him. "Can we take a quick break?" I said to Tara and went over to Donnie.

His jaw twitched when he saw me, but what did he expect? He knew I'd be here for tutoring and he was in here almost every day. "Please, I really don't want to speak to you." He wouldn't even look at me.

"What happened after you hit him? Are you going to get excluded?"

He sighed. "Nathan claimed it wasn't a big deal and Mr. Antonio loves me so no. I'm on report though."

"Oh. I'm sorry… again."

"Look, I really don't want to talk to you. I'm not going to say it again."

"Fine!" I said and stomped off back to Tara, making sure to keep my head down over my work so I wouldn't have to look at him. Nathan had to go to minor injuries to get his nose set but I wasn't going to text him to ask how he was. He would be back by now but I hadn't seen him. Probably sulking in his room and coming up with a better cover story for his mates.

It really annoyed me how he'd said he could have me whenever he wants. No doubt that was what provoked Donnie, literally the least violent person I knew, to hit him. Honestly, I'd slapped Nathan myself for less. I don't know whether Donnie thought what he said was true or not but it was obviously meant to rile him up. It was so disrespectful to me, though, and I doubt Nathan cared about my feelings when he said that. Anything to get a rise.

I had to relay the story of what happened to the girls in my room and although Bea was annoyed with Donnie for hurting her brother, Donnie seemed to be the one with whom the sympathy lay. The way they saw it: they agreed that what Nathan said was out of hand and he did somewhat deserve what he got. "Yeah but Donnie was really short with me afterwards. I've apologised twice and he still doesn't want to talk to me."

"He probably felt like you played with his feelings," Hannah said. I knew she'd say something like that but I hadn't meant to lead anyone on or pretend there was something there when there wasn't. Since Rosie's party I hadn't once made any sort of move on Donnie and neither had he, so I didn't see what the big deal was. "I'm not responsible for his feelings," I said. "And it's obvious to everyone that me and him aren't ever going to happen."

Two days later, I got a text from Steven telling me to go down to the art rooms even though I didn't have art that day. He said Mrs. Hayes wanted to speak to me about something. He was already down there for a 3D design lesson but he stopped answering my texts so I guessed he was busy with his lesson. If Mrs. Hayes still thought she could change my mind about my coursework theme, she was wrong.

I knocked on her office door but when she answered she didn't invite me in like I thought she would but instead started walking towards our art classroom. "Please," she said as we walked, "tell me you already took pictures of your competition submission."

"Of course I did," I said, confused. "It's as good as finished."

Mrs. Hayes looked grim as she pushed open the door to the little backroom that opened off the main art room where we were keeping our submissions. She flicked the light on to brighten the dinginess of the room and I realised immediately why she wanted me here.

I saw my sculpture lying separately on a table, not where I left it. It had been cracked into two pieces like it had fallen from where I'd put it on a shelf but I'd been so careful setting it there and I'd been so sure it could balance well. I'd even put it against the corners where the wall met. How could this have happened?

"It fell?" I stated the obvious, feeling crestfallen that I'd have to make it all over again if not able to stick the pieces back together again. The split was more or less down the middle. The two pieces might even be able to be stood up and support themselves. Perhaps it wouldn't be too difficult to fix.

"Steven says he heard someone in here a little while ago and heard it crash so he came in but they'd already ran out the door." She gestured to the door in the back of the room. It wasn't even a door anyone really used much.

"He didn't see them?" I asked.

"No, they must have come in and out through that door. *Why*, I don't know. No one should be in here unless they're storing pieces for the competition. It isn't being used for anything else."

"I don't get how it could have been knocked down," I speculated. "It was tucked away here, in this corner." I pointed to where it had been and realised that the model that was right next to it had not moved as it might have been pushed aside if my sculpture had been accidentally knocked off. I went over for a closer inspection.

"Look," I said. There was a very fine layer of dust around where my sculpture had been placed but it hadn't been disturbed as it would have been if it had fallen off the shelf. "It was picked up. Why would anyone pick it up and run off after they broke it?" I was angry and in my anger, the answer came to me. "Unless someone broke it on purpose."

"Nathan Horne," I burned.

"You were involved with him weren't you? Heard you had a fight. Do you think it might be likely he did break it?"

"How would - how do you even know that?"

"Teachers gossip too, you know… have a think about what you want to do and I'll see if I can help you out with your submission. There's still time to completely redo it if that's what you choose. I know you're more than capable."

Chapter 25

Nathan was lucky I couldn't find him all morning. I checked the sports pitches, peeked in the gym and even asked some poor passing twelve year old to look in the changing room for me but he was doing a very good job of avoiding me.

My annoyance was so great that I decided to bunk off my lessons that day. I should have gone to English for an hour before lunch and maths afterwards but Hannah needed no persuading to skip English since she'd failed to bother to do the reading we were supposed to have done. "In my defence," she said. "Who the fuck does Chaucer think he is just spelling shit however he wants? It's worse than Shakespeare. No one can read that rubbish without a translation."

"Chaucer's work was supposed to be revolutionary," I countered. "It's hard to read but at least it was in English rather than French like most work from that time was."

"I literally do not care. I'm dyslexic and he's rubbing it in."

I laughed. We'd walked into town to Nandos and the spicy aroma was not making me feel guilty for not being in English at all. We'd made a little detour to the book shop first. "Retail therapy always helps," Hannah had said. The both of us were suckers for books more than anything else. My bag was in fact weighed down by three books more than I left school with so it was a little later than usual that we were eating lunch.

Maybe as revenge for teasing Hannah about her not bothering with the English texts, she started hitting me with jokes about getting my chicken at a medium heat whereas she had opted for extra hot just for dramatic effect and I pretended I didn't see her eyes water after only the second bite and several drinks refills.

"Dessert?" I asked when we were finished. It was nearing two o'clock now.

"Don't ask stupid questions," Hannah scoffed at me and promptly ordered two salted caramel brownies. It was nice, I mused, that we had managed to slip back into our old friendship after it blew up so badly. There was a time when I thought we'd never see eye to eye but I know she was in the right about the whole Donnie thing really. I just didn't want to hear it at the time.

I had barely stuck my spoon into my brownie when my phone pinged with a message. *Finally*, I thought. Digging my phone out of my bag, I expected to see Nathan's name followed by maybe an apology, possibly an explanation, or at least tell me where he is and why he hasn't had the balls to answer me. It wasn't Nathan though. It was the other idiot.

Mr Barnes wants to know where u r because this is the second lesson today you haven't registered for apparently.

I resisted the urge to roll my eyes. **Having a me day w Hannah. You'll be glad to know Nate has pissed me off good and proper by wrecking my art so if you see him, make sure you give him another bruiser from me thanks.**

His reply came so quickly I'd barely swallowed my mouthful of brownie. **Understandable, I'll let Barnes know. Don't you think he's got bigger problems right now though? Give it a rest for a bit even if he does deserve it.**

"What the fuck does that mean?" I showed the texts to

Hannah who couldn't understand where he was coming from either. "They *hate* each other. How can he side with me one second and say it's understandable and then tell me to give it a rest?"

"What problems has he supposedly got and why would Donnie care?"

I shrugged. "Stupid. They say girls are the ones that don't make sense." I decided it was best to ignore him. I knew he didn't really want to talk, as he'd told me several times now. He was only asking because Mr. Barnes wanted to know, and I'd probably get reprimanded by Dean Smith later for skiving but whatever. What was she going to do, put me in another detention? We're adults, near enough.

When we got back through the school gates, I saw Donnie from a distance emerge from the maths classroom behind a throng of third form girls and head towards the library. I knew our paths were going to cross and I tried to make a detour but Hannah groaned and tugged me back. "Don't be a pussy, you don't even have to talk to each other. Just make conversation with me."

So I did. And I picked one of my favourite topics: whinging about Nathan Horne.

"Nathan is the pussy; not me. Where is he hiding, anyway?" I checked my phone both to see if he'd bothered to message and also to avoid eye contact with Donnie as we passed him.

"He's still at the hospital," a voice said from behind me. It was Donnie speaking, obviously.

"What do you mean 'at the hospital'?" I asked. Now I looked at him, I could see he looked absolutely awful. "Have you been crying?" I asked before I could stop myself. His eyes were red. What could have happened that was so bad it had actually made Donnie feel empathy for Nathan?

Tactfully, Hannah quickly made an excuse about having to

meet Megan and ran off but I knew she'd want to hear all the details later. I was beyond confused. I suddenly felt guilty that I'd been harassing Nathan all day when he couldn't reply because something had happened to him.

"Are you free right now?" he asked and I told him I was. Even if I wasn't, I had to know what had happened that was so bad it had actually affected Donnie himself. The 'don't talk to me' stance seemed to have gone out of the window. Maybe they'd had another fight. I looked at the split skin on his knuckles but they looked like they were only from when he hit Nathan the other day.

He wouldn't say a word until we got to his room. He said he wanted to sit down first. He did look like he'd had a long day and there I was having bunked off all day, screwing around at Waterstones and Nandos.

"What happened?" I asked as he turned his back on me and unloaded his bag, putting books back in his desk drawers. I stood there like a lemon, not sure if I was welcome to sit down and also burning to know why Nathan was in the hospital, as annoyed at him as I was.

His back shook and I heard him choke on a sob before he wheeled around and pulled me tight into a crushing hug. I patted him awkwardly on the back, still completely not understanding what he was upset about.

"You have no idea do you?" he cried. "I thought that's why you said you were taking time to yourself."

"I really… I'm so confused. What happened to Nathan?" He was acting like it was completely obvious and it was taking everything I had not to start getting short with him if he didn't start explaining soon. I led him to the bed where he collapsed in a fresh heap of sobs.

"It's not about Nathan, it's Rosie!" he finally spluttered. Rosie? What did she have to do with anything? Donnie was almost inconsolable. I'd never seen him cry but this was worse than I'd ever seen him or ever imagined seeing him.

"What about Rosie?" I asked, still wondering how we'd gone from Nathan to Rosie in a heartbeat.

"She…" He choked and pressed his palms into his eyes. I took a few tissues from the box on his bedside table and offered them to him when he'd collected himself slightly. "She's in the hospital." He burst into more tears and my heart sank. Something really bad must have happened for him to be so upset. As much as I desperately wanted to know what happened and if she was ok, I realised it was best not to push him right now. He'd tell me when he's ready.

I waited for him to calm down and wiped his eyes with more tissues. "She texted me," he eventually gulped. "In the middle of the night when I was asleep. She must have texted a few people. She was saying goodbye."

"What do you mean saying goodbye?" I was going blank, just listening, taking it in but feeling awfully distant like the unconscious part of my brain was understanding before the rest.

"She said she'd been struggling with mental health and…" He fell into my arms again. "I had no idea," he whispered. "No idea. I've barely talked to her in years." I let him cry into my jacket and felt tears prickling myself. "She slit her wrists," he said so quietly I almost didn't hear. But I did. And a wail left my lips as I hugged him harder. "I di- I didn't see the message until I woke up and I ran." He hiccupped. "I ran to her dorm but she wasn't answering. I thought she was…" He trailed off and couldn't finish.

"It's ok," I said, trying to be reassuring while in shock myself. She had to be ok. I lay his head on my lap and clumsily smoothed the hair out of his blotchy face. "She'll be ok." I wiped my own tears on my shoulder.

"Dean Smith found me," he said a few minutes later. "She said she'd gone to the hospital in the night. Nathan had got there in time. He was awake. It was like four o'clock, she thought no one would be awake to stop her."

"But he was," I whispered. It made sense now. The way Nathan had been keeping secrets about her for months and months, telling me it was none of my business. She'd been struggling all this time and only he knew. This had all happened just down the corridor last night and I had no clue. I'd slept right through it. She never confided in me. We were friends, I thought she would be able to tell me if she needed help. If she was sending out goodbye messages, I thought I would get one. She hasn't spoken to Donnie in forever and he got one.

"Everyone else she messaged was put into isolation in the office," he explained. "When we found out she'd been stabilised I said I'd go to my lessons. I thought it wouldn't affect me that much." It clearly did. Even if they weren't so close now, they used to be. Even if I still hated her, I would still be upset. We're only human.

Now I thought about it, I hadn't seen any of her friends all day either. "Why didn't she message me?" I asked, not actually expecting an answer.

"Be grateful she didn't. You wouldn't have wanted to go through what some of us went through."

Obviously I wasn't upset I missed out on the terror of it all but I was upset that she didn't think to include me in her farewells. I didn't want to sound conceited, I didn't want to make what she went through all about me but *why* couldn't she have tried to talk to me or someone before she took such drastic action. Why would she pick Nathan of all people to confide in. He's useless at keeping secrets unless they're from me and he's useless at being helpful.

But he did save her. For that I had to be grateful.

"You said she's stabilised though?"

"Yeah, she'll be ok." Physically, at least, but I wondered

more about her mental state. If she'd try to do anything again. There was nothing left to say and we lapsed into a long silence until he sat up. His soft fingers brushed my skin as he wiped tears from the corners of my eyes.

"She'll get help," he said. That had to be something. She'd been bottling everything up until it spilled over but now she'd get actual support. She'll get better in time. She needs actual professionals not Nathan who, as we both know, already struggles with his own problems.

"I have to tell you something," he said and I thought I was about to get an insight into why Rosie had chosen to message him. Did they have some little secret that he was willing to divulge with me? But it wasn't anything of the sort. "It was me who broke your art sculpture."

I wanted to be angry with him. I wanted to yell and ask him why and break something of his. I didn't do any of those things. It wasn't the time to rip into him when he was already lying in pieces, broken over what Rosie had done.

"It's ok. That can be fixed too."

Now I wondered why I had jumped to the conclusion that it had been Nathan. Both of them were angry at me. Nathan was just usually the one that acted more recklessly. He was the one that knew about my sculpture. He'd seen the picture of it while I was writing up about it on the laptop. But Donnie had been there too. I'd assumed he was paying no attention to me but of course he was. He always was.

"Don't you want to know why I did it?"

"Why did you do it, Donnie?" I sighed.

"Because I love you. And there you were with someone else saying they can have you at their will. I found out you were playing with my feelings when I'd been trying to tell myself to get over you ever since you kissed me. I knew it was too good to be true. I was kidding myself thinking maybe you were doing the same thing. Maybe neither of us were going to make the first move once we were back in school."

"It's not like that," I said, knowing it was going to break his heart, hearing what I had to say. "I'm happier on my own. I sometimes get caught up between the two of you and I don't know how I feel and we all get hurt and I don't want to do that to you again."

"You don't need anyone else, I know that. That's what I love about you: you make your own way but... that's also what I hate about you. That's why I did it. I'm sorry I did. I regretted it."

"I can't be what you need." I knew he wasn't really interested in talking about the sculpture. It was more what it represented. The same thing to me and him but also different. For me it was a project on self love; to him it was a project about how by loving myself I didn't need to love him.

"I'll help you fix it," he said.

"No." I thought about it. "I think maybe I'll submit it as it is."

It has more of a story behind it now. It tells of friendship as Rosie and Steven helped me make it. It tells of my heart split between those two boys. It tells of a lot of things that aren't quite whole and need working on in a few places but mostly it tells of me.

Epilogue

Rosie got pulled out of school by her aunt and I only briefly got to say goodbye. Things were worse than they seemed and now the lid had been opened, it became clear just how much help she needed. She got admitted to a clinic down in Devon where her aunt could keep a closer eye on her. I resolved to pay more attention to my friends after that. It scared me how I thought I knew her when I really didn't know her at all even after seeing both sides of her as the bitch and the friend.

I got to visit in the Easter holidays. She said she wasn't coming back. I understood. I wouldn't have wanted her to come back if she couldn't handle it. I took an art magazine with me along with some other little gifts. "Look at the tabbed page" I told her. She smiled for the first time when she opened it to the page. It had a picture of my love heart project still broken cleaved down the middle as I'd submitted it. I hadn't won any prize with it. It wasn't that special but it had won an honourable mention and I'd got to give a short interview about it.

'To Rosie', it was dedicated.

My parents were so proud. Even Pippa was enthusiastic although she didn't really understand the meaning of it. Dad was growing on me, I hated to admit. I'd lost the energy to keep pushing him away after Christmas and he was doing a really good job with Pippa. My suspicions about him seemed to be unfounded. He treated Mum and their baby like he was his treasure. Yes, it was a boy, Jack, that Mum had several months later and although I'd resolved to keep a close eye on Dad and his behaviour, he doted on his whole family. As long as he raised Jack to be a better man than he was, that was all I could ask.

I'd have to go and finish my second year at Darwin before going to university but after the art competition, I'd already found myself in correspondence with a whole load of them who were interested in me. I didn't see Donnie or Nathan over the summer but we talked on the phone as friends do, but as much as I reassured Donnie that that's all we'd ever be, I did still have another year to fuck things up in good teenager fashion.

Printed in Great Britain
by Amazon

63786765R00138